"Joe," said David severely, "don't you go to smoking around the house any more. She don't like it."

"She needn't trouble herself," Joseph replied angrily. "The less she thinks of me the better I am pleased. If you think I am going to give up my rights in my own house, you are mistaken. I'll smoke as much as I please, and light my pipe in the kitchen if I choose. You've sat in that kitchen and smoked whole evenings yourself. You needn't be so holy all of a sudden. It is just as I expected. The minute you get a woman in the house everything has got to be turned upside down to suit her. If you're going in for that sort of thing I'll clear out. And as for my part, I shall do all in my power to make it uncomfortable for her, for the sooner she gets out of this and back to her city home the better I shall like it."

IN THE WAY

Grace Livingston Hill

BANTAM BOOKS
TORONTO · NEW YORK · LONDON · SYDNEY · AUCKLAND

IN THE WAY

*A Bantam Book / published by arrangement with
Author's Estate*

Bantam edition / November 1985

ISBN 0-553-25253-4

Published simultaneously in the United States and Canada

*Bantam Books are published by Bantam Books, Inc. Its trademark,
consisting of the words "Bantam Books" and the portrayal of a
rooster, is Registered in U.S. Patent and Trademark Office and in
other countries. Marca Registrada. Bantam Books, Inc., 666 Fifth
Avenue, New York, New York 10103.*

PRINTED IN THE UNITED STATES OF AMERICA

O   0 9 8 7 6 5 4 3 2

IN THE WAY

CHAPTER I

The kitchen looked unusually dreary that night. It was raining and the two young men who called it home had thrown down their wet coats on chairs to dry before the fire when they came in. Their heavy boots also had been drawn off and looked out of sorts and out of place in a dark pool by the door. The stove needed blacking and the fire was sulky. In the sink were piled the dishes of the entire day, still unwashed. They were not many to be sure, but they added to the general air of desolation. Two blackened pipes on the mantel-piece lay in the one cleared space, the rest of the shelf being occupied by a miscellaneous collection of years. On a hook behind the cupboard door there hung a faded checked gingham apron. The owner thereof had been dead nearly a year, but the apron had never been taken down, either because it had never been noticed, or because the boys had not known what to do with it. It could scarcely have been a pleasing object to them, but they had not been accustomed to much that was pleasant in their lives so far, and hardly thought to try and make it for themselves.

The table was set for the evening meal without table-cloth or much regard to the fitness of things. A baker's loaf of sour, puffy-looking bread lay on the bare table. A paper containing a slab of cheese was on the other side. A knuckle of ham on a plate and the molasses pitcher completed the array, with some miserably made tea in a tin teapot. It was a very uninviting-looking table, and yet these two preferred it to having their premises invaded by hired help, or to going out to board. They shrank from any more changes. They ate in silence, for they had worked hard all day and were hungry.

At last the elder of the two shoved his chair back from the table and sat thoughtfully gazing across the room.

"Joe, she wants to come here!" he said, still looking thoughtfully about the dismal room.

"Who're you talking about?" said the younger a little crossly, helping himself to another slice of ham. He had been working all the afternoon in the rain, mending the cowhouse roof, and the supper tasted good to him. "I wish you'd ever begin at the right end of a thing, Dave," he went on; "you always plunge into the middle, and it takes half an hour to get at your idea. Where have you been this afternoon, and who are you talking about?"

"Ruth," said David.

"Ruth?" said Joseph, showing by his tone that he was scarcely enlightened.

"Ruth," said David again.

"Oh, Ruth!" said Joseph, a kind of dismay and consternation in his voice. He laid down his bread and molasses and sat back in his chair. "What in the name of common sense does she want to come here for?" he asked after a minute.

"Because Aunt Ruth is dead," answered David, like a lesson he had been saying over to himself to be sure he had it right; "and because she is alone and is our sister and we are her brothers."

"Well, where's all the money that was going to be left her? Is it dead too?"

"I don't know about the money; she doesn't say as to that."

"It must be gone or she wouldn't want to come here. Why doesn't she do something and stay where she is? After being away from home all her life, she can't expect to be taken care of now."

"Joe," said David rather sharply, bringing the front legs of his chair down with a thud, "she's our sister. What would father say to hear you speak like that? She doesn't say anything about money, but I don't believe she was thinking of that. She seems to want to come to see us. Maybe it's only a visit she wants, but anyway she is coming. She isn't even going to wait to see whether we want her. She is going to start to-night and will be here to-morrow morning."

Joe answered this announcement with a long whistle of astonished disapprobation.

He reached for the letter David handed him, and drew the smoky kerosene lamp nearer him to read it. His face grew dark as he read it slowly. It was a letter fair and dainty enough for any brother to be glad to read. Written on heavy, creamy linen paper, in even, graceful lines and curves, a sort of initial of the lovely writer herself.

But Joseph threw it down angrily when he had finished, and flung back his chair roughly from the table.

"I guess I'll clear out of this ranch for a while, and let you enjoy your company to yourself," he said, rising as if to carry out his threat.

His brother rose also, and laying a rough hand kindly on his arm said: "No, you won't do any such thing, Joe; you'll stay here and behave yourself, as you promised father you would do, or at any rate as I promised father I would see you did. She is our sister, and you have got to do your duty toward her, whether you like it or not." Then David took one of the two dirty pipes from the mantel, and lighting it sat down by the stove, with his stockinged feet on the hearth. Joseph followed his example, and for a few minutes there was silence, save for the sound of wind and rain outside.

"Pretty place this is for a girl," said Joseph, taking the pipe out of his mouth to speak; "she'll come around messing up everything, and the way she's been brought up she won't know how to do a thing."

David looked about the room again in a troubled way. It was the same room he remembered in his boyhood, aye, even his babyhood, away back where that shadowy memory of his mother moved about; but the old kitchen had a brighter look in those days. What made the difference? Then when mother had gone and Aunt Nancy had come, the room had seemed well enough; father had lived there and seemed contented. After father had died, Aunt Nancy had kept the room about the same, until her death, nine months ago, and nothing had been changed since.

His eyes wandered to the gingham apron behind the door. He slowly brought his feet down from the hearth, and going over to the cupboard took the apron down from its

hook, and carefully rolling it up put it in the stove. Then he
sat down and went on smoking. The action stirred up
something in the younger brother's memory which made
him uncomfortable, and in spite of the rain he announced
his intention of going down to the store awhile. David said
nothing, and Joseph went about some noisy preparations,
drawing on his boots with a heavy thud. Then he threw
open the door, and was greeted by such a gust of wind and
torrent of rain that, after scowling out into the darkness for
a minute, he slammed the door and came in, pulling off his
boots and sitting sulkily down again by the fire.

David roused himself to wash the dishes. So much he
could do toward clearing up. "I suppose I shall have to get
some one to fix up here," he said, looking hopelessly
around.

"What for?" said the irritable Joe. "If she don't like it, let
her go home. We don't want her, anyway. There's other
rooms in the house besides this; she can stay in them and
keep out of here. As for eating, let her get her meals over to
Barnes'. We can't cook for her, and 'tain't likely she knows
how herself."

"Look here, Joe," said the elder brother turning slowly
around, the cold greasy dishwater dripping from his great
red hands; "you are hard on her. She never knew she wasn't
Aunt Ruth's own child until after Aunt Ruth died, three
weeks ago. It was part of the agreement, you know. Father
thought it best for her to have a mother. Aunt Ruth said she
wanted her to grow up loving her as her own mother. I
never could quite see how it was right and fair not to tell
her, but Aunt Ruth made a good deal of it, and father
thought it would be just as well, for she would have
everything money could buy—you know Uncle Hiram was
pretty rich awhile before he died, until he lost a good deal
in a failure of some kind. She was a pretty little thing when
I saw her."

Here the dishwasher folded his arms and leaned back
against the sink. "You know father sent me there with a
message the year before he died, and he told me not to tell
any one who I was, but Aunt Ruth. I wasn't to let Ruth
know I belonged to her, if I should happen to see her,
because he said she had never even heard of me. I didn't

kind of like the idea, then, for it seemed as though she would feel ashamed of me if she knew I belonged to her, and I went there feeling all out of patience with a girl that was letting herself be fooled in that way; but you know she was a baby only a few days old when she went there, and how was it her fault?

"Besides, I don't believe they brought her up near so stuck up as I thought, for while I waited in the great big hallway she came flying down the stairs just like a robin, and asked me to please sit down till her mother could come. Then I heard some one call her Ruth, and so I knew who she was, and she answered, yes, she was coming, and went away. But before she went she smiled at me, and said it was a cold morning outside. It seemed sort of funny to think she was my own sister, and if mother hadn't died, or things hadn't turned out as they did, she would have been here instead of there, and like as not she'd have been washing these very dishes now, instead of my doing it."

"Well, you needn't count on getting her to do them to-morrow night, Dave, I can tell you. City girls never do those things. They're afraid of their hands. She'll be a precious nuisance; that's what I think. How old is she now?"

"'Bout a year and a half younger than you."

"H'm, they're always silly at that age. I wouldn't let her come if I was you, Dave."

"She's on her way by this time, so I can't help it," said the elder brother imperturbably. He stood still, the dishcloth in his hand, thinking of the bright little figure in blue and white, with flying golden hair, that had tripped down the stairs and given him the chair so graciously; and then he looked hopelessly about that room and wished he knew how to make it pleasant for her coming.

The brothers did not sleep well that night. David had an uncomfortable sense of responsibility upon him which he was in nowise able to discharge, much as if an elephant had suddenly found himself inheritor of the proverbial china shop. What he, a quiet, awkward farm boy, was to do with a full-fledged young lady sister, fresh from the city, was more than he could fathom.

He arose early the next morning, as was his custom, and went about his usual duties, or "chores," as he called them, with the problem still unsolved. Joe, meantime, was angry and dismayed. Though it was by no means a pleasant day for such work, he announced his intention of "gettin' the timber off that upper wood lot," which was at some distance from the farm proper, and would require all day. Therefore, he took a cold bite in his pocket, shouldered his axe, and was off before David had realized that he would be left alone to receive their guest, when he had entertained some thought of sending his younger brother to the train to meet her.

Her letter had been a brief one and to the point, with an undertone of eager sisterly love and longing for some one who belonged to her, in her loneliness; and this on the second reading reached her elder brother's heart and made him wish that their father was alive to give her what she wanted. He felt himself utterly unable to do so.

Out of deference to the expected guest he forebore, as his brother had done, to eat his breakfast from dishes, this morning, but took a cold hurried lunch from the pantry shelf. He tried to think as he ate, what his father would have done, but it seemed impossible; and again, as he had done many times before, he decided that it was a bad business to give up one's children to some one else to bring up, even though that one was the rich wife of your own brother and the mother of the child was dead. Doubtless Ruth had had a much pleasanter life in her luxurious city home than she would have had in the old farmhouse with only her rough father and brothers and old Aunt Nancy for company; but now that those who had guarded her life were taken away, what was to become of her? He gave it up and went out to his work again. There was a certain amount of work about the farm that must be done every day no matter what happened, and he was glad that it was so.

When this had been done he harnessed the old horse to the light spring wagon; smoothed his hair; put on a coat—an unusual addition, except in cold weather, for merely a ride to the village—and drove slowly toward the town and the railway station. It did not occur to him to put on a collar. That was an amount of dressing not indulged in, except on Sundays or extraordinary occasions, by the people with whom he had been accustomed to associate. Half-way to the village, and almost overcome with his sense of the nearness of the station and his expected guest, he halted the old horse suddenly, thinking of his collarless condition, and half turned the wagon around again toward home to make it good; but the color mounted to his cheek as he remembered the crowd that would be at the station—always, to meet every train—and he turned the astonished horse's nose back again with a jerk, going on more rapidly toward the station.

It was bad enough to have the gaze of those curious eyes, and the ridicule of the lazy tongues leveled upon him while he met his city sister, without having a collar on. A collar was always an embarrassment to him, and for that reason alone he had several times meditated giving up going to church on Sabbath mornings since his father's death; but the power of habit and his father's steady example still held him to that when there was no reasonable excuse.

There was no need to fasten Old Gray lest she should be afraid of the cars. She was not afraid of anything in this world now, and so David drew up in front of the long, low station, that had done duty for many a year, and swinging one leg over the wheel to the platform, which was about on a level with the floor of the wagon, he sat surveying the crowd of loafers assembled for their daily excitement of watching the New York train come in.

He had sat in just that way many a time waiting, with no particular end in view except that he happened to be there at that time, and it was interesting to see who would come and who would go. Now it was different, and the commotion in his breast made him wish himself at home. In a few minutes all the eyes would be leveled at him, and the wonder and surprise would be about him and his sister. How strange that word "sister" sounded to him, anyway! He had never really thought of her as belonging to him, and he was conscious of almost wishing at that moment that she did not. Then the distant whistle sounded, and he lounged out of the wagon and stood waiting with the others.

There were not many passengers to alight at the small village. One or two drummers, a merchant returned from a trip to New York, and an old grandmother come to visit a swarm of grandchildren, who were all down to meet her.

After these, preceded by an obsequious porter from the parlor car carrying her immaculate luggage, came a dainty young woman. She had golden hair, which escaped from the imprisoning shell combs into little sunshiny rings about her temples, and her eyes were large and blue, keen and bright, yet tender. David's eyes were blue too. She was dressed all in brown, very plainly indeed, and yet it seemed extraordinary to Summerton, for they seldom saw a dress or a coat so perfectly made. The oldest grandchild, who was herself approaching young womanhood, wondered what in the world there was about her simple hat that looked "so awfully stylish," and began studying it, if perchance her last year's might be made to serve in somewhat similar fashion.

Ruth Benedict walked the entire length of the platform to the dingy station, and had her baggage deposited on the grimy, much-cut benches, paid the porter a shining quarter, and then looked about for her brother. She had not discovered him in her walk down the platform.

He meantime had been sure that this was his sister, but he could not bring himself to speak while that important black porter was in attendance, and the blood mounted in rich waves to his face as she passed him. He turned his eyes the other way lest she should divine who he was and speak. She, meanwhile, knew not what manner of person to look for. She knew he was a farmer, but at least she expected a collar, and so she passed him by at the first glance; but something in his face, as he turned during the bustle of the moving train to slip around to where she stood, attracted her attention, and she looked again, a smile lighting up her sweet face, the same smile he remembered of her childhood. That smile enabled him to get over the embarrassing ground between them and reach her side without the painful interval he had expected.

"Are you David?" she asked eagerly before he reached her, and then without waiting to give him time for more than a nod in reply, she put up her pretty lips and threw one arm simply and gracefully about his neck and kissed him.

David felt as though he never had been through such a trying experience in his life, and would rather be killed outright than go through it again. He was painfully conscious of the watching eyes. He dared not turn toward them to see what they thought. He had a faint hope that the outgoing train had attracted the attention of most of them, but it was only a hope. Ellen Amelia Haskins, the eldest granddaughter, was taking notes with undivided attention, and she immediately began to give abroad news.

All Summerton knew that away back in the years somewhere there had been a baby sister in the Benedict household, who had been adopted by the father's rich brother, but they had almost forgotten the story. Now, even as David hurried his sister to the waiting wagon behind the station, it was revived, as Ellen Amelia's excited voice proclaimed in tones which might have been heard by the occupants of the wagon, had it not been for their absorption in themselves, that she "just betted Dave Ben'dic's sister had come to make a visit, 'cause she kissed him," and she added, "and he looked real kind of handsome and majestic bendin' down to encircle her slight form," and she giggled softly to herself and remembered the last week's story in the "Fireside Companion."

David Benedict did not stay to hear what might be said. He whipped up Old Gray as that animal could not remember to have been whipped since the last hired man got married and went away, and the wagon was soon hidden down the road behind the great elm trees at the corner.

CHAPTER II

Ruth felt not a little dismayed to find her brother present so unpolished an appearance, but she tried to remember that it was early morning and she knew nothing of farm life. Doubtless he had left his morning work to meet her. Her artist's eye decided that he was handsome in spite of no collar. The Summerton girls had not known enough to discover this as yet. They looked more upon the outward adornment than upon the true man, and could not recognize him except accompanied by well-oiled hair, flashy necktie, and perfumery on his handkerchief, which was to their nostrils a perfect cover for a barnyard odor on the boots or onions on the breath. Besides, David was shy and awkward and never gave them any attention. Joseph, the younger brother, was much more to their liking.

Ruth, sitting beside her silent brother trying to get acquainted and feel her way into his heart, felt her own sink in a lonely, homesick way, and began to long again for the dear ones who were gone, whose constant care had made her life so bright. But she turned her attention to the country about, frankly admiring the river views and the waving fields of grain. It was indeed a lovely drive to the Benedict farmhouse, and Ruth began to dread its ending.

She had been curious to know what her old home was like, but something began to warn her that she would be disappointed. She had read of and seen some beautiful old farmhouses, painted white with green blinds and with lofty columns supporting the front roof. She had imagined that her home would be something like this with a velvety lawn in front and a dainty white hen here and there walking carefully over it, while at the back there would be a row of shining milk cans, and some peaceful cows musing not far off. That was her idea of farmhouses in general. Now she began to feel that there might be some mistake about their all being like that. Since they had left the station they had passed no such homes.

They presently came in sight of some spacious barns, well coated with red, and a little farther over a large old-fashioned rambling house, of color so dingy that no one might tell what it had been in former days. The front part of the house seemed to be closed, at least the weather-beaten blinds were shut. There was no smoke coming from any chimney except the back one. The front porch had a fallen-down appearance, which gave an expression to the house of a person with the corners of his mouth drooped sadly. This porch was an old-fashioned "stoop," with a narrow seat on either side too, instead of a wide, airy piazza stretched across the front of the house. The front dooryard was overgrown with tall grass and a few straggling pinks and bachelor's buttons here and there, while the rose and lilac bushes had tangled their branches across the path to the steps, according to their own sweet will.

Ruth wondered idly how the people could ever reach the front door, and felt sad at the air of abandonment and desolation. Then she saw Old Gray turn in at the great unpainted gate of many bars, and knew that she was at home. Somehow the tears were very near her eyes, but she bravely pressed them back and tried to be cheery and find something to admire. Strangely enough the old flat stone in front of the worn, much-chipped old green kitchen door with the quaint brass knob was the first thing that caught her eye.

"What a beautiful flat stone that would have been to play on when I was a little girl," she said impulsively, feeling that she must say something or break down; and then she realized what a silly remark that was to make. But some One wiser than herself was guiding her words that day. She could not have said anything that would so have warmed David's heart to his sister as that. He had a feeling that she must of course consider her life and her bringing-up as above that of her brothers, and when she actually spoke as if she would have liked to share their childhood joys in the old plain home, he felt as if he loved her at once. The old flat stone was dear to him for memory's sake. He could even remember so far back as when he used to sit on it, in his little gingham apron, and his mother would come to the door and give him a large piece of warm gingerbread, standing there a minute to watch his enjoyment as he ate, and saying in soft tones, "Mother's dear little boy."

His heart was so soft over Ruth's words that when he awkwardly helped her out of the wagon he had an impulse to kiss her. He restrained it, of course. All his life training since his mother died had been to restrain any such sentimental impulses as that, but the impulse had made his heart warm, nevertheless. It is a pity he did not give way to that impulse, for Ruth, suddenly ushered into that dreary kitchen, and left alone with the injunction to sit down and rest herself until her brother put out the horse, felt such a rush of desolation come upon her as almost overpowered her.

She sat down in Aunt Nancy's old rocking chair and buried her face in her hands. What did it all mean? Was there nobody left who cared for her? Did her brother not know what to do with her? Was she an unwelcome guest? That had not occurred to her before. Now it brought a sickening loneliness. She had been rash, after all, as her old lawyer friend had told her, in rushing off to brothers she did not know without any warning to them or any chance to hear from them. Yet she had thought when she prayed to be guided that her direction had been to come here. Could it be that she was mistaken? Perhaps her own desire for the love of some one who belonged to her had made her mistake her desires for God's guidance! Then came another thought. Perhaps he had wanted her to come here after all, and though there might not be comfort for her, still he might intend that there was something she could do for her brothers. Perhaps they did not know Jesus Christ.

Her heart went out in great longing for them. She wanted to be sure that they were Christians. If they were Christians, then surely there would be a tie between them even stronger than blood. If they were not, then she must stay and try to lead them to Christ. She slipped down on her knees beside the old calico-cushioned rocker and asked her Saviour for help and guidance, promising to try to do whatever he wanted her to do here in this home, no matter how hard it might seem, if he would only stay with her and help her. Then she got up, resolutely wiped away the tears, and looked about her. She forced herself to take in every detail of that room. It did not take long, for the kitchen had not much in it. She even walked over and looked at the chromos of bright red and pink roses framed in pine cones, hanging on each side of the little high clock shelf, and took in the fact of the smoky kerosene lamp, realizing that there would be no gas in this house.

Then with a glance out of the window, to make sure David was not at the door, she went over to the pantry with swift determination. David had told her during the drive that Aunt Nancy was dead, and that they were living alone, and she began to wonder how they lived. Did they board, or what? She stood in the door in wonder. The great piece of ham, the half-loaf of bread, the broken cheese, and bag of crackers told a pitiful tale to her. She applied the tip of her nose to the baker's bread, and then straightened up suddenly with an involuntary "Ugh!"

Something of her amazement, disgust, and pity, mingled, must have been in her face as she turned at a slight sound behind her and saw her elder brother standing hopelessly in the door. He would not willingly have had her see that pantry. He had fixed it all, out in the barn, while he unharnessed Old Gray. He would go right over to the Barneses and take board for his sister, and then he and Joe could go over and call upon her often and keep her from being lonely. The old house was no place for her, and of course she could not eat there. It was all well enough for him and Joe to get along on anything, but such a dainty bit of flesh and blood as their sister must have better fare. Accordingly he had stopped in the process of unharnessing and come into the house to tell Ruth his plan for her and ask if she would like to ride over there with him at once, and have him take her trunk over with them.

Shame filled his face at sight of her discovery of his awkward attempts at housekeeping. He would have resented her going to look in that pantry if she had not been his sister, and even as it was a kind of anger began to rise in his heart, and he would soon have been ready to say with pride, "It's none of her business how we live. She has no right to poke and pry into things." But Ruth turned with tears in her eyes and threw her arms about her brother.

"Oh, you poor, dear David!" she exclaimed. "How you have needed me! And you have been trying to keep house for yourselves. I see it all now. I am so glad I have come. I was afraid at first that you did not want me; but you do need me, don't you? Tell me you do, for I am so hungry to be loved and needed. And I'm glad I came to make you comfortable. You are glad too, aren't you?" and then she hid her face in his coat and cried.

He stood helpless before her tears. He was really frightened. He had never seen a woman cry before, and began to wonder if he ought to go for a doctor; but just when he felt the most helpless, she lifted a face all smiling through her tears and kissed him.

Somehow David felt as though she were more really his

sister after that, as if in some subtle way a sympathy had been established between them. He was willing to let her do anything she wanted to now, and he felt as if he would stand up for her against the world. He made her sit down while he explained his plan for her boarding, but she only laughed a silvery laugh.

"Now, David, my dear brother, did you suppose I came here to be a summer boarder with the Barneses, and have you come and call on me occasionally? No, indeed! The Barneses are well enough in their places, and I shall be glad enough to call on them some time in the future if they don't see fit to call on me first; but just now I have not time. There's a great deal to be done in this house before dinner. I came here to find my brothers, and I find they need me a great deal more than I supposed they did. What time do you usually have dinner? and where is my other brother?"

"But what do you mean to do?" he asked helplessly. "You can't eat here," and he looked about on the kitchen which seemed, with her bright presence in it, to have a great many more defects for a kitchen than he had ever seen before.

"Why can't I eat here, I should like to know?" asked the sister brightly; "I guess I can if you can. But I must go to work, or there won't be anything fit for either of us to eat. That bread in there is very sour. I wonder you haven't got the dyspepsia. Do you mean to say that you and Joseph have been living in this way on such food as that ever since Aunt Nancy died? You poor dear! Now, let's get to work. We must have everything nice and cheery before Joseph comes. That fire looks as if it was almost discouraged. Can you make up a good fire for me? I'll have to learn how to operate that stove; our range was different. But if you'll fix the fire real rousing and bright, and bring my trunk in and unstrap it, I'll fix things up all right. Where is my room to be?"

David did not know how to answer all her questions. He felt that some one had come at last who knew what she wanted and his part was only to obey, so in bewilderment he brought her trunk in and deposited it in the room she selected. She had resolutely refrained from looking about her much as she went through a portion of the rest of the house. The kitchen was enough to deal with at first, and too much dreariness would take away her self-control. A room with four walls and a bed was an absolute necessity, and beyond that she would not see anything until she had done all she could in the kitchen. She kept her eyes strictly upon their work, while she rapidly took off her traveling dress and donned a neat gingham, enveloping herself in a large kitchen apron. It was the apron she and her dear adopted mother had made for her to use in cooking school a year before, and the tears came to her eyes as she fastened it, with the memory of all the sweet words and looks sewed into the garment with the dainty stitches.

"Darling, this apron will be with you in many a time of need and stand you in good stead," he mother had said. "You may find times when you will prize it more than any pretty dress you have. I hope this apron will wear to help you do great good and achieve great things in the culinary line." These had been that dear mother's laughing words as she handed her the finished garment. Ruth brushed the tears away and rushed down to the kitchen. There she found a bright fire roaring away in the stove, and David standing by it looking about in a dazed way as if he wondered what was coming next.

"Now the next thing is to find out what there is to work with," said the new housekeeper eagerly. "David, have you any yeast? I want to set some bread the first thing."

"Yeast?" said David; "no, we haven't had any yeast in the house since Aunt Nancy died."

"And David, where do you keep the baking powder and the salt?" called Ruth from the pantry.

"You will certainly have to go to the grocery before we can have dinner," she said, emerging from her investigations. "If you will go to market I will write down a list of things we need right away. I'll try to have some kind of lunch for you when you come back. I cannot make bread without yeast and I cannot make biscuit without baking powder."

David brought the potatoes from the cellar and saddling the horse made ready to go on his errand, not much relishing the thought of the sensation he would make, returning to market with a basket so soon after the arrival of his sister. However, he hastened away, and Ruth locked the door securely and went to work. It must be confessed that while she was a brave girl in the city, here in the country she felt the least bit timid at being left alone in this strange house for an hour. Who could tell what awful tramp might come? However, she made up her mind to be so busy she would not think of it, and sending up a prayer for help, she went in search of a knife to peel the potatoes. It was fortunate that there' was so much to be done, else the desolation of the whole home, without even an attempt at comfort, might have made her heart fail her, till she must have returned to the lovely home in the city she had left behind for love of two unknown brothers.

The work of setting the table did not progress so rapidly as it might have done under other circumstances. In the first place, the table received a thorough scrubbing, as the two young men had not thought it necessary to wipe off any stray molasses drops for many a day. They had supposed a table was an article of furniture that would clean itself in some way. Then a table-cloth must be searched for. Napkins she did not find, but supplied them from a few she had brought in her trunk. She also placed in the center of the table a daintily embroidered bit of linen, and then after surveying the general effect, decided that it did not fit into its present surroundings. There would need to be great changes made in that room before the doily would belong there. In fact, it seemed to be incongruous with the immediate proximity of the cook-stove.

Ruth wondered furtively if there was not a dining room in the house, but forbore to reflect much on the subject, resolving to consider the question at her earliest convenience. Then the dishes came in for investigation. They were thick, and some were cracked and ill-smelling. Up on the top shelf were a few bits of rare old china, perhaps some of her own mother's wedding gifts. She wiped these off tenderly, and washed such of the others as she considered necessary to the meal, not being entirely satisfied with the result of David's dish-washing. The table at last was set. She stood back and surveyed it a moment. It did not look much like the elegant table to which she was used to sitting down daily, with its fine linen, solid silver, cut glass, and china, and the various forks and spoons considered necessary in polite society for the different courses, but it was neat and inviting looking.

Next she turned her attention to the menu. There was not much variety available until David returned from the store. There were eggs and potatoes, and cheese and crackers, and plenty of milk and cream, and—yes, there was the ham. She despised the very thought of ham herself; but probably David liked it, and she would sacrifice her feelings and cook him a bit, for he must be very hungry after all these months of his own housekeeping. So she toasted some of the cheese, after grating it on the crackers, creamed the potatoes, made a puffy brown omelet, and crisped a bit of the ham by way of decoration. She had everything ready, and was just making a cup of most delicious coffee as her brother rode into the yard.

To understand David's feelings when he opened that kitchen door and saw that table, you must be a man and keep house for yourself for a few months. In spite of the fact that many of the so-considered necessities of a good meal were missing, and that there was no bread, the young man considered it the best meal he had eaten in years. In fact, he was not sure but things tasted better than they ever had in his life, except perhaps that gingerbread his mother used to make.

He told Ruth so, and her eyes grew bright and her heart beat fast with the pleasure. She felt well rewarded for her efforts. She resolved also, if possible, to have some warm gingerbread very soon for David, and meanwhile she started some bread with the yeast which he had brought, which she was sure would be delicious. She was an expert in the art of bread-making.

But the work of regulating that kitchen was by no means more than begun, so though she had been somewhat weary before lunch, she went to work again as soon as David had gone out.

The washing of the dishes proved to be not so rapid as she had intended it to be. She unceremoniously dumped the ill-smelling dish-cloth into the fire, and washed all the others out in scalding water before beginning. Then when the dishes stood shining from their bath in boiling water, dry already, because allowed to drain scientifically, she attacked the china closet. It would never do to put the dishes back into such a state of hubbub. She stood a moment reflecting, and then put all the remaining dishes into the hot suds and washed off the shelves. Of course boys could not be expected to know how to clean house, and evidently this one had not been cleaned since Aunt Nancy's death.

When that cupboard was cleaned and the dishes in shining order, her excitement had reached such a point that she felt she could not rest till the mantel and clock shelf were also cleaned of their rubbish. And it was while she was engaged in cleaning off that same mantel that she came on something which made her heart almost stop in dismay, and for an instant she felt as though she must turn and flee out of that house and away from that place as fast as she could go.

CHAPTER III

It was not dirt, nor insects, nor a revolver, nor a serpent, nor a whiskey bottle. It was only David's black, ugly pipe. But it gave her such a throb of disappointment and disgust, that she found herself trembling and weak, and obliged to sit down to regain her strength.

She had been brought up very rigidly with regard to the questions of temperance and tobacco. Her adopted father had never smoked, and her adopted mother had taught her that it was a vile and filthy habit, not only making the persons addicted to it disagreeable nuisances, but making them dishonor and defile their bodies, the temples of the Holy Ghost. Ruth had thought and read a great deal on the subject. She had tried and succeeded in turning every member of her large Sunday-school class of boys against the habit. She had been an enthusiastic member of a club of young Christian women who were banded together pledged not to select their friends from among the young men who smoked, and never to consent to walk the street with a young man who was smoking. It was in her eyes a disgrace. Now to find that one of her own brothers— perhaps both—smoked, was terrible. The blood rolled in waves over her fair neck and cheeks at the disappointment and shame and disgrace of it, and the tears would come in spite of herself. To have her brother wear no collar had been a surprise, but a collar was not a vital matter. This black pipe was.

It required a moment's prayer before she could calmly return to that mantelpiece. What to do with that pipe was a serious question. She hated to touch it. She had never touched a pipe or cigar in her life. After some consideration she got a newspaper, and by help of a burnt match, shoved the pipe to the paper and laid it on the floor in the corner where no harm could come to it. She would have liked to destroy it, but she knew that would do more harm than good, and besides, it was not hers, and she had no right to do any such thing. However, during the remainder of her work that afternoon, she was reflecting on what course she should pursue with regard to it, and many were the prayers for guidance that she sent up.

As she worked and prayed her heart grew calmer. Perhaps, after all, it might have belonged to some hired man; she would try to think so for the sake of her own peace of mind, at least for this afternoon. Happily it did not occur to her to think that it might have belonged to her own father. There was too much to be done for her to dwell upon details. She had set her heart upon having a cheerful room for her two brothers to come home to that evening.

She viewed the contents of the pantry with utmost scorn, and doubtless gave those two young men more pity than they deserved, for they had fed upon such fare so long that it was not the hardship to them to eat such things that it would have been to their dainty sister.

It may have been her compassion which led her to plan a rather elaborate supper, considering her recent arrival and the state of the kitchen. For though she was somewhat weary with traveling, her nerves were keyed high to

accomplish what she purposed. She arose from her knees
where she had been washing the oilcloth under the stove
by the door, and stood thinking a moment. Then she shut
her lips firmly and rapidly went to work making a custard
and some gingerbread. After all it did not take long to do
things when one had the will. When they were in the oven
she went back to her housecleaning with renewed energy.
Given nerves, a quick brain, and a pair of deft and willing
hands, great changes can be wrought in the course of an
afternoon. David came to the door once, from his work, to
ask if she was lonesome and if there was anything he could
do, and looked about helplessly on her work and went away
bewildered. He had a dim idea that this was not exactly the
way to entertain a city young lady on the first day of her
arrival; but she seemed determined, and what could he do?

She had promised to call him if she needed anything, and
by and by she did open the door and ask for his help a
moment. She had ventured into one of the unused rooms
on the ground floor; it seemed to have been a bedroom, and
she called David to know if he would mind if she took the
large rug made of rag carpet from the center of that room to
spread in the kitchen. He was entirely willing she should
do anything she pleased in the house, and awkwardly
helped her to shake it and arrange it under the kitchen
table. Then he stood a moment irresolutely by the door
wishing he knew something else to do, but finally went out.

Ruth worked hard. It grew late before things were in the
order that pleased her fastidious taste. It was growing dark.
She wondered why Joseph did not come, and yet was glad
he delayed, and finally she stood a moment and gave a last
look at her completed task before she slipped away to her
room to smooth her hair and remove the traces of toil from
face and hands and dress.

Everything was immaculately clean. The lamp chimney
shone with cleanliness, and the light glowed through a
rose-colored crape paper shade she had hastily improvised
from a roll of paper in her trunk. The table was set decently
and in order, as nearly like that of her city home as she
could compass with her present material. There was a plate
of delicate, puffy white biscuits suggestively near the
golden honeycomb David had brought in that afternoon

from one of the hives. The bread had been started so late that it was just now beginning to send out a wholesome odor from the oven, so the biscuits had been made in a desperate rush at the last, when the cook found that the bread could not possibly get itself ready for supper. The roasted potatoes had their brown coats just ready to crack open, and covered closely on the back of the stove was the meat, which had been gently simmering all the afternoon, till it was tender as could be, and browned to a nicety with a savory gravy about it. The coffee gave a hint of its aroma also.

It is necessary to understand the details of this first supper of the united family in the old home, that you may be able to enter into the feelings of the young man who entered by the back kitchen door not two minutes after the fairy who had wrought all this change had departed to her toilet.

Joseph had toiled hard all day doing work that might have waited until his brother could help him. Gloomily he had eaten his dry, solitary lunch on a log, glaring at the brightness of the day with a fierce expression of dislike. Occasionally he wondered how David was managing at home. That he would get rid of the unwelcome young lady sister in some comfortable way Joseph never doubted. The old farmhouse was no place for her. What could they do with her there? David would either send her back where she came from, or get her a place to board near by at some house in the village until something could be done with her.

Life had been hard and disagreeable enough before without this rude breaking in upon the poor comfort of their solitude. Joseph felt a fierce rebellion at the unfairness of Providence in so ordering things, and said to himself two or three times that it wasn't of much account to live anyway. He had indeed reached a stage of his life where he was dissatisfied with his surroundings. He did not know that his restless, unhappy feelings came from a longing for a higher, richer life. He had been brought up to this; how should he know there was anything better? To work hard all day he did not grudge, and in a way he enjoyed the evenings he occasionally spent in the down-town grocery; but David

kept a pretty steady watch on his evenings, and the ones he
spent in the village were not so many as he desired. No
other avenue of amusement was at this time open to him,
unless indeed he went to church. There had been a time
when he haunted the church steps during the progress of
any meeting or entertainment or supper, but since he had
outgrown his Sunday-school class at the time of the death of
his first and only teacher he had dropped that amusement.

Life on the whole looked dull and uninteresting to him.
He had fierce, wild thoughts of plunging off into a city
somewhere and doing as he pleased, though that was
impracticable, for he had no money aside from his share in
the farm, and his early training had at least given him a
horror of tramps. He worked doggedly on in the gathering
shadows until the darkness put a stop to his labors. Even
then he was as slow as possible about gathering up his tools.
He would not go home until every possible chance of
seeing the intruder was gone. David would surely have
disposed of her by this time, he thought, as he dragged his
weary, unwilling feet homeward.

He was growing very hungry, for his hasty lunch had
been meager and his day long and filled with hard work.
Fortunately he did not approach the house from the side
where the kitchen windows shone bright in the rosy light of
crape paper and clean window-glass, else he might have
disappeared into the darkness again, who knows where?
and for how long, who can tell? Instead, so sure was he that
David had managed things somehow by this time, that he
came in as usual through the back kitchen door. He paused
in the shed a moment before he laid down his heavy tools,
and listened. He heard nothing. All was quiet. Only the
sound of David's voice in the cowyard not far off, as he
spoke to the cow he was milking, and the ring of the milk-
pails as something hit against one of them.

The light under the crack in the kitchen door guided him
as he hung up his old coat and put away his tools. He was
glad David had lit the lamp before he went out. Strange he
was so late at milking, but probably he had been so busy
getting their sister off somewhere that he had only just
come home. Now that she was fully disposed of, he thought
to himself perhaps it had been a little mean of him to go off

and leave everything to David in that way. Not that he would do otherwise now, but he felt a little compassion for his brother. It was the penalty he paid for being the elder brother.

Then Joseph pulled off his heavy, mud-covered boots, set them by the shed door, and walked on to where the crack showed a little cheer. He threw open the door and stepped in. Coming from the darkness into the unusual brilliancy of the room blinded him, and for a moment he stood winking and trying to see. Gradually the changed room dawned upon him one corner at a time. He noticed everything, even to the details of the delicious supper prepared. He was dazed. Could he have made a mistake in the dark and gone out of his way into another man's house? Was he in a dream? What was the matter? Had David gone and hired a housekeeper, and was the obnoxious sister then in the house, and were they waiting supper for him?

Before he had time to think further or even to move from where he was standing, the opposite door opened and the sister came in. She was a trim little figure in a plain, dark-blue dress and a white apron. She saw her brother at once. Some women are gifted with being able to read men at a glance. Perhaps too, some words that David had spoken, or more, the words he had not spoken, about this brother, had helped her to know what to expect in him, and she had made up her mind to win him if possible. Her greeting was as sensible and sweet and winning as could be desired by any brother, no matter how crusty he was feeling.

"Oh, this is Joseph, isn't it? I'm so glad you've come, for supper is all ready, and the potatoes are horrid if they are not eaten the minute they are ready." And she reached up and kissed the bewildered, embarrassed, uncomfortable young man just as if she had been accustomed to kissing him every day all the years of her life.

He was painfully conscious of his old brown jean shirt and his stockinged feet, especially as the weekly darning had been neglected for many a long week. But she, with a cultured woman's instinct, understood his embarrassment and covered it by cheerily bustling about at her supper, telling him to hurry and get his hands washed, and asking if she could not find his slippers for him. David came in just then, the full brightness of the room bursting upon him for the first time, and his heart leaped with a new kind of joy he had not imagined was possible. Was it going to be a happy thing after all to have this high-bred sister live with them? Was it possible there was in the world for them as much brightness as this kitchen contained, to be lived in every day in the week, all the year around? He had supposed it was only rich city people who had things so kind of comfortable and cheery looking.

Then presently they sat down to that supper table. The meat and potatoes vanished rapidly, for the two young men were hungry. Only the cook did not partake very freely, but her nerves were too highly strung, and she was too weary to eat much. The Benedict boys discovered that their sister could cook. She was so lately the pupil of a famous cooking school that it had been easier for her to prepare this somewhat elaborate repast under the circumstances, than it would have been for most city girls who had indeed been taught to cook, but who had not had the opportunities for every-day practice which her wise foster-mother had given her. So Ruth thanked God for her ability to cook as she watched the great pile of puffy biscuits disappear rapidly. For the brothers did justice to the supper, the like of which they seemed never to have tasted before.

There were embarrassments connected with the meal, and Ruth was glad that they were hungry, in order that they should not feel quite so awkward. Instinctively she felt that she was on sufferance with her younger brother, and perhaps to some extent with the elder also. She dared not stop to think of it, or she would have broken down and cried. It seemed too dreadful to have come all this way to find brotherly love, and to be all alone in the world, and then to find that one was not wanted. Her better sense told her that she was needed there, and some heavenly influence seemed to say God had a work for her. She tried to remember that she had but just come, and they did not know her nor know what to do with her.

She must make a place for herself in their hearts first. She must at least show them what she was and had to give them, and then if they did not want her she could go away; and so she put aside the pride which kept coming up to trouble her at the thought that she was not wanted, and

calling to her aid all those winning ways that were hers by
nature, as well as of grace, she set herself to win her
brother Joseph. With glowing cheeks and bright eyes,
looking first at one and then the other brother, and with
well-chosen, pleasant words she told bright bits of things
that had occurred on her journey. She made them laugh
several times, which was a great help.

They forgot for the moment that she was city bred, and
that they must have a care for the way they managed their
forks, articles which had sorely oppressed them during the
beginning of the meal, for Aunt Nancy's training in the table
etiquette had seldom included the use of the fork in
preference to the knife. David even ventured to respond to
her bright talk occasionally, and secretly voted her unusually jolly for a girl. Joseph seemed silent, almost shy,
watching the new sister furtively, enjoying the good cheer,
but wearing an air that said as plainly as words could have
said, "I'm not to be fooled into liking you by all this."

At last the evening was over, the preparations made for
the morning meal, and the weary young woman was at
leisure to rest and think.

It was in the quiet of the bare room upstairs, whose dull
ingrain carpet, helped out on one end by a breadth of faded
rag carpet, seemed to intensify the dreariness. The only
other furniture was a plain old bed of the kind known as a
cord bedstead, two wooden chairs, a wooden table, with
wash-bowl and pitcher, and a small, cheap, gilt-framed
looking-glass hanging over it. There was a closet in the
room, and a green paper shade at the window, and the lamp
which she had brought up with her and deposited on a rude
wooden shelf over the chimney shed a dull, desolate light
over all. Ruth's tired nerves gave out at last, and she sat
down in the wooden chair by the door and cried. Why had
she come here after all? Her lawyer had begged her to
write and find out about things, or let him come on ahead
and survey the land. Her many friends, and her foster-
mother's as well, had opened their hearts and homes to her.
A dear old friend of her mother had offered to make her
home with Ruth, in case she preferred remaining in the old
home, which was hers to do with as she pleased. But she
had refused them all and had come here, stubbornly

perhaps, but feeling that it was what Christ would have her do. It was what her own father and mother would have had her do, as well as what would please the dear ones who had for so many years occupied the places of father and mother in her heart. Had it all been a mistake? Ought she to have waited? Did she then have no call from God to come? Should she have stayed in the city?

There were many things she might have done to feel that she was of use in the world. Not that she needed to earn her living, for she was amply provided for as far as money went, but she might have gone into city mission work. She could have given her time to church work. She was a graduate of a school for physical culture. She could have given some time to teaching and helping poor overworked girls to a better physical life, and so have led them step by step to a better spiritual life through this influence. She might have organized classes in cooking, or dressmaking, or millinery, among young women who were too poor to afford to go to the schools where such things are taught. She had delighted in all such things herself and was one of those people who can turn their hands to almost anything. The father and mother who now were gone had made it their pleasure to see that she had the best instruction in any line which seemed to please her. She thought now of the many words of praise she had received for this or that little service which she had performed well, and how others had envied her varied skill. She had not thought much of it then, because anything she tried to do always seemed easy to her. Now Satan came to tempt her with the thought that she ought not to bury these talents up here in the country, when they might be reaching hundreds, instead of just two young men who really did not want her to stay. Then something seemed to say: "But they are my brothers, and if I have any talents I can use them here as well as in the city. Jesus Christ knows what is best for me to do, and he will show me what I must do next. I will ask him."

She knelt beside the ugly bed and told all her troubles, asking that she might be guided in the way he would have her go; that she might be humble, and not seek to do work he did not want her to do; that the Lord would bless her brothers, and if possible give them some love for her. Then

she rose and went about her preparations for the night with
the tumult in her heart stayed. Even the creaking of the
cord bed did not serve to rouse the evil thoughts again,
though it certainly was not pleasant. She fell asleep
wondering whether she would always care about little
things and be so annoyed by them, and if eating with one's
knife and wearing no collar would be barriers of the true
love that ought to exist between brother and sister,
supposing that there was no way to get rid of these little
annoyances. She was distressed with herself beyond measure that she noticed these things. Why was it that she
noticed them so much more than if they had been in some
of her Sunday-school scholars? True, these men were her
own flesh and blood—her brothers. Yes, it was pride after
all. But the others were her own brothers and sisters in
Christ. She was God's, and he would take care of it all, she
thought; and then fell asleep.

CHAPTER IV

Joseph spoke but little at breakfast, and went off to work
soon after the meal was completed. David seemed to Ruth
much changed. He had had time to reflect and get himself
out of the maze of unexpected problems into which he had
been plunged by Ruth's letter and arrival. He showed great
kindness, even tenderness and thoughtfulness, with regard
to her comfort. He said at once that they must have some
help in the house, and spoke cheerfully about his desire to
have things bright and pleasant for her. He even went so far
as to tell her that he had never dreamed there could be so
much comfort in any home as she had brought to theirs
during the few short hours since her arrival.

Ruth flushed pink over his praise, for she recognized that
it had been hard for him to say these things, and that to

him, hardened and roughened by his outdoor work, she seemed a very dainty, fashionable creature, more to be looked at than used, and that, in a way, he was afraid of her. Still she felt that this feeling was wearing away with him and that they would presently be as frank and friendly as though they had always known one another. She decided that David was a true gentleman, and she divided the word into two parts when she said it softly to herself while she washed the dishes, and she put an emphasis on the word "gentle," with all its ancient, courtly, noble meaning. Yes, it was going to be very easy to love him as a brother, she felt. As for Joseph, he was very interesting, and she felt sure the love would come. No need to worry about that. They were brother and sister, and all the tenderness of that relationship would surely come by and by. Her troubles seemed to be lightened by the morning light and she felt more hopeful of the future, and thus fell to planning.

She had discovered in her talk with David that the idea of hired help had been a great bugbear to the brothers on account of the extreme familiarity with the family which all the Summerton girls who "lived out" expected. They dreaded it. David in particular seemed to stand in horror of having Eliza Barnes or Jane Myrtilla Fowler sitting at the table at every meal and speaking to him as "Dave Benedict." He had also tried in a helpless kind of way to explain to his sister how utterly unlike her these girls were and how incongruous it would be to see them sitting across the table from her. David had an innate delicacy about him which was more than mere worldly pride. Ruth laughed brightly at the idea that there would be anything out of the way in her eating at the same table with the said Jane Myrtilla if need be, but secretly she saw exactly how unwise it would be for them to try to have another element in their already mixed household. Matters must be simplified as much as possible if they were to find a common level for all three to live upon. It would not do to have a stranger always about who might possibly report to the entire town anything which was said at the table by any one of them. Ruth sat down perplexed. Something must be done. She must talk it over with David. The house needed cleaning. There would be hard work to which she was unaccustomed, which even if she felt competent to do might end by making her ill.

A bright idea suddenly occurred to her. Sally, the cook, of whom she had taken a sorrowful leave but four days before, had been in her foster-mother's family for twelve years. She had been rescued from a life of trouble and taken in by Mrs. Benedict, and she felt a gratitude which knew no bounds. She had clasped the young girl in her arms in a reverent kind of way as she bade her good-bye and said, "Yeh dear little thing, yeh! Miss Ruth, if ye'll jist say the word only one time and wroite me, I'll folly ye to the inds of the earth." Now, it was but four days since she had left and she was going to her sister's to stay till she had found a suitable place. Perhaps it was not too late to secure her. Ruth thought over all the possibilities, pictured Sally, used to large rooms, elegant furniture, and fine cooking, placed in the plain farmhouse, and decided what she would do. She would put the matter before her plainly and let her decide for herself. Ruth ran to the door and called David. He came quickly from the barnyard, where he was busy about some work, thinking to himself how very pleasant it was to have some one there to call him.

"David, isn't there some woman who will come in to clean house and go home to her meals for a few days? Or can we get along for a few days almost anyway, you know? I have a plan."

David thought a moment and finally decided on a good, strong colored woman who might be induced to go out by the day for a short time. Then Ruth unfolded her plan. David was somewhat dubious about introducing another unknown quantity into the household, but he was already beginning to have unbounded confidence in the young woman who was at the helm, so he gave his assent to her proposition. Ruth then went in to write Sally, while David prepared to "hitch up" and take the letter to the office.

After Ruth had dinner well under way she took a survey of the house, trying not to feel the chill of desolation as she entered one after another the great bare rooms. It made her shudder to feel the cold air that struck her even on this warm day in late summer as she opened the closed rooms. She threw open all the shutters and let the sunlight stream in from garret to cellar, even over the sacred haircloth furniture in the well-guarded "front room" which Aunt Nancy had carefully kept just as it had been when she came, and which, since the mother's death, had not been used. There was a wax cross with clambering, impossible flowers, under a glass globe on the marble-top table. There were several thread tidies in elaborate patterns on the haircloth chairs and sofa. The small box stove that was supposed to heat the room had a grim, leering effect, with a few cobwebs draped across its front. The yellow paper shades had stiff baskets of fruit pictured on them by way of decoration. The ingrain carpet was a bold attempt in crude reds and greens. Beside the glass globe on the center table, there was a large old-fashioned family Bible, and on it lay a red plush album with a looking-glass on the upper cover. It looked absurdly new and out of place amid the old-fashioned atmosphere of the room. It had been Aunt Nancy's purchase of a traveling agent for whom she felt sorry, and she had excused the unwonted extravagance by saying that "the woman needed help, and an album was a handy thing to have in the house, anyway." It was about the only luxury that Aunt Nancy had ever permitted herself to purchase in the whole of her lifetime, for she was of a saving disposition and had been brought up to economical habits.

There was a framed wreath of hair flowers under glass and there were some portraits on the wall, queer old-fashioned photographs and daguerreotypes in oval gilt, or frames of ancient pine cones and varnished coffee berries. The faces were faded and the hair and dress were of years before. It made them seem unreal. She wished she knew which were her own father and mother. It was so strange a position, hers, not to know the look of the faces of those who had been the source of her being. With a sinking sensation as if everything were slipping away from her, she reached out her hand to the Bible and read a part of the ninety-first Psalm:

"He that dwelleth in the secret place of the Most High shall abide under the shadow of the Almighty."

There came a warm thrill of joy to her heart, and it was as if her Master were speaking sweet words in her ear. Here was a message for her, and perhaps then she was wanted just here to live and work for him. If she were under the shadow of the Almighty, then surely no earthly shadows could ever fall upon her. It was hers to dwell in the secret place of the Most High if she would. She dropped upon her knees and asked for strength to dwell in that sweet secret place, and then again for guidance in this her much-hedged-about path.

Then Ruth deliberately sat her down to face the question of this bare, old-fashioned, unattractive house—almost uninhabitable it seemed to her refined taste, used to having everything arranged in comfort and harmony. In the first place, the furniture was not abundant, and what there was of the stiff, hard kind. How could she ever make this home attractive and comfortable for her brothers and pleasant for herself? Some of the furnishings had suffered through much use and some through neglect. The boys had not been careful housekeepers. How could they have been expected to be? The rag carpets were musty from long dampness and lack of air in the rooms. Ruth leaned her head against the hard haircloth back of the only arm-chair the room contained and closed her eyes, thinking wearily and hungrily of the soft carpets in rich harmonious colorings which covered all the floors of the home she had left, and of the easy-chairs and pretty curtains, and oh! all the pretty belongings of a comfortable, even luxurious, city home. She had helped to select many of those home furnishings, and her heart ached for a sight of them even after one day's absence. If she only dared bring them here, or some of them, but no—and here she sat erect. Was it possible that she was so bound down to mere things that she could not give them up for a time? Her brothers might be seriously offended if she should propose such a thing. Besides, she had put the house, furniture and all, into the hands of her agent to rent, and it was doubtless by this time rented. She had burnt her bridges behind her and must not look back.

David's step as he came through the hall from the kitchen in search of her roused her effectually. Had he returned so soon? She smiled as she heard his hesitating voice calling her by name. He scarcely felt that he had a right to speak to her so familiarly. A thought of sorrow that it should be so between own brother and sister came to her, and then she met him in the hall. He had brought her a letter, and as she took it a swift hope passed over her that maybe the Lord was calling her in other directions, that this letter contained an answer to her prayer. She tore it open hastily, while David stood awkwardly by, watching her, not knowing whether to go or stay, and half fearing himself that this letter might in some way snatch this new-found sister away from the gloomy house. He was beginning to be thoroughly glad she had come, even so soon.

But no, she found that there was no call for her to come back to the city. Instead, it was a letter from her agent saying he had an opportunity to rent the house at a good rate unfurnished, if only she were willing to have her goods stored. He desired to have an immediate reply as to whether she wished him to close this bargain or not, and awaited her orders concerning the furniture, in case she chose to have the articles taken from the house. He added in a postscript, that as they had so often talked over the matter of renting unfurnished, and decided it was best to rent furnished under the circumstances, he feared she might consider that he had taken a good deal upon himself to consider the matter at all; but the fact that the parties wishing to rent were such exceptionally fine tenants and willing to pay so high a rent had made him feel that possibly she would wish to change her mind.

Ruth read the letter through twice, standing there in the hall, and then sighed and wished she had some one to advise her, and so looking up met the clear admiring eyes of her brother fixed upon her. Why, to be sure! David could advise her, and was it possible this letter was in answer to prayer for guidance? Was it put in this way that it might be easy for her to bring her own furniture here without offense? Without more ado she handed the open letter to David and sank upon the lower step of the staircase saying, "There, David, tell me what to do?"

Surely God's Holy Spirit was guiding her every action. She could not have done anything which would have more completely and quickly won the heart of her brother than to thus freely and frankly give him her entire confidence. It changed the face of matters quite materially in his mind.

He was no longer being condescended to by an angel who had suddenly dropped down and might as suddenly and mysteriously disappear, but he was being looked up to as a brother by one who needed help, advice and protection. His heart warmed instantly with the thought that he would protect her always from everything just so long as she would let him. Then he read the letter. Ruth watched him as he read and decided again that he was handsome. There was a look and bearing about him which reminded her of his Uncle Hiram, who had been known to her all her life as her father. She wondered if he did not resemble their father.

David had a few questions to ask. Did she know what the rates of storage in the city were? Were they not very high? Was she attached to the furniture? Would she like to have some or perhaps all of it about her? Would it not make the old farmhouse seem more homelike to her? He had a dim recollection of rich blendings of color and soft luxury of which he had caught a glimpse on that memorable visit to his Aunt Ruth's, and a fine instinct told him that the haircloth furniture and rag carpets must be a decided contrast. Her face flushed and her eyes grew bright with eagerness as he asked this last question.

Oh, she would like to have her things here; might she? She clasped her hands in her eagerness and came and stood shyly by his side, looking up at him. Was he sure they would not be in the way? Would he mind having her put them in place of some of the present furniture? She did not want to do anything which would hurt his feelings or Joseph's, and if he was attached to the things he had been used to all his life, she was perfectly willing to live just as they did. (At this instant she made up her mind to really like that red and green ingrain in the parlor, if it was necessary in order to win her brothers' love.)

But David was in no wise offended. He was pleased at the idea of pleasing his sister. He knew their things were old and ugly and that probably if she had lived at home they would have been different; but Aunt Nancy's taste had been severely plain and they and their father had never thought, if they had known how, to get better. It did not matter anyway for just men, he said a little sadly and added: "But if you will stay and brighten up this old place for us—if you think you can stand it here and not get lonesome—why we'll do everything we can to make it pleasant for you. Joe is a little backward and he'll hold off for a few days, but he'll be acquainted with you in a little while, I guess, and then he won't seem quite so shy and sullen. He's not much but a boy anyway, you know, and he's always been inclined to be stubborn and have a way of his own. Maybe you can help make him different. I think father always had some idea of giving him a better education than could be got here, but things didn't go so well on the farm the last few years before he died and he couldn't. There was an old mortgage to pay off that kept him down all his life. But Joe and I paid the last cent on that two months ago, and I guess we can afford to paint the house and fix up a bit if you can stay with us. Things need to be different for a woman. Do you think you can stand it?" he asked wistfully.

"Of course I can," she answered, brushing away happy tears that his words had brought to her eyes. "David, I came here to find my brothers. I don't care about things. But I should like to bring the furniture here, for I think I could make it cozier for you and Joseph, and so if you are sure you don't mind I'll send for them to-day. But see here, David. I have not come here to be a burden on you. I am not penniless. I'm to bear my full share of everything if I stay."

It was then that David sat down upon the stairs beside his sister, and they had a talk that was more like what a talk between brother and sister should be than Ruth had been able to hope for. She went back to her dinner-getting and David to his farm-work, with happy, light hearts. Ruth sang about her work:

"Wherever he may guide me,
    No want shall turn me back,
My Shepherd is beside me,
    And nothing shall I lack.
His wisdom ever waketh,
    His sight is never dim,
He knows the way he taketh
    And I will walk with him."

CHAPTER V

Ruth stood in the doorway of her brother Joseph's room. She was trying to plan what changes she would make, and what articles from the city home should be put into it. She felt like a fairy about to wave her wand and bring beauty over everything, and she was as excited and happy over it all as a child with a new toy. The bare room had given her a heartache. That any human being should have so dreary a place for the only spot which he could call his own seemed very pitiful to her brought up amid a wealth of beauty. She would delight to make it all different. Joseph had been told that his sister was to bring her furniture to the home, but he had not seemed to manifest much interest in it. He was still very reticent with his sister, to say the least. Indeed, he sometimes seemed harder to win than ever. Ruth could not understand it. She wondered about it now, as she stood in the door of the desolate room and planned how she would change it. Perhaps David might have explained his brother's actions if he had thought about them at all. In a measure, Ruth herself had had a hand in bringing about a dogged determination to have nothing whatever to do with her more than was absolutely necessary. It had happened in this wise.

During the frank, free talk which Ruth had held with her brother David, after the arrival of that letter about her house and furniture, the brother and sister had opened their hearts to one another in a way that each would have thought impossible an hour before. Ruth, as the talk concluded, made up her mind that she would find out the truth about that horrid pipe.

"David," said she at last, lifting her clear, sweet eyes to his face, "I found something when I was clearing up that troubled me very much. I was so afraid it belonged to some member of my family. I do hope it doesn't. Do tell me it was the property of some hired man. I can't bear to think either of my brothers uses it. Wait! I'll get it," and she slipped out to the back kitchen where she had deposited her paper, and brought it with very gingerly fingers.

David took it anxiously and opened the paper. Then the rich red blood rolled from neck to forehead. He was ashamed before this sweet sister. Never before had the old black pipe seemed obnoxious. He had always looked upon it as a friend in his loneliness, a thing as pleasant as anything which came into his life. But suddenly, without ever having heard an argument against smoking, without even reasoning on the subject, he seemed to see this little bit of filthy clay through the eyes of the young girl who stood beside him, and he felt a disgust for it and for himself that he had ever had to do with it. David's was a fine nature. It is not many men who would have felt this instinctively; others might have come to the point through reason or conscience or reverence for another's protest persistently made. This man saw in a flash, by the revelation of the curl of disgust in the delicate lips, and the eager pleading in the earnest eyes of his sister, how a more refined being such as she was might look upon this subject, and before his reason grasped it he had surrendered to what seemed grandest, noblest, and best in life to do. He might have a struggle with himself afterward to carry out his purpose—doubtless would—but certain it was, he would never willingly smoke again. He answered very little. His downcast eyes convicted him. He folded the paper together with a hasty movement.

"I am sorry about it. This shall not trouble you any more," he said, and strode away to the barnyard; but the look he gave his sister as he said those words made her feel glad and proud of her brother, though she could not explain why.

But this was not the end. When Joseph came home that night his elder brother was on the watch for him and called him to the shelter of the barnyard. Now David was not so wise in his dealings with the brother but four years younger than himself as he might have been. Perhaps it was because he felt the load of anxiety so heavy upon him as he remembered his dying father's request: "David, you look after Joseph. He's not so steady as you, you know. Don't you let him get astray." And David had tried to carry out his father's request; but Joseph bitterly resented being interfered with, and it was not always easy to keep him in the straight path.

"Joe," said David severely, as they came in the shadow of the great barn, "don't you go to smoking around the house any more. She don't like it. She'd be perfectly horrified if she saw you with a pipe in your mouth, and if you dare so much as bring out a pipe to light it around where she is you'll be sorry, that's all. You had better give it up. She'll be sure to smell it on your clothes, and I know by the way she looked when she brought mine to me that she hates it. She'll never think anything of you if she finds out you smoke."

David wanted to make his speech very intense, and so he had gone on saying the most unwise things that could be thought of. By the time he had come to this climax his younger brother was exceedingly angry.

"She needn't trouble herself," he replied angrily. "The less she thinks of me the better I am pleased. If you think I am going to give up my rights in my own house, you are mistaken. I'll smoke as much as I please, and light my pipe in the kitchen if I choose. You've sat in that kitchen and smoked whole evenings yourself. You needn't be so holy all of a sudden. It is just as I expected. The minute you get a woman in the house everything has got to be turned upside down to suit her. If you're going in for that sort of thing I'll clear out. There's places enough I can smoke, if the house gets too hot for me." Here his brows were drawn in an ugly, threatening scowl. "And as for my part, I shall do all in my power to make it uncomfortable for her, for the sooner she gets out of this and back to her city home the better I shall like it."

With this parting hit he had betaken himself to the house where he had eaten his supper in silence and then departed to the village grocery. He meant to carry out his intention of smoking in the kitchen if he chose, but he preferred to think it over in the pleasant jovial atmosphere of the village grocery before he decided what line of action he would pursue. The supper had certainly been a good one and he had been hungry after the long day's work. Neither had he quite the face to carry out his threat that night; the new sister was so bright and smiling and ready to do anything or get anything for him. There came too an almost irresistible longing to give up and be a part of all this coziness which had come to the old farmhouse, only he was too stubborn to relent. At the grocery he was accosted by various welcomes born of curiosity. "Hello, Joe," said some of his intimate friends who helped him to smoke the evening away. "Got company at your house, ain't you?" and in the question many things were expressed: curiosity, a decided wish to know how the land lay, eagerness for a bit of gossip and willingness to join in laugh or ridicule of the new guest if that was the mind of the brother. But Joseph did not give them much satisfaction.

He did not quite understand himself and so was not ready with his usual caustic sarcasms at the expense of anybody for them to laugh at. He said "Yes!" short and sharp and the company of loafers, young and old, understood that the door to that conversation had been shut; nay, rather, slammed and decidedly locked in their faces for the evening. They set to work to study Joseph in their dull way to find out what mystery of like or dislike there might be behind his manner, but could not determine. He was silent for the most part, unless there was opportunity to turn a joke against one of them and then his words were sharper than usual, fairly making some of his victims writhe.

He had come as yet to no conclusion except that he would do as he pleased; but the days went by, two or three of them, and he still continued to work in that far-away wood lot. He smoked a good deal during his lonely morning and on his homeward road, taking a fierce delight in thus defying his brother's urgent advice, but as yet he had not attempted to bring out pipe or match in the presence of his sister. If it were necessary in order to defy David he would have done it, but unless provocation should arise he would hardly have the face to do it. Nevertheless, he came to the table with the strong odor of tobacco about him and Ruth understood that her younger brother smoked, and thought and pondered how she might win his love that perchance she might get him to give up this habit some day.

And she stood in the desolate room. It was large and square and bare. To one not used to beautifying empty places it would have seemed a hopeless task to make it other than it was, but Ruth enjoyed the thought of what a change she would make. She puzzled her brows at first over what should go into it. There were rooms of various coloring in the city home. They had all been thought out with the exquisite taste that belongs to refinement and carried out as only those who have a well-filled purse can do. Perhaps just as beautiful effects might have been reached by a much less expenditure of money, but in this case there had been money and everything had been good, enduring, and beautiful. There was a room in sunset tints of rose and mauve and cream, whose carpet of soft coffee and cream color was scattered over here and there with tiny rose-pink buds and leaves. The furniture was curly maple and all the dainty accompaniments were pink and white. Ruth tried to imagine these things occupying the empty desolateness before her, but Joseph with his heavy muddy boots did not seem to fit into the delicate colorings. It might seem too fancy for him. She must choose something quieter. David said he was working in the woods; then maybe the woodland colors would seem more homelike to him. She did not want to startle him with a vivid contrast between his present room and the one she meant to make; no, only to soften and sweeten and brighten everything and make it a real home and not a mere spot in which to stay a few hours. She would choose the fern and moss carpet with all the wood tints blending and a hint of summer sunshine through the green. He would feel more at home with the woods about him. Then the windows should be draped in soft sheer white muslin, fastened back with green, and there should be ferns growing in a pretty green and brown jar. In that corner where the clothespress made a deep nook in the wall she would put the low bookcase that turned a corner and had the queer little niches for favorite books hidden behind the green curtains that had faint shadows of ferns in the pattern of their silk. She would be careful not to put too many fancy things on the bureau, and the pincushion should be severely plain and useful looking, and not the much be-ribboned and be-laced affair that belonged to the original room in the city.

She went on planning, seeing everything take its place in the room. She even chose, with great care, a few choice books and a picture or two which she thought would interest him. There must not be too many chairs, else he would feel the room too full if he was used to this bareness, and the main object in it all was to give him a spot in which he should delight. Would he, could he, appreciate it all? The tears almost dimmed her eyes at the thought that she might fail, and she knelt beside the one wooden chair the room contained and asked the Holy Spirit to guide her in her selection and furnishing of this room. What! ask the Holy Spirit of God to stoop to the selection of a chair or picture, to trouble himself with the texture of a carpet or the pattern of a curtain? And yet these things have more to do than we think with the influencing of human lives. People who live in a house made beautiful by refinement and taste, even though they may not have much money with which to carry out their pleasure in such taste, are nevertheless more able to appreciate beautiful words and high thoughts and holy living, than those who live where harmony is not and where colors and shapes are forever at variance. There is an education and an uplifting in beautiful things and in quiet, peaceful, restful surroundings, which does not count for naught, else God would not have made the world so beautiful.

Ruth, as she rose from her knees, began to think she would have to pray in every room in that house before anything could ever be done with it. And then she brushed away a tear that would come from the longing for the dear ones gone, and a weariness of fear and hope in the life that was before her. Would she ever win this brother for Christ? For neither he nor David was a Christian, she was now certain. She felt alone in a strange and alien land. David was growing dear to her. Perhaps this work she was undertaking was too great for her, an unskilled girl. She might do more harm than good. Perhaps she had been audacious to attempt it. Should she leave it all and go back where people knew and loved her, and she could work, and not feel afraid of defeat?

These thoughts would come to her almost hourly, when she had met some new obstacle in her task. But indeed, there was so much to be done during the days that she had little time to reflect, and it was only at night in the stillness of the ungarnished chamber that she could ask herself these questions. It was always her Bible then that brought her some answer. Now it would be, "Fear thou not for I am with thee; be not dismayed, for I am thy God: I will strengthen thee; yea, I will help thee; yea, I will uphold thee by the right hand of my righteousness." Again, she would turn to this verse, "Ye have not chosen me, but I have chosen you and ordained you, that ye should go and bring forth fruit, and that your fruit should remain; that whatsoever ye shall ask of the Father in my name, he may give it to you."

"And when He has said that to me, why should I not ask him to help me select the right carpet for Joseph's room?" she asked herself.

CHAPTER VI

At last there came an answer from Sally the cook. Yes, she would come gladly and would be there soon. Ruth's heart was set at rest about her housekeeping. When a few days later Sally arrived, strong, capable, willing, and warmhearted, Ruth relaxed the high strain she had been under and began to think that things would really settle down into something like order pretty soon. The house had been thoroughly cleaned from garret to cellar by the woman David had secured for the purpose, and a good deal of the drudgery had also been taken from her, but she had felt she must do all the cooking herself, for the woman seemed not to know how to do things in the right way, nor, what was worse, to care to learn. She had a way of her own which she considered was the only way, and Ruth found, like many another, that it was easier to do things herself than to try to teach another.

So with Sally's coming came an opportunity to rest a little and look about this new home of hers. She knew it indoors pretty well now, but had hardly ventured out at all as yet. She began to wonder how long it would be before she would go to church and know the people and be known in the village. Two Sundays had passed, but on the first she was so thoroughly exhausted by her unusual efforts at housecleaning that she did not feel able to go; and the second it had been so exceedingly stormy that the subject had not been mentioned. She did not know yet that it had never occurred to either of her brothers as a subject of conversation. They seldom went any more themselves. She had yet to bear the disappointment of that discovery.

A day or two after the arrival of Sally, there was some business to be done at the county seat, not far away, connected with the farm and the sale of some cattle. Heretofore David had been the one who had taken these trips, which occurred once or twice a year. It usually kept him three or four days, or sometimes a week. This year when the matter was spoken about, Joseph declared that he would go. He told his brother quite gruffly that he would not stay there with those two women, and besides, he thought it was his turn to go; he could sell the sheep quite as well as David. Now, David had been not a little troubled about leaving his sister alone just now, fearing lest Joseph might make her uncomfortable by his silent, unpleasant way, so, while he was somewhat anxious about the way in which his brother might perform the business part of the trip, anxious also as to where he might spend his time during his absence and what companions he would choose, he nevertheless saw no other way but to let him go. Indeed, Joseph was so determined, that his brother felt sure he would go away somewhere if he did not consent. So it was settled that Joseph should take the trip.

Ruth upon hearing that he was to start in three days hastened to carry out one of her own plans for which she had been waiting her opportunity. After consultation with David she dispatched a letter to a firm in her old home, which very soon brought her a large package by express. Her orders had been explicit, and she knew well the man with whom she was dealing, so that the contents of the package was exceeding satisfactory. Joseph started early the next morning, and about an hour afterward there arrived from the village paperers and a painter.

David seemed as interested and happy over the plan as if it were his own. He hovered near while Ruth talked with the painter, and helped him to mix and match tints, and while the package was opened and the paperers went to work with scissors and paste on the smooth rolls of paper. Ruth had ideas, and was very particular. The village painter declared to one of the paperhangers that he never did see such a queer style in paintin' in his life, that he s'posed he'd got to do the way that girl said, but it would look mighty queer, accordin' to his notion. Nevertheless he worked, and so did the others, as the strange young woman with the sweet voice and determined mouth ordered, and, behold, by night there was a change wrought, the like of which Summerton had never seen before.

It was in Joseph's room where the changes began. That was the fun of it all, to surprise Joseph when he should return. If only the furniture would come before his return. David and Ruth went up to survey after the workmen had finished and gone. To David it was a marvel. How could paper and paint make so great a change? The ceiling was a sunny cream tint, plain and simple, shading at the edges into a deeper yellow sunlight, bordered with maidenhair ferns, which by some mysterious skill of designers fitted the ferns in the border of the paper on the walls. The tint of the walls was a soft, hazy green, like the suggestion of an orchard bursting into leaf, and a deep dado, about which Ruth had been explicit in her orders to Browning & Co., was massed over with palms, so lifelike as to almost deceive the eye. Ruth intended when it was all finished to have a real palm standing in just the right place by this dado, to increase the distance and make the room look as if it stretched away to endless groves of palm. But to David, whose imagination had not been cultivated, it was sufficiently wonderful as it was. The woodwork had a beautiful blending of the cream and sunny tints, which the reluctant

painter had charily acknowledged "Wa'n't so bad, con-
siderin', only nobody in earth ever see the like before. It
was somethin' new, certainly, though fer my part I prefer
good, solid, substantial color all through." The floor glis-
tened in a border of hard-oil finish, sufficiently deep for the
green mossy rug that was to lie over it.

Said David, as he stood spellbound: "This fits you, Ruth.
You ought to have this room yourself and let Joe take
another. You can't ever get anything as pretty as this for
anybody else."

But Ruth laughed in her pleasure, and said she had
plenty more plans for the other rooms, that his was to be
even prettier than this. And then she wished again the
furniture would hasten on its way, and she ran away to give
some direction for breakfast.

And the furniture did come the very next morning. They
told each other that it was really wonderful for it to arrive
from such a long distance, considering how long freight was
sometimes on its way. They forgot to take into account that
the man who had sent it on was a friend, and had spoken to
another friend in a freight office, which had hastened things
a little. They forgot also that the Holy Spirit was guiding
the whole affair, and that perhaps God wanted Ruth's plan
for Joseph to succeed even more than she did. We have a
habit of thinking our nice little plans are all against God's
way, and of asking his help much as if we expected he would
naturally refuse or let something hinder them. We forget
that if we are letting him guide our lives in everything, it is
very often his own gracious Spirit which gives us the
thought of these plans, and it is God who has given us the
intellect and skill to plan. Even when he lets our plans fail
apparently, it may be that their very failure has been their
success in his eyes.

David had tried to arrange for the freight to be brought
from a quiet little station two miles up the road, from the
village, that the whole neighborhood might not know
everything that was going on, but it had proved impossible.
For some reason the cars could not be left on the right side-
track. So through the eager little village the hauling wagons
toiled back and forth, back and forth, an incredible number
of times, emptying the great freight car. Mrs. Chatterton

could hardly get her work done that day, so afraid was she that she would lose count of the wagon loads, but when the night came her record was correct, she was sure. Not much satisfaction had she from her watch, however, for everything was so carefully packed by professional packers that its shape and design were hopelessly covered. A crowd of boys and older men, and even a few curious women, had made errands down toward the station, that they might see these city things nearer, and some papers were picked a little just to see the woodwork on a bedstead or the upholstery on a chair. There were great stories afloat, and much wonder. But there was nothing to go on but hearsay and surmise. David was always "close-mouthed," the neighbors said, and they did not like to ask him questions, and Joseph had gone to the fair to sell sheep. If Joseph had been home they felt sure they might have found out something. One old man with a ragged, discolored beard, where a river of tobacco juice ever and anon flowed down, even said he shouldn't wonder if there was trouble up there with that highflier of a city girl, or Joe never would have gone; he never went before, and this was reported as true by the postmaster to three friends of his as he sorted over the mail to go east.

But at the farmhouse there was eagerness and pleasant hard work. David got his own necessary work out of the way as soon as possible that he might help. As the loads came in they were deposited here and there, out of the way, in rooms that were not to be used immediately, and Ruth selected the things she wanted for Joseph's room at once. David opened the boxes and helped to uncover the swathed furniture, and carried up and arranged. He did not wish to trust the men with this more than he could help. Some things he found pretty heavy, however, and was obliged to have help, so he kept John Haskins.

Perhaps that was a providence too, for John Haskins was brother to Ellen Amelia, she who had admired the hat of the city lady at the station the day she arrived, and Ellen Amelia's heart was delighted, and her life was brightened greatly by the wonderful account of velvet carpets and downy chairs, which her brother John gave at the supper table. It may be that John's vocabulary was hardly suited to

convey exactly correct impressions of all he had seen, and it
may be that where he could not remember he drew somewhat on his imagination, but on the whole the account was
a good one and eagerly listened to by the entire Haskins
family, including the New York grandmother, who was
pleased to be able to explain the uses of some articles
described, though she was hardly familiar with them in her
own home. But city people have opportunities, which gives
them an advantage sometimes, and it pleased her to be able
to air her little knowledge. As for Ellen Amelia, her
"Fireside Companion" had just come, and she had finished
reading "The Disguised Duke; or, From Poorhouse to
Palace," by the fading light, when her mother called to her
for the fifth time that the table must be set that minute.
And now her dreams were being carried on into realities by
John's account. It did her good to think that there were such
beautiful things in the world, and that they had come as
near her as to be in Summerton. Thenceforward it should
be her great desire to get into that house and see all those
beautiful things. Perchance there might be something
there which she could carry out in cheaper form at home.
For Ellen Amelia was not all dreams. She was ambitious,
and in her way she was not unskillful, but the poor child
had few opportunities of any kind.

Meanwhile at the farmhouse things were growing interesting. Out of the chaos of the morning was evolved a room
so beautiful that David as he went and came, bringing this
and that at his sister's direction, fairly held his breath. The
old cord bed was replaced by one of white and brass, and
from this and that chest and bureau and packing box, Ruth
brought linen and blankets and white drapery and made
the bed, all white and lovely. The corner bookcase was
there with a few books and a statuette and vase. Ruth
unpacked in a reckless way. She was determined to have
that room done before Joseph came, no matter how much
she broke all laws laid down for movers and unpackers. She
pulled a box of books all to pieces to find one which she
knew was there and which she wanted Joseph to read
sometime. She would have a certain picture for his room.
She would have driven a less interested helper than David
distracted with her searches after certain little things,

which in the natural order of things might have been waited for till they turned up. Ruth wanted that room complete, and David was none the less an eager boy at play than she was a girl. There was a large, soft, luxurious couch covered with green plush, which looked like a mossy bank, and this accompanied by its many soft silk pillows was established near a window, and by its side a small flat-topped desk on which was a reading lamp with whitelined green shade. The palm was there, for Ruth had had some of the choice plants from the greenhouse sent on, and all the windows were draped in soft white swiss.

David, while he put up the little brass rods for the curtains and sawed and fixed a heavier pole in front of the closet door to hang a heavy dark green portière where the door had been missing for many a year—so long that the reason for its disappearance had been entirely forgotten— wondered in his heart if he would have been a different being if he had been surrounded by such things sooner; wondered what Joseph would think, whether he would be offended or pleased; resolved to give him a lesson if he were not pleased; and wondered again what poor, economical Aunt Nancy would have said to all this luxury in the old farmhouse. He remembered the dazzling plush album in the parlor and smiled to think how tawdry and common it seemed to him now, though in former years he had looked upon it as an awesome treasure.

They stood back at last and looked at the finished room. Everything was in its place, even to the articles of toilet.

"It is beautiful, beautiful!" said David. It stirred something in him as he gazed at it completed that he did not understand. It made him long for higher, nobler things. It opened possibilities that he had not dreamed of. It made life seem rich and sweet, and, did it speak to him of heaven and his mother? Was not heaven something like this? It came nearer to his ideal than anything he had ever seen before. Perhaps it might stir Joseph with the same thought and make him want to be better, to please that mother who was up there, somewhere, among palms and songs. He closed the door softly as they went out as if they were stepping from some sacred place. As he lay awake that night in his own bare room he liked to think of that lovely spot and know it was near. It made heaven seem a fair reality and even a possibility for him. "And now what next?" he said the next morning with almost as eager a look on his face as Ruth wore. They had each been that morning for a silent peep at Joseph's room, just to see it by the daylight, finished, but neither guessed it of the other. Ruth had knelt a minute there and breathed a prayer that the Spirit of Jesus might hover over that room and influence the life of the occupant, and David's wish for his brother, unuttered, had been perhaps no less a prayer for him.

"What next?" said Ruth gayly. She was growing happy. David and she were comrades, and they had accomplished one purpose together; now they were ready for more. It was beautiful work, albeit there was a sad side to it which her brother had not thought of yet. She was unpacking and putting about the things which she had laid away in sadness and tears. Everything was full of associations of the dear ones who were gone, for whom and by whom and with whom they had been purchased. It was hard to keep back the tears sometimes and yet she felt that this was the very work those dear ones would have liked the precious things to be put to, so she went bravely and even gladly on with her work. There might be tears for the quiet of her own room, but she must have only smiles here, for the old house had been gloomy long enough, and she was come that she might help to win home to heaven and Jesus the two brothers, so long strangers to her.

"We will work at the parlor I think, and in there," pointing to the large room adjoining the kitchen, which had been so long a dusty, unused bedroom. "If you don't mind I want to make a lovely dining room out of that, with a library in the front room beyond. The little room adjoining the parlor would make a nice retreat for my piano and a couch for you to lie on and listen to the music sometimes, if you are willing to cut the doorway a little wider so that it will take in the fretwork archway that used to be between the parlors at home. It is in the hallway at home. This is the only place I can think of where it would fit prettily."

David assented eagerly. He would cut any number of doorways, if she wanted them, though it did puzzle him a

little to know what fretwork was. However he held his
peace, for he had confidence in the present architect.

"I want to keep all signs of work from the halls and
kitchen and the places where Joesph usually goes, so that
his room will be a complete surprise. Shall we leave our
own rooms till the last? Then we can work at them at our
leisure?"

David agreed and they went to work. The painters and
paperers were kept close within certain rooms. The trans-
formation in the old house went on, and so did the village
tongues.

Mrs. Chatterton ran in to see old Mrs. Haskins and took
her knitting. Ellen Amelia hovered about with her paper in
her hand and her hair in curl papers. She was going to a
church supper that night.

"They say," said Mrs. Chatterton, as she picked up some
stitches she had dropped, "that there's great doings goin' on
over to Benedicts'. I guess that girl's a piece. That aunt and
uncle 't adopted her must have been awful rich. I guess
you'd be surprised if you knew how many loads of furniture
I counted at my window yesterday, and 't ain't all there yet,
I heard."

"Well, I guess she's used to havin' things mighty stylish,"
responded the New York grandmother. "John, he says she
has pictures painted right onto the walls, of trees and
things, and she's fixed something in the room, he don't
know what, that made the sunshine streak right in on
anything she wanted it to shine on, even though 'twas a
dark day. I s'pose it's one o' them new kind of Eddysun
things you read about. They do most anything now."

"You don't say!" said Mrs. Chatterton, pausing to take in
this great wonder and pack it away for further transporta-
tion. "One o' them Edsun machines fer makin' sunshine!
Well, I ain't sure but I'd like to have one. Well, she's got
some funny idees about paint. My son's wife's brother did
the paintin', and he tried fer all he was worth to 'dvise her
'bout things, but she would have her own way, an' a mighty
funny one it was too. I wonder what Joesph'll say 'bout it all
when he comes back. Strange he went off so sudden, ain't
it? I wonder if he knows."

And that night Joseph came back.

CHAPTER VII

Joseph was cross. He had not enjoyed his trip so much as he had expected. Somehow everything with which he had come in contact had made him discontented, and as he came in sight of the farmhouse he scowled at it and hated it. Perhaps he added a little hate with the thought that it contained the sister who had come in to interrupt the quiet and have her own way. He did not want to go in but neither did he wish to go anywhere else, and besides, he must make report to his brother at once of the result of his trip.

David met him as he came around to the back door and gave him a hearty welcome. Indeed he could hardly keep the light of the secret upstairs from shining in his face. He had a fear lest his brother should read the story of the new room in his eyes before he went in. He got Joseph's report in a few words and then turned away. He wanted his brother to go upstairs at once, as he was sure he would; so he went to attend to some small unnecessary matter among the milk pans, that he might not seem to be watching him.

Joseph went upstairs. It was growing dusky outside, and Ruth had taken advantage of the moment that her brothers had been talking together, to slip upstairs and light the lamp which shed its soft green glow over the new room and even shimmered unusually under the crack of the door. Joseph paused in wonder at it, and looked up and down the hall to see if in his pre-occupation he had made a mistake and was standing in front of the wrong door. Then he threw the door open and gazed, first in wonder, then in dismay, and then in anger. What was all this? the door of a palace open before him? He made one step across the soft rug and looked down and then brushed his eyes to see if some cobweb were across them which hindered the vision. It was beautiful, it was wonderful, but it did not belong to him; and in his present mood he desired to be alone in his own room. Where then was that old retreat? Had it been spirited away? Oh! with a flash he understood it all now. During his absence my lady Ruth had pitched upon his poor room as the only one she wished to occupy, and had arranged it with her own things to suit herself. Their house was not good enough for her. She had taken his room without his leave. She might at least have told him before he left and given him some notice of where his bed had been moved. He was intruding upon her room it seemed, when he had but thought to go to his own. Well, he should not trouble them further to tell him where his things were, and he shut the yellow cream door with a slam and thundered down the stairs and out at the kitchen door, shutting it also with a heavy jar. If they chose to thus ignore his rights he would show them he could get along without their help. What he meant to do he was not sure yet, except that he would not sleep in that house that night. And he wished them thoroughly to understand that he was angry beyond recall. He went with long strides down the walk and out the gate to the road, but he turned his face away from the village for once.

David, standing behind the shed door, watched him with dismay. What had happened? Was Joseph displeased at the change in his room? Had they then failed after all? Notice that he classed himself with his sister in the enterprise. He had gone over completely to her leadership. He turned and went in the house. Ruth stood in the kitchen by the pleasant, attractive tea table, with a look of mingled fear and dismay. Fortunately Sally was upstairs putting on a clean apron preparatory to waiting upon the table, for though they had not yet established the dining room, things were beginning to be served in some sort of order, such as she was used to in the city.

"What is the matter, David? What has happened? Doesn't he like it?"

There were tears in her eyes and David felt at that moment as if he would like to go after his younger brother and chastise him severely. He had no business to be such a bear.

Ruth went on: "I had just lighted his lamp and slipped over to my room as he came up the stairs and opened his door. He stood still a minute and then he shut the door very hard and went downstairs. I came right down after him, but he isn't anywhere around."

David tried to comfort her as best he could. He did not quite understand what was the matter with Joseph, for he had been sure he would be pleased. But yet, on general principles Joseph was often displeased. He seemed to be always out of harmony with himself and with everything about him.

But Ruth was not easily consoled. She ate little supper that night, though David did his best to keep up a show of eating himself and to talk cheerfully. Joseph did not come back. Ruth went soon to her room and wept. By and by she slipped upon her knees and tried to pray, but it seemed as though she had set her heart so upon the success of this her plan, and had been so sure she was being guided by a higher Power than her own, that she could not rally from the shock of finding that it had failed. She never doubted that it had failed, and that Joseph was exceedingly angry that they had meddled with his room, and had gone off, perhaps never to return. She had little creeping thoughts of doubt as to whether her prayers had not all been in vain, though she put them aside and would not give place to them. But it did seem strange that she should have been living with such a firm belief in that promise, "Whatsoever ye shall ask in my name I will do it," and now had come this failure. Then she remembered the first part of that verse again, and it became to her like a rebuke for doubting her Lord. "Ye have not chosen me, but I have chosen you, and ordained you, that ye should go and bring forth fruit, and that your fruit should remain." Surely she had forgotten. She had not taken up this work for God, but he had led her to it, had put her into it, and ordained that it should be as he wanted it. Nothing could really fail of what he had planned, and he had promised that it should bring forth fruit, the fruit he wanted, and that it should be fruit that should remain; not just the kind that blossomed and formed and then fell off with the first wind of storm or blight that came along. He was able to make good come out of even

this failure, disappointment though it was for her. She dried
her eyes at last and went to bed, first looking out of her
window in the vain hope that she might see something
moving down the road to the gate. Oh, if her brother would
but return, she would replace his old room just as it was, if
he wanted it so; she would beg his pardon for having
displeased him. Then she turned away from the window
and tried to hum

> He holds the key of all unknown,
>   And I am glad;
> If other hands should hold the key,
> Or if he trusted it to me,
>   I might be sad.

She sighed as she thought of what to-morrow might bring
of certainty about Joseph, and then the hymn answered
her:

> What if to-morrow's cares were here
>   Without its rest?
> I'd rather he unlocked the day,
> And, as the hours swing open, say,
> "My will is best."

Then she laid her soul down to rest saying:

> Enough; this covers all my wants
>   And so I rest;
> For what I cannot, he can see,
> And in his care I safe shall be,
>   Forever blest.

Out there, not many feet away from her window, over in
the great hay barn, lay the young ingrate who had so torn
the peace of mind of his family. He had stolen softly back
after walking about two miles, for the exertion of his day's
trip made him feel suddenly weary, now that the first heat
of anger had worn away. He would not go back into the
house, neither would he go to the village. He wanted to lie
down and rest. The sweet hay in the great barn was easy of
access by a little side door of which he carried the key, and

so, while his brother and sister were worrying about him, he was sleeping heavily from sheer weariness. When the morning broke he rubbed his eyes and wondered where he was; and then it all came back to him, but his own stubbornness came as well. He was hungry but he would not go in and eat. It was early. He found some old clothes which were almost unused, a coat and a pair of overalls which he had kept in the front of the barn for occasional service, and with these he arranged a working suit; and taking a wash and a drink at the pump and his tools from their places, he went breakfastless to the wood lot to work. It did his angry soul good to have this revenge of feeling that they had driven him from home and to his work without food. Of course this could not go on forever, but while he worked he could think and decide what should be done. He felt pretty certain that he would go away somewhere, and that at once; but he wanted to think his plans over a little more before he put them into execution. And so he chopped angrily away at the trunk of an old tree and thought and grew hungrier and more stubborn with each hour, and the autumn sun rose high and clear, but it brought no cheer to him. It seemed to him now that all the universe was against him and was exulting in the fact that it was so.

Ruth did not know what to do with herself. To take up the work of finishing the house where they had left it the day before was impossible. Her heart was no longer in it. She would much rather have packed up all her things and sent them back to the storage house, replacing the old furniture now. All the plans seemed wrong. David at her earnest request had started out immediately after breakfast to see if he could find a trace of Joseph. Ruth was restless. She wished she were a man and familiar with her surroundings that she might go also. She tried to work at this and that, but her restless spirit would not be put down. She went from one window to another, and the tears were very near the surface. If she could but go out and search and in some way make amends for what she had done. She felt certain that she would break down and cry outright if the morning went on much longer and David did not come with word. She would go out and see if she could not find him.

Suddenly the remembrance of her bicycle came to mind. It had not yet been unpacked, and was at that moment in its crate in the front room, which was to be a library, behind all sorts of boxes and chairs and tables. Could she get it out and uncrate it? She knew enough about the machine to put it together, when once she had it out, she was certain. At least she would try, for it would give her something to do with a purpose. This standing about and waiting was intolerable. Her vivid imagination through the night had conjured up all sorts of things that Joseph might have done, and she blamed her own sweet services for him for it all.

She went at once to the front room, armed with hatchet and hammer and screw-driver. It proved a work of time and strength to get the crate out of the tangle of furniture, and when at last this was accomplished she found the task of uncrating no easy one. But at last the machine was out and put together, and oiling it hastily she ran upstairs to put on her bicycle suit. With a few hasty directions to Sally, who had learned not to be surprised at almost anything her young mistress undertook, she started on her way, knowing no way in the whole place and having no fixed idea except to go somewhere and to find her brother Joseph. It was a lovely, clear, cool morning and the roads were perfect for a ride, but she took no thought of that. She rode steadily and rapidly, looking about with eyes which searched but saw not much of what she looked upon. Indeed, so hurried and earnest was she that she did not take her usual care to look about her and take her bearings that she might return without any trouble. She only thought about her errand. Down the road toward the village she started and rode as far as the Chatterton house, but then she reflected that David had probably gone on to the village to search and she would better go elsewhere. A long stretch of smooth, much-traveled road led off to the right just beyond the Chatterton place, so without much thought she turned upon it and flew on.

"For the land sake!" ejaculated Mrs. Chatterton, glancing up from her darning at the front sitting-room window, and dropping her lapful of stockings she hastened to the kitchen windows which looked on the side road to get a further view. Eliza Barnes, who was helping Mrs. Chatterton for a few days while she got the apple butter and mince-meat for the winter out of the way, dropped her dishcloth and went to the other window to see what it was that so interested Mrs. Chatterton.

"My land!" said she, her mouth open, her hands on her hips. "A girl on a bicycle! Don't she go it though? Who can she be?" Eliza was not favored by living on the direct road to the village and therefore did not know who the young woman was.

"I ain't sure, but I rather suspect it's that new Benedic' girl. I told 'em I thought they'd find she was a highflier. The idea! It isn't considered decent; but I s'pose them city folks do anything they please. She hasn't got no kind of a ma now to tend to her and you can't expect two boys to hold her in; besides, I heard Joseph was away from home and I see David a driving like mad by here an hour and more ago. She's just waited till they got off, that's what she's done. Somebody ought to tell David; such disgraceful goin's on! What would their poor father and mother say if they could rise up in their graves and know it all? It's a mercy they can't, I declare."

"Wal! she don't look any diffrunt from other folks as I see," said Eliza with admiring eyes as she watched the lithe, graceful figure disappear up the road. "I've heard say they dress just awful for riding, but her dress looks all nice and proper and she sets up as straight as a needle. I mus' say I think it would be fun," and Eliza went back to the greasy kettle she was washing with a sigh of envy. Eliza was always on the lookout for fun, and precious little of it ever came in her way.

"H'm!" ejaculated Mrs. Chatterton severely, looking over her glasses at the preserving kettle on the stove. "It's lucky for you you've got a mother then. Look out that apple butter don't burn. It seems to me you've got a pretty much of a fire on," and she shut the door and went back to her darning.

Meanwhile, all unconscious of the impression her first appearance was making upon the villagers, Ruth rode on. She was almost in feverish haste to get somewhere and get home again. She seemed to feel that she was riding straight to Joseph, and who shall say she was not being guided? On and on she went and coming to a turn to the right and still another she whirled around them hardly knowing that she did so. She passed a handsome farmhouse after this second turn, where some men were working near the fence, and one called out to her something she could not hear. But the tone had been unmistakable and she felt sure that the words were such as she would not wish to hear. She was frightened; her cheeks burned; and her heart beat so fast she could scarcely breathe. For the first time since she started it occurred to her that perhaps it was not safe to ride alone in the country, that bicycles might not be so common here as at her former home. She had been so accustomed to riding when and where she pleased that it had not even occurred to her to ask David whether girls rode here or not, and if it had, the question would have had very little weight with her, her wheel had become so much a part of her by constant use. Now to her confusion, her cheeks flamed crimson. Her nerves were in a quiver before she started and her hard, strained ride with the one purpose in view had not served to calm them. She did not wish to hasten her speed or to take notice of the presence of the men in the least, but they, thinking perhaps to have a little fun, added to her nervousness by sending with a low-spoken word a great fierce-looking dog after her. He came with long, low bounds like some wild animal after its prey and burst upon her with a portentous growl farther down the road from behind a hedge. She had to give a quick turn here to avoid running into him and her frightened heart beat wildly. She was terribly afraid of dogs.

She could scarcely manage her wheel. It was just at the brow of a hill and she put on all speed and fairly shot down that hill, the sound of the dog's deep growl seeming to follow her even after that had become impossible by the distance between them. But now she kept on faster and faster, feeling certain that she was pursued. She heard the sound of the ringing of an axe in a wood she had to pass, but that only added to her fear. Here was a new danger to be encountered. She would put on all speed possible and drive past, and it might be the user of the axe would not perceive her till she was beyond reach; but just as she came to the

center of the very space whence had come the sound of the
axe something happened. What it was she never quite
knew. A great boulder was in the road. The wheel struck it.
The handle bars which she herself had fastened on turned
in her hand at this sudden wrench, and the saddle which
she had supposed securely fastened turned under her. In
vain she threw all her weight upon the pedals. It was too
late. She had attained a fearful speed. She suddenly felt
herself helpless. She seemed blind with fright and could
give but a little gasping cry for help, as she was flung
violently in the dust of the road.

It was very strange. She had never fallen before in all her
riding, except a little tumble or two when she was learning.
And now to fall in disgrace before some country loafers who
only wanted to laugh and jeer at her at best—to fall when
there was real peril, when she was far from home and—oh,
that dog! Her mind seemed in a whirl. Then she lay there
as if stunned in the dust of the road, her eyes shut. She
could faintly hear footsteps crackling over dried twigs and
some one jumping the fence by the road. She knew that he
was coming and perhaps that terrible dog was almost upon
her. Perhaps his hot breath would burn her already hot
cheek, and that awful growl would freeze her very blood
she was sure, if she should hear it in her ear. She could not
help herself now. She would not open her eyes, let come
what might. She remembered that God was guiding her
and she sent up a cry to him for help in her dire need. Then
she felt a touch, a gentle, almost reverent touch, upon her
forehead. She opened her eyes and looked up. It was her
brother Joseph.

Now Joseph had worked hard that morning. He had
perhaps accomplished more in a given time than he had
ever done in the whole of his life before. It is marvelous
how well and rapidly one can work when he feels that he is
acting the part of a martyr. He was considering himself very
ill-used indeed. Self-pity, when it is left to work, getteth to
itself thousands more like unto itself, and Joseph had been
having a real nice gloomy time all alone out there in the
wood lot. He was cutting a tree quite near to the road. Not
a soul had passed since his work began, to interrupt his
meditations. He was growing very hungry—no supper and
no breakfast. He straightened up and felt his back. It was

stiff and ached. Something must be done, for he did not feel
that he was willing to longer undergo this state of discomfort. He was certainly not called upon to do so under the
circumstances. He would go away at once, somewhere—
anywhere. Where? He paused and leaned on his axe,
looking up the road.

Then had come that flying vision: wheels, a dark blue
dress, soft hair, the waving of a great dog's yellow tail as he
wheeled and gave up pursuit, and then the almost immediate catastrophe right before him. He did not know
who or scarcely what it was, but he went to the rescue.

CHAPTER VIII

"Oh, Joseph!" said Ruth, her pale face lighting up. "I have
found you. You'll forgive me, won't you? It was all my fault;
David only helped. You won't be angry any more. I really
thought it would please you to have your room fixed in that
way. We wanted to surprise you; that was why we didn't ask
you first; but I see now it was very wrong of us, for of course
you were attached to the old room as it was. Say you'll
forgive me, do! I wanted so to have you love me!" She was
lying in the dry grass at the side of the road, whither her
brother had swiftly and tenderly borne her. She was dimly
conscious of intense agony in her ankle, but she could think
of nothing until she had Joseph's full forgiveness.

There were real tears in her eyes now. Joseph stood
staring down at her in amazement, hardly able to take in
the meaning of her words. That his sister would suddenly
drop down before the wood lot in this unexpected manner
was astonishing enough, but that after such a ride and such
a fall she should be able to speak was incredible. Her tears
melted him at once. He was not used to women's tears. His
heart went out to her. Her peril had been so great that it

overshadowed everything else, and he did not yet know how badly she was hurt. She made no attempt to rise, but only pleaded with him about the room.

"Bother the room!" he said gruffly, trying vainly to get the huskiness out of his voice. "There ain't anything to forgive. You may have all the rooms in the house, if you want them, and welcome. Are you hurt?" and he stooped anxiously to lift her again.

But she looked eagerly up at him.

"Have all the rooms! What do you mean, Joseph? Was that what you thought? That I had taken your room for myself without asking you? Was that it? Tell me! Oh, you poor boy! I don't wonder you were angry. But Joseph, listen. I never dreamed of such a thing. We were fixing the room up for you. Did you think I would want to take your room away? But I don't blame you; you and I are not acquainted yet. I only wanted to make it just as pretty and pleasant as I could for you, and I had the things and didn't know what else to do with them, and David said they might as well come on and be used; but I'll take them all out and fix it back the way it was if you prefer it that way. It won't take long, and I'm so sorry."

Her nerves had been completely shaken by her excitement and fall. Indeed the poor child had been working beyond her strength for two weeks, in her eagerness to get things done just right, and there had been no one to restrain her. As she talked she could not keep the tears from rolling down her cheeks, she who never cried before people. She remembered it afterward, and rebuked herself for her weakness.

Joseph straightened up and looked at her.

"You fixed that room for me?" he said, such utter amazement in his voice that his sister almost laughed afterward with joy to think of it. She had the pleasure of her surprise after all in thinking of the expression on his face then.

"You never fixed that all up for me," he said stupidly, looking down at her as if she must be a little out of her head. "Why I'm just a—just a—— Nobody ever does things for me."

"Yes, they do, Joseph! David and I do," she laughed, her

tears shining like a mist before the sun, and she caught one of her brother's great rough, red hands and kissed it.

He felt a queer kind of a sensation in his own eyes then, and to cover it he stooped once more and said:

"We must get you home. Where are you hurt?" She took his help then and tried to rise, but now the terrific pain in her ankle asserted itself, and she turned quite white and sank back again. "Where—what is it?" questioned Joseph anxiously.

"Oh, it's my ankle, and I suppose it might be a sprain. I have always thought it was so silly for people to get their ankles sprained, and now I've done it. Oh, it hurts dreadfully, and we're a long way from home, aren't we?"

"Well, not so far but what I could carry you, I guess, only I'm afraid it'll be hard on you; and what'll we do with this concern?" pointing to the down-fallen bicycle. "It ain't very safe to leave it here if you ever care to see it again. I guess I'd better leave you long enough to borrow a wagon."

"Oh, don't!" said Ruth, rising again with sudden energy, which sent the pain shooting through her ankle. "I'm afraid that awful dog would come again," and she shuddered at the thought. "If you think you can screw those handle bars on tight, perhaps I could get on and manage with your help to ride it home. I suppose it was very reckless of me to start out when I had screwed things up myself. I never put it together before."

Joseph stooped and raised the fallen machine. It was almost as mysterious a thing to have to do with as a young woman. He had never seen one save at a distance before. There was but one in the village, and that was owned by a youth who spent his time away from home, at college, almost entirely. He was not a young man of Joseph's immediate social circle either.

With Ruth's directions he was able to make all the repairs necessary, and finally, with much care and not a little pain, Ruth was placed on the saddle, her lame foot held in as comfortable a position as possible, while with her brother's help and her one well foot she was able slowly to propel the machine. It was a slow and painful ride. They took down the bars of the woodlot fence, and went by a little, winding, unused road, which led among the trees, but straight across

lots to their home. Ruth was at least shielded from the eyes
of the village gossips, and thus her downfall and untriumphal
return were not proclaimed from the village house-
tops. Mrs. Chatterton missed a moral for her sermon on
bicycles, and Eliza Barnes watched in vain for the spinning
figure down the road,

David was just driving into the gateway as they reached
the barnyard entrance, and he could scarcely believe his
eyes to see the prodigal brother steering the despised sister
on a machine, which to David's eyes was a very strange
sight indeed.

"You turn right around and go for the doctor," called
Joseph peremptorily, as soon as he was within hailing
distance. "She's had a fall and hurt her ankle. No; I'll carry
her up," as David jumped from the wagon in dismay and
ran to help. "I've brought her this far and I guess I can do
the rest. You go quick."

The command was given so decidedly that David turned
meekly and obeyed. He hurried the horse as much as
possible, but he turned his head once for the astonishing
sight of Joseph with Ruth gathered tenderly in his arms
striding across the dooryard. Ruth waved her hand to him
and tried to smile as she called, "It's all right, he just didn't
understand"; but the pain was so bad she had to close her
eyes and keep still.

A mother could not have been more tender than those
two brothers were during the days that followed. The
doctor came and fixed up the poor swollen ankle, encouraging them by saying it might not be so bad as it looked. Then
they hovered near her and could not do enough for her, and
even neglected their work to stay with her. It would seem
as if they were just awakened to the fact that there was
something else than work in the world worth living for; for
love, the love of a brother for a sister, was growing in their
hearts that had been empty so long.

Early that evening Joseph went to the village on an
errand. The doctor had called again and recommended
some lotion for bathing the hurt ankle, and Joseph offered
to go for it. Ever since morning he had seemed to take
David's place in ordering about things and in doing all he
could to make his sister comfortable. He had a feeling as if

he had been the cause of her suffering and he must take the responsibility of caring for her. David was quite astonished at him, and sat down now beside Ruth's couch to talk things over with her. The large, easy, leather-covered library sofa had been hastily unpacked by David and pushed into the kitchen for the benefit of the invalid, because she utterly refused to be sent off upstairs away from everything. She was quite happy in spite of her hurt. She was rather glad than not that she had fallen, now that there was such a change in Joseph. It was worth a ride and a fall any day to gain a brother like her younger one, for when Joseph's heart was once touched there was a great well of good there, and he bestowed freely where he chose to do so.

While they talked and arranged some little matters, going on with their plans where they had been left the day before, Joseph went with long, free steps to the village. It was a very different walk from the one he had taken the night before. Indeed it never occurred to him to mark the contrast between himself to-night and twenty-four hours before. His mind was busy over his sister, who, as far as he was concerned, might have just come into his range of vision. Heretofore she had been an imaginary being whom he hated, because he fancied she was in his way and perhaps disliked him. There in the dark on this lonely country road he remembered her words, looks, tones, and her tears. These were things he would not have dared even think about in the daylight or in the presence of others, for he was very much afraid of any sentiment. Indeed the least tendency in that direction was something so new to him that he scarcely believed in it at all. He decided that he had been a fool the night before and metaphorically kicked himself all the way to town for his bearishness and boorishness about that room. It suddenly occurred to him that though he had been about the house nearly all day, he had not yet revisited his room, nor seen it enough to tell what it was like. He tried to recall what he had seen at his first glimpse, but the veil of anger was between and he could tell nothing, except that there had been a green glow and a look like a glimpse of paradise to it. An eager desire to see it at once took possession of him and he hastened his steps. His errand at the drug store completed, he went to the post office to see if there was any mail. He and David had not been used to getting letters nor going often to the office, but since their sister had arrived there had been something for the Benedicts almost every mail. They were growing accustomed to going to the post office every day as a matter of course.

The grocery, in the front of which the post office was located, was ill lighted by smoky kerosene lamps. At the back end, beyond the counter and a little hidden by the dusty post boxes and the little stamp and letter window, there was a sprawling box stove and around it at all seasons of the year, no matter whether there was a fire or not, was usually gathered at this hour of the evening a number of loafers, young and old, spitting, smoking, and talking, with loud guffaws of laughter interspersed. They were all there tonight. Joseph recognized one or two voices and he drew his brows in a heavy frown. Ruth had told him of the men who had called to her as she rode and frightened her so terribly. He knew at once who they were and that two of them were at that moment at the back of the store.

They were talking loudly and laughing as usual. One of these two seemed to be telling a story of something he had seen that day. Joseph, as he waited for the tardy postmaster, who was interested in the story and came unwillingly with his head turned to hear the rest, could not help but catch some of the sentences. There was something being said about a bicycle and a girl—and—could he believe his senses? He straightened up like a spirited horse that has been angered. Amid the loud laughter that followed the close of the story, there came like a sudden thunderclap a swift, stinging, stunning blow across the grinning mouth of the teller, which caused him to suddenly fall backward into one of the store chairs and made his head ring and his eyes see many constellations. There was startled, utter silence in the room. Joseph, in part by his strange moods, his alternate deep silence and witty, sometimes cutting, sarcasms, and in part by his unusual physical strength, had gained a supremacy over the rest which made them almost afraid now as he stood tall and strong and straight before them, with folded arms and lowering brows looking down at the dazed man before him, waiting until he should come to his senses sufficiently to hear what he had to say. Joseph was conspicuously without his pipe that night. The fact gave him an added dignity.

The young man in the chair was Bill Brower. His brother Ed stood on the other side of the stove. They were two of those who had made remarks to Ruth as she rode by their place that morning. The Browers were rich farmers, and took a good many airs on themselves, though it was whispered about that the father was very "near." The three young men, sons, were rapidly going to the bad. Their mother, poor soul, had never had much control over them, and their father did not care so long as they worked and did not spend too much of his money. He was not over-good himself.

Joseph had never liked these two young men. His sarcasms had oftenest been directed against them, and well he knew they dreaded his tongue; for they were dull in a way, and not able to make quick reply or get the better of him before others. They hated ridicule as only coarse, weak natures can. Now Joseph stood above Bill Brower and looked down in scorn as the other tried to recover from his blow and show some fight. Joseph placed a firm hand on his shoulder, with menace in his face, and said:

"No, Bill; don't you dare to stir or answer me back. I have just one thing to say to you. I want you to understand that the young woman you were talking about just now is my sister and that you will be sorry if you ever mention her name in my presence again. You are not fit to be in the same world with such as she. Remember, I mean what I say, and you will be sorry if I hear of you ever mentioning her again in any but a respectful manner. And you'd better look out how you even do that!"

Then Joseph walked away and there was silence in Summerton grocery till he had well turned the corner and was out on the pike toward home. Bill Brower managed to pull his scattered senses together after a few minutes and talked a little in a threatening way, saying he would "have it back on Benedic'," but the others only laughed at him. They were easily turned this way or that and had ever despised Bill Brower and held Joe Benedict high in their estimation. It did them good to see a blow well deserved and well planted.

The records of the remainder of that evening in the grocery would not be interesting. The postmaster and storekeeper yawned and shut up store earlier than usual by a half-hour, for his usual entertainers and story-tellers had dropped out one by one. Nevertheless, the story of what had happened hastened on fleet wings about the village, a scrap of it here and a scrap of it there, pieced together by the village gossips who attend to such affairs, till it got all mixed up and meant an entirely different meaning from the truth.

Meanwhile Ruth was being borne by four strong arms upstairs, and the brothers and sister were taking together a complete survey of Joseph's new room. They established Ruth on the green sofa, while David took his younger brother about showing him this and that feature of the new room as though he had been a fancy house furnisher and upholsterer from the city. Joseph admired in words stronger than his brother had ever heard him use before in praising anything. He told Ruth it was too good for him and she must have it all and let him take some other room, that it just fitted her; but she, with happy face, told him all her plans for the house, and together they arranged to complete the work begun. Joseph was intensely interested. He had never been in a room like this before. He had not had even David's experience of the time when he went to the city to see his aunt and take that message before their father died. His highest ideal of a room was the stiff haircloth and ingrain of the Summerton parlors to which he had access.

Ruth selected one of Frank Stockton's incomparable stories and read to her brothers a little while to finish the evening, and they both declared they never had had such a good time in their lives. They laughed over the book and made interested comments, which showed they were no fools, and Ruth enjoyed the reading as much as they. Then as it grew late they planned to go at the new work in the morning, while Ruth should lie on her sofa and direct and read to them.

Ruth, as she closed her eyes to sleep that night, thanked God and took courage. A sprained ankle was not so bad if it was the price of another brother.

CHAPTER IX

The Reverend Robert Clifton, pastor of a month's standing to the principal church of Summerton, was in consultation with his deacons. He had not really been at work for more than a few days, for though he had preached Sundays in his new charge he had been away during the week most of the time making arrangements to move his mother and young sister to the parsonage from their old home in a neighboring city. Now, at last, the parsonage was habitable and the mother and sister would arrive in a few days. He was anxious to get to work. It was his first charge and he meant to do his best in every way. He must be a good pastor as well as preacher.

They were meeting in the gloomy little room back of the church known formerly as the "lecture room," now in process of being rechristened by the title of "ladies' parlor," at the suggestion of Mrs. Brummel. The Brummels were rich and had their own way. Their only son owned the only bicycle in town until Ruth's came, and was off getting a college education. Mrs. Brummel had given a rocking-chair with one spring broken, a marble-topped table for which she had no use, and a set of "Lives of the Martyrs" in an ancient hanging bookcase, which was apt to collapse at some critical moment if the books were not balanced just so; these to carry out the illusion necessary to a parlor. She also cut up her old piano spread that the moths had eaten, and had her daughter Georgiana embroider crewel sunflowers in Kensington stitch in the corners, to spread over the reading desk when the ladies met to sew.

The minister sat in the broken rocking-chair. It had been given to him out of deference to his office. As a matter of fact not one of the deacons enjoyed the broken spring. The

minister was uncomfortable, but he took it as a part of the
ills of life. He was trying to get at the boundary of his parish
and find out "who was who." He had early discovered that
the Brummels, and Browers, and one or two other families,
were people to whom the deacons thought it well to pay a
great deal of attention, and that the Barneses did not matter
so much. It gave him a desolate feeling to find so mercenary
a spirit among the chief men of his church. What if the
Brummels were worth more money than the Barneses,
were not their souls of just as much value in the sight of the
Master?

"Now then, there are one or two other places I want to
know about, Brother Chatterton. There is a house just a
little back from the road, about a mile I should say beyond
your house, up toward the Barnes place. Who lives there?
Do they belong to us or to the other church? I can't find out
about them."

"Why, that mus' be Benedic's," responded Deacon Chatterton, without much interest in his voice. "You needn't
trouble about them. Oh, they go to our church when they
go anywhere, but they haven't been for a long spell back
now, not much since the old aunt died. They're mostly
dead, all 'twas any 'count, anyway. There's only the two
boys left now and they ain't like other young men. One of
'em's gone to the dogs, I guess, pretty much, and the other
might as well be for all the account he'll ever be to the
church. Oh yes, they've got a good farm, and I guess
they're doin' pretty well at it, but they never go anywhere
and they live there alone. You can't do nothin' with 'em.
They used to come to Sunday-school awhile back, but they
grew out o' that."

"They live entirely alone? Does no one keep house for
them?" The minister was curious about them. For some
reason they interested him. He had a passion for going after
lost sheep and bringing them back. Part of his seminary
training had been work among young men in the slums of a
city. He would like to try for these two, but he must know
more about them before he went.

"Oh well, no, they ain't egzackly alone now," spoke up
Deacon Haskins. "There's a sister o' theirs come on from
way off somewhere. I don' know how long she 'ntends to

stay, but I should say she's set her stakes pretty deep, for she brought a whole raft of things along with her. She's livin' with them and she has a garl to do her work, so they ain't alone now."

"They might a good deal better be, in my opinion," put in Deacon Chatterton with emphasis. "Ef there was any ruin left to 'em, they'll go to it now. From what I hear she's a regular piece. She's one o' those new bicycle girls." He spoke the words in a low convicting tone, much as you would speak of a ballet-dancer in some low theater, and they conveyed to the new minister a meaning deeper and darker than even the good-hearted, narrow-minded deacon had any conception.

"Yes," said Deacon Hobbs, shaking his head regretfully and sighing a funereal sigh; "I'm afraid she's pretty bad. There's a story come straight from headquarters about her and those Brower boys, and we all know what they are. I'm sorry for the sake of the young women of this locality—yes, and the young men too—that she's come among us." And he sighed again.

"Now, brethren, don't be too hasty. We don't know her as yet. Let us wait till we see more of her."

It was Deacon Meakins, kind, sweet-spirited, always ready with a good word for somebody, everybody, who spoke. He was a thorn in the flesh to this body of good men, for they loved a little gentle gossip as well as did their sisters, and he was forever putting in with some meek reminder of mercy, or a word in favor of the one who was being discussed. They rose and began to button their coats, for the evening was chilly. It was time to depart if Deacon Meakins had begun.

But Deacon Chatterton felt that he was called upon to have the last word, in this case especially.

"Brother Meakins," he said severely, "isn't it enough that she has been an inhabitant of this town for now over two months, and not once has she made her appearance inside a church? I have it on good authority from two or three members of the other church that she has not been there."

"Yes," said Deacon Hobbs; "it is a pity, a great pity. Her folks were very good, respectable people. Her father was once a deacon in this church."

"Well, brethren," said Deacon Meakins apologetically, "you know she has been confined to the house by a sprained ankle. Dr. Stormer seems to have a very good opinion of her, so far as I have heard him say. Perhaps she might be helped in some way, you know, brethren."

"Yes, and how did she get her ankle sprained, Brother Meakins?" said Deacon Chatterton with a severity that he evidently expected to be convincing.

"Dr. Stormer never says much about his patients. It is not to be expected," said Deacon Hobbs, and then he turned the lights out and they all went out into the crisp autumn evening.

The minister walked along in the starlight silently. He was puzzled and troubled. Here was this case of the Benedicts in whom he had been so interested. It was complicated sadly by this wild, gay sister. From what these men said, she was evidently one whose influence was to be dreaded, to say the least. It would not do for him to allow his name to be mixed up with hers. He must move very cautiously. It was a case where a woman would be a great help. His mother was a shy, quiet woman, who had always been sheltered, and who had loved to stay at home with her children. She could not help in a case like this. And his sister! He sighed. She was bright and gay and pretty, but she had no wish to help. She was not even a Christian; she must be sheltered from evil influences herself. She must yet be won to Christ; and he had no earthly help apparently. If he only had a wife, one who would love the work as he did, and would know just how to go to work for such a girl as the Benedict sister, one like—here he stopped and would not go on, even in his thoughts. She was far away, and far above him. But how strange that this name should be Benedict! Well, life was a queer puzzle, anyway. It was no use to try to think it out. He fitted his night key to the parsonage door and tried to shut out his troubled thoughts as he shut himself in. He sat down in his study chair and drew his hand wearily across his eyes. He had started out that evening eager and interested, his spirit glad, rested, ready for work, but somehow he had lost his enthusiasm already. What was the matter? He reached his hand to his study table for the Bible and it opened of itself to the first chapter of Joshua, perhaps because that was a favorite place of his. He wanted help and here it was.

"Be strong and of a good courage: for unto this people thou shalt divide for an inheritance the land, which I sware unto their fathers to give them . . . Be not afraid, neither be thou dismayed: for the Lord thy God is with thee whithersoever thou goest."

Surely he was not presuming to take these words to himself, for if he believed anything in life he believed firmly that the Lord had called him to the ministry as much as he ever called Joshua to take Moses' place at the head of the children of Israel. If this were not so he was committing sacrilege to try to preach at all. The words comforted him. The Lord who was leading would provide a way and would keep his promise. He was with him, even if he had no earthly helper. God would take the place of mother and sister and wife if need be. God would care for it all. There came to him the words of a hymn or a poem, he could not tell which, that he had heard recited in a young people's prayer meeting by a sweet girlish voice. He had met the girl once or twice and talked with her for a few moments, and he knew that her life must fit such words, and so they had meant more to him than they would have done otherwise, and when he had chanced to find those words in print he had committed them to memory.

He was not in love with the girl. He had never given time to thinking of such things, nor indeed to knowing girls very much. She was very young, and he had met her only once or twice and talked but very little with her. That was four years ago, before he was through the seminary. He could not tell if she even knew his name. But she had seemed like an ideally happy Christian, and had left a pleasant fragrance in his memory which he had used occasionally for a womanly ideal when it had been necessary for his thoughts to have one to fill in with somewhere. But he was not at all sentimental, nor did he often think of her. The words of the verse were these:

> Bear not a single care;
>   One is too much for thee.
> Mine is the work, and mine alone;
>   Thy work—to rest in me.

It was strange—and yet nothing is ever strange that happens to God's people, for he knows the whys and wherefores—that he was reminded of her again the very next morning as he stood at the front window of the parsonage looking idly out at the village street that stretched away into blue misty mountains whose feet were already wreathed with the last autumnal tints. He was wondering whether he should venture to call at the Benedict farm that day or wait until his mother came and try to persuade her to go with him. He had just made up his mind that he would pray about the matter a little while and see if any light came, and perhaps he would be guided to go there that afternoon or the next day. He was sure he would be shown the way.

A lady was walking slowly along the street, stopping now and then to gather a lovely crimson leaf from the flagging. She walked as if she was waiting for some one and was not in a hurry. Now and then she turned her head in the direction of the stores as if looking for something. She glanced up curiously at the houses as if they were new to her; not with a steady stare like a person who had never been there before, but with a well-bred interested glance, that had such a touch of pleasant admiration for all she saw. The minister hardly knew that he was watching her till as she came nearer she turned her face and looked full up at the upper windows of the parsonage. In truth she was admiring the dainty ruffled curtains which the minister's mother had selected with great care, and thinking to herself, "Some little woman with good taste lives there, I'm sure, and perhaps she and I will be great friends," and then she turned her face away and looked for more leaves and walked slowly on and did not see the minister at all.

And Robert Clifton looked at her full face and thought how like it was to that other face he had remembered, in purity of outline and with clear earnest eyes. He made up his mind with the moment's glance he had that the woman looked as *she* would look when she grew up. She had been a girl with floating hair four years ago, and dresses not quite touching the ground in full-grown fashion. By and by she would be a woman, and then she would look like this woman and he would like to meet her then. Would she keep her childlike trust in Jesus, he wondered? And then he began pondering where she might be and what her life was now, and half forgot to wonder who the passer-by had been, so brief had been his sight of her. He noticed in a moment that a surrey went by with a young man driving, and that farther up the road it stopped and picked up the lady and that they drove on. "Some one from West Winterton," he murmured to himself and turned to go to his almost completed sermon. A sermon was still an arduous and serious undertaking with him. He wanted this one to reach hearts. Without knowing it he had written it with the Benedict boys in mind. He did not know them, but he had imagined what they were. He did not expect to have them present, and yet his sermon was an earnest plea for Jesus Christ to just such young men as he imagined they were. But there were young men who were like that, and they would be present in some numbers to hear the new minister preach, and the sermon was not written in vain, in spite of the fact that it did not fit the real Benedict brothers.

Before he took up his pen he settled one matter. He would go and call on those two young men before the week was out. He would do it for the sake of that sweet girl face, a vision of which he had just beheld. She had once said to him that she thought God gave us our fancies and preferences for some real reason, and that if we could disconnect them thoroughly from our own way, we would usually find that they led to some work for him when we were on the lookout for it. She had not expressed it in just that way, but more simply and girlishly. It had impressed him at the time as being a very unusual thing for one who was not more than a little girl to say, but he had heard that her mother was an unusual woman. That might explain it. At any rate he made up his mind to try and follow out this fancy.

Here the minister resolutely locked the door of those thoughts and dipped his pen in the ink.

CHAPTER X

Through many perplexities and prayers Robert Clifton had arrived at a decision with regard to his proposed visit to the Benedict farm, viz., that before another Sunday passed it should be accomplished; and so the first bright afternoon he took his way down the long, dusty country road lit up along its edges with faded autumn tints and a few late, brave, scarlet leaves. He was going in fear and trembling, yet he hoped much from this visit. He had planned it with a view to reaching the entire household if possible, and yet not at a time when there might be danger of his meeting that bugbear of a sister alone. It would be best not to do anything which might make talk in a country village. He had wisely learned that fact early in his career. The two young men he was reasonably sure to find at or near the house at this time of the day. He had been utterly unable to decide what he should say to them when he reached there. He had planned conversation after conversation, but the unknown quantity represented by what the Benedict brothers would probably respond to his first sentences was so uncertain that he finally gave it up, and with a prayer that his lips might be guided and that his ears might hear a voice behind him saying, "This is the way, walk ye in it," he started on his errand.

Arrived at the place he was surprised to find as he walked up the front path to the door, that painters seemed to be preparing to paint the house. He had understood that things were somewhat run down and that the young men did not care to keep them up. Perhaps his sister had money; and he sighed to think of the possibilities of what that sister might be. The old-fashioned knocker did not give back the empty comfortless echo he had somehow expected, but it sounded forth his arrival as if from cheerful, well-filled rooms that had no need to shrink and be sad at the approach of a stranger.

Sally the cook responded to his knock. It had not been exactly within the range of her province in the city to answer the door, but things were different out here, where none of her associates would know of her condescension, and besides there were so few visitors. So she smoothed her hair before the little glass in the kitchen and tied on a wide, long white apron which hung on the identical hook which poor Aunt Nancy's had adorned for so long and went with quiet, trained footsteps to the door.

Robert Clifton was somewhat taken aback at the sudden appearance before him of a city-trained servant. For the instant he thought she must be the sister, though her age was somewhat more advanced than he had been given to suppose Miss Benedict's to be, and he afterward remembered finding something incongruous in the thought of Sally's dignified proportions mounted on a bicycle.

It must be owned that he was somewhat embarrassed, and just escaped addressing Sally as Miss Benedict, but caught himself in time and asked if Mr. Benedict could see him for a few moments.

Now Sally had determined in the depths of her soul that if she was obliged to be door maid as well as kitchen maid, she would make the most of her opportunities and impress this country village with a sense of high station of her young mistress, so that she really succeeded in quite overawing the young minister with her airs, as she told him that Mr. Benedict was not in, but she would see if Miss Benedict knew if he would be back soon, and would he give her his card? Then from a tiny stand she produced the silver salver, and the Reverend Robert Clifton could scarcely find a card, so astonished was he at the difference between what he had expected and what he had found.

While he waited in the lovely reception room which had once been the cold and deserted parlor of haircloth and red-and-green ingrain, he had ample opportunity to observe the many evidences of refinement and taste spread all about him. Everything was beautiful, luxurious, comfortable; evidently purchased by one who knew how to do such things. Mechanically his eye took in the fact that the heavy rugs spread in the wide oak hall were real Oriental. He could see an upright piano through a veil of fine bead *portières* and a glimpse of an inviting couch with pillows, in the room opening out of the parlor, and across the hall a pleasant vista, a library furnished with luxurious leather-upholstered couch and chairs, with a large reading table and shaded lamps, books, a low bookcase running around the wall. He could hear a canary singing in the room beyond the library. He wondered vaguely what sort of young woman would appear and rapidly began to change his mental picture of her. She must be a woman of the world, and if so, she would be doubly hard to reach and help, and he would need to take the more earnest care of his own good name. He began to fear he had done wrong in coming alone and to wish he had heeded the advice of Deacon Chatterton. Then there came the soft rustle of a dress down the stairs, and a light step at the door, and Ruth Benedict stood before him.

Ruth had looked at the card curiously when it was brought to her. Had her servant been one from the village she would at once have been informed that the visitor was the new minister; but Sally did not move in Summerton society and shunned gossip of all sorts. Ruth recognized the name at once as belonging to a young theological student whom she had met several times at the home of friends during a summer visit. He had interested her because he seemed in earnest, and had also disappointed her in some respects because he had not seemed to have thought seriously about a great many questions which to her were very important ones. Now her quick brain at once jumped to the conclusion that this student had finished his educational course and was a full-fledged minister, and was probably occupying the position of pastor in Summerton. She had heard David say that there was a new minister and that he was a young man, and she had hoped that he would call on her brothers and would have a good influence over them. Indeed she had planned it all out nicely how he and his wife would be such helpers in her schemes, and would perhaps invite them to the parsonage and make friends of them. She was very anxious for her brothers to meet some

earnest, Christian, cultured young men. But she looked
doubtfully at the card.

Would this young Mr. Clifton be the one to do them
good? He was bright, she knew; indeed some had called
him brilliant. He was a Christian—she had felt sure of that
when she met him—and that he had chosen his profession
because he felt that God had called him to it, but—she
drew a sigh and went downstairs breathing a prayer.
Perhaps after all Mr. Clifton had changed some of his
theories. She remembered very distinctly how it had
troubled her to know that a young man, who was so soon to
be a minister, had deliberately sat himself down to read a
comic story in one of the current magazines on his return
from the Sunday morning service, and how later in the day,
when the subject had come up for discussion, he had
defended his action by saying that he did not believe the
Lord wanted us to be long-faced, and that the "sabbath was
made for man and not man for the sabbath." He also said
that his mother and several of his dearest Christian friends
always read whatever they pleased on Sunday, and so long
as it was a good thing it did not seem to him that the
Heavenly Father could object. He added that their profes-
sor in theology in the seminary told the students that he
had often read novels on Sunday evening after his most
earnest services, in order to give his mind as entire a
relaxation as possible.

Ruth had sat quietly in a corner, a very young girl, not
supposed to be taking any part at all in the conversation;
but her eyes must have expressed wonder, and perhaps
disapproval, for as he raised his eyes he caught her clear
gaze, and with his pleasant smile had appealed to her with,
"What do you think about it, Miss Ruth? Isn't that a wise
position I have taken?"

She had not expected to be asked her position, but,
though taken by surprise, she answered quietly as she had
been taught to do, just what was in her heart.

"I cannot judge for any one else," she had said simply.
"For myself I feel as if God made the Sabbath for me to
enjoy him in, and not to enjoy myself. There is a verse in
Isaiah that settled the question for me two years ago."

The young theologue was pleasantly interested. He

asked for the verse and listened respectfully to her answers to his questions. She had repeated the verse in a matter-of-fact tone much as if she had been reading a bit of a letter from a dear friend. It seemed to have a new light to the young man as she spoke it: "If thou turn away thy foot from the sabbath, from doing thy pleasure on my holy day; and call the sabbath a delight, the holy of the Lord, honourable; and shalt honour him, not doing thine own ways, nor finding thine own pleasure, nor speaking thine own words: Then shalt thou delight thyself in the Lord; and I will cause thee to ride upon the high places of the earth, and feed thee with the heritage of Jacob thy father: for the mouth of the Lord hath spoken it." He had hinted that these words belonged to the old dispensation and that we were no more under the law but under love, and she had laughed a happy laugh. "Oh, I don't feel that it is a law at all," she said, "because I love him. It is merely a statement of what he would like to have me do. When my mother asks me to do something or says, 'Ruth, it would please me very much if such and such a thing were done,' I don't feel like going around saying my mother has made me do this thing, or commanded me to do that. But it is just as binding on me as if it were a law, for I know it is what she would like to have me do. Besides it seems to me as if God had put the words in just that way to make us see that it is meant for a law of love as well as written in tables of stone. It says not 'if you don't do these things I will punish you,' but 'if you do them then shalt thou delight thyself in the Lord.' I should think that must be the highest, most restful happiness there could be, to be perfectly delighted in the Lord and have him delighted in us."

Their conversation had been interrupted just then and they had not seen each other since, but Ruth had carried away a troubled feeling. Her reverence for and her ideal of the high calling of the ministry had been very great. It troubled her that one who professed to believe that in Jesus Christ alone could true rest be found, would try to rest his own brain from preaching the message to others by reading worldly papers and books, some of which were written by men who did not believe in Jesus at all. It seemed to her that a minister should know the way to find true rest from anything in Jesus, else he could not point it out to others. There had been other discussions too, during those few weeks when she had seen him occasionally, that gave her a feeling that he was worldly in a great many ways. But the Ruler of all was leading and she could trust it with him.

Ruth had the advantage of her visitor, for she was reasonably sure who he was before she saw him, while it had not occurred to him that she and the other Miss Benedict could be identical.

"Mr. Clifton, this is a pleasant surprise, to meet one who is not a stranger when I am in a strange land."

There was sweetness and modest grace in tone and movement. The young minister was utterly bewildered for a moment. She stood just as he had planned she would stand in the years to come, his ideal of Christian young womanhood. How had she attained to it so soon? She ought to be but a little girl yet.

But she was standing there to welcome him and he must gather his scattered faculties. All thought of the Benedict brothers, so hard to reach in hermitage and isolation with their wild, worldly, bicycling sister, drifted away from him. The surroundings were such as to make him forget. He greeted her warmly. He was eager to know how she came here and what it all meant, and he must answer her questions about their mutual friends. It took him some time to understand the situation, and he began to wax indignant in his heart at his deacons and their wicked gossip. Surely some one must be greatly at fault that such terrible things could be said. He wondered what her brothers could be about that they allowed it, and what indeed could have started it in the first place, and then wondered again if he had not made some great mistake and gotten into the wrong house; and yet it was scarcely possible that he could have made such a mistake. Presently Ruth gave some light on the subject, however.

"I am sorry my brothers are neither of them in," she said. "They told me they had not met the new minister. I want them to meet you. I am sure you can help them"; here she looked anxiously at his face to be sure whether she was sure. "They are neither of them Christians," she added sadly. There was an answering sympathetic light in the minister's face which reassured her, however, as she went on. "I have been so sorry not to go to church. Day before yesterday was the first time I have been outside of the yard since my accident. I had the misfortune to fall from my bicycle and sprain my ankle."

Ah! here was the key to the story. He would ferret out the rest and have it explained fully. He asked a few questions about the matter, and then, that she might not think he had a special reason for his earnest inquiries, he changed the subject.

"Miss Benedict," he said earnestly. "I have always thought I would like you to know that you once helped me very much on a certain subject, and indeed I am not sure but on more than one, for I found it reached to many things when I once began to think about it. Do you remember a certain brief discussion on the subject of Sunday reading and conversation? And do you remember repeating to me that verse in Isaiah as your answer to my question what you thought about the subject? Well, that verse stayed with me. I could not get away from it, and in spite of the fact that I had settled in long before that I had good ground for the position I then held, I could not get rid of the feeling that I was doing wrong and grieving my Saviour every time I gave myself over to enjoying a secular book or paper on Sunday. In vain I used my former arguments. In vain I told myself I was reading this or that for the spiritual good I could get from it. I could not help seeing that that was merely an excuse I was hiding behind, and that the reading was being done for my own pleasure, more than anything else. I was brought to see then that I did not love my Bible so much as I ought to do, and that my excuse used heretofore that I had not time to devote to its study as I ought, was a flimsy one, for I did have some time on Sunday, if not for study, at least to read, and get rest and refreshment and joy and new strength. Then I saw that the Bible had not been all those things to me at all, and I set about changing the matter. Now I stand in an entirely different position from what I did. I do not say nor think that it is wrong to read anything other than the Bible or some strictly religious book on Sunday, but I do say that I have not time enough for my Bible now and cannot afford to lose one moment of the precious rest it brings me on Sunday, when I am weary with my work, and I believe that was what He intended the book and the day should be to us. I want to thank you for bringing that message to me."

Ruth's face shone with the joy that comes with the knowledge of having helped another human being. Her heart was relieved about another matter also. There was no mistaking the true ring to the minister's voice. She felt sure he would be a helper for her brothers. Before there was time for any answer a step came across the hall and David entered.

CHAPTER XI

David wore a collar now almost all the time. It had come about through the influence of the beautiful things with which the old house had been filled. He did not feel at home among them without a collar, and so he was gradually becoming accustomed to its stiffness. It is true he always took it off as soon as he reached the solitude of his own room and gave a sigh of relief, but he nevertheless put it on the next time with less reluctance. As soon as his farm work was done and he could come in the house he put on the collar. As for Joseph, he took to collars and the like much more naturally. He had at one time had longings toward a glass scarf pin and oiled hair, but having little use for such things his longings had not met with much encouragement. But David dressed as a distinct mark of respect for the new sister and the new order of things in the house. So Ruth was not ashamed of the appearance of her brother when he entered the room to meet the minister.

He did seem somewhat surprised to find a stranger there, it is true, for visitors at the Benedict farm had been few in the lifetime of the boys. But David's welcome was cordial, and Ruth noted with pride that he did not seem to be embarrassed by the young minister, but talked well. She thought that Robert Clifton's face expressed some surprise and admiration at David's intelligence. She sat by listening and praying and watching the two. Would they become warm friends and mutual helpers? She saw that they were mentally measuring one another, and that each was at least pleasantly impressed by the other. She wished that Joseph would come in, and excused herself once to go in search of him, but he was not to be found. However, just as the minister was going out the front gate he met Joseph coming in, and with his naturally frank, pleasant impulse he greeted him and introduced himself. It was but a moment they stood together within the fast gathering twilight, but the younger man went into the house with his heart completely won over. He had not been in a state of mind to resist, and the new minister had a very winning way with him.

Joseph was in a softened mood these days. Ever since Ruth had been hurt he had been different. All the repressed child-love that had found no expression seemed to be stored up in his nature, and was seeking an outlet. Now he poured it upon Ruth. They had been a happy family during Ruth's temporary confinement to the house, and though they did not know it, the two young men had been growing in knowledge of many kinds so rapidly as to astonish any one who had known them well before. It is wonderful what a refining influence a few pictures and books can have upon a human soul. Ruth was delighted, but yet her heart was heavy, for though she had been able to reach her brothers in many ways, there had not been one little minute when she felt she had done anything toward influencing them to come to Christ. It is true she recognized that she was gaining an influence over them that might help her in the future, but she was anxious to have them one with her on this great vital question at once, that she and they might grow together. She had been pained to discover that the subject of church-going was very doubtful, so doubtful that it often did not come up as a question at all. She knew that they would be willing to accompany her, at least one of them at a time, perhaps as soon as she was able to go, but she would so much rather have had them go from love of it, or at least from habit. She had wondered so many times what sort of a minister the Summerton Church had, that it was a great relief to know at last who he was. Somehow she felt a great deal more certain of his help for her brothers since that earnest speech of his about Sabbath keeping. To be sure it was no way to judge a man, by his theory on some one subject, but still it was, in a way, an index to his character, and as he had said, led off into other subjects. Still she had seen men whose ideas of right and wrong fitted hers exactly, and who were by no means fitted to be helpers to young men who were not Christians.

Therefore Ruth prayed much during the Saturday that followed the minister's call at their home, for a blessing on the Sunday with its services. She had arranged with both of her brothers to accompany her to church. They had acquiesced as a matter of course. If it pleased her to go to church they were entirely willing. Indeed on Joseph's part there was not a little pride connected with escorting his beautiful, well-dressed sister to church. He hoped the Brower boys would be there, and if they dared once to even so much as look in her direction, and he saw them, woe betide them. David wanted to amuse his sister in every way possible, and his only fear was that she would find their church a dull place. However, there was also an element of interest in the person of the young minister with whom both brothers had been pleasantly impressed. They would like to see if he could preach. He had talked with them so well and freely, just as if he had always known them and had worked beside them. At least David so put it to himself as he thought over his conversation with Robert Clifton.

Sunday morning dawned bright and beautiful. There had been a sharp frost during the night and the air was clear and crisp.

Ruth somehow felt very happy as they drove down the long white road, so smooth and hard and straight. She had just come from communion with Jesus and her face was shining with the peace in her heart. She had been enabled to leave all her cares and perplexities to him who was guiding, sure that he knew the way and could not make a mistake.

The minister had spent much time upon his knees that week. It seemed to him that he could not pray enough. As the week neared its close and the Sunday services were at hand he began to realize the awful responsibility of speaking the word of God to the people. He was beginning to know some of his young people now, and to be personally interested in them for their own sake, and as he had inquired about this one and that, he had been pained to learn how few of the younger ones were members of the church. He had been told that Summerton was a hard field and indeed he feared from what he had seen that it would so prove itself.

He had laid aside some of his cherished sermons which seemed to him the best fruit that thought and study could produce through his brain, and had written a plain, simple, earnest appeal to sinners from the text, "What think ye of Christ?" He had written it out fully, but he felt that he would not have to read it, for every word of reason and exhortation seemed burned into his soul, and he wanted to speak from his heart to his hearers. The more intellectual sermons would have their place by and by, but he wanted to find out now what each one of them thought of Jesus Christ. He wanted to know what those two Benedict brothers thought of him; and what the two low-browed men in the back seat thought, and what some of the pretty giggling girls thought; and what the elder members of his church, both men and women, thought. Did they think enough of Jesus the Christ to enter into the work heart and soul for his church, bringing all the tithes into the store-house and proving the Lord of Hosts for a blessing such as there should not be room to receive? One might almost have called his mood exalted as he entered the house of worship and made his way to the little study which occupied a small space at one side of the pulpit and opened into the "ladies' parlor."

Deacon Chatterton and Deacon Meakins stood in this doorway talking and the former stepped up to hand him some church notice.

"By the way, Deacon Chatterton," said the minister, "and you too, Deacon Meakins, you will be glad to learn, I am sure, that there is some mistake about what was said of the

Benedicts. I called there this week and find that Miss
Benedict is the adopted child of a very dear friend of my
mother's I have met her before, and her character is beyond
reproach. She is an unusually remarkable Christian, and
has been brought up by a woman whose life was one long
sermon. I shall rely on you two brethren to correct any
absurd report that may have been spread abroad. It is very
strange how such a thing could have started. You will find
the young woman a great help in church work, I am sure.
She was a power among the young people in her former
home. She has come among us to stay, she tells me, and will
bring her letter at once to this church."

"But—but—the—the—bicycle!" gasped Deacon
Meakins anxiously. He wished to have the whole trouble
cleared from doubt at once, and he had himself seen the
bicycle coming from the freight car, though he would not
have told the other deacons so for a good deal.

"I don't understand, Deacon Meakins," said the minister
anxiously. He wanted to be alone for the last minute before
the bell should cease tolling and he thought he had
explained fully. "What had the bicycle to do with it?
Certainly she rides, she told me so herself; but very many
young ladies do that now in the city. My own sister has had
a wheel for some time. It is perfectly respectable."

The bell ceased to toll, and the minister's quiet moment
was gone. The two deacons went to their seats pondering,
one of them relieved in his righteous soul, the other
wondering whether they had chosen their minister wisely,
after all, if he was going to uphold such things as bicycling
for young women. But do him the justice to remember that
he forgot all about it when the sermon began.

Ruth Benedict dawned on Summerton, and between her
and the new minister the attention of the Summerton
congregation was quite divided.

It would have been a study in human nature if the
thoughts of the different people could have been pictured
that morning. It might have somewhat discouraged the
earnest minister, and perhaps so disheartened him that he
would have given up at once and missed the blessing, for
there were some souls ready for the message, and it bore
rich fruit in the days that came after.

Ellen Amelia Haskins happened to sit near and almost behind Ruth Benedict, and her admiring eyes were scarcely taken away from the black velvet hat with its drooping plumes and the sweet oval of the earnest face before her. Once she turned to watch Joseph and David a moment, to try if she could see how they felt, sitting beside such a creature and calling her sister. It was the nearest to a romantic story that had ever come into her life, and she was enjoying it to the full. An intense longing filled her soul to get nearer to this wonderful young woman and know more of her. For a few moments she studied the black velvet hat to see if it was possible to use that dark red velveteen she had intended using for big puffs to her sleeves in any such way. She wondered how the brim took on such a pretty curve and felt sure she could manage it if she only had some of the mysterious stuff they made hat frames from; but the wonderful feathers were beyond anything she had ever seen in Summerton and she gave up the hat with a half-envious sigh and let herself drift off into enjoyment of the whole lovely figure of the stranger.

Joseph had walked in with haughty mien, straight and protecting, beside his sister. He gave a glance over his shoulder to see if the Brower brothers were there, and when he discovered them sitting with lowering brows sullenly back near the door, he made himself a little straighter, if that were possible. Only toward the end of the sermon did he listen to what was going on. Then an illustration caught him and held his attention to the end; and when the final amen was pronounced he confirmed his first decision that the minister was "something like it," whatever that meant. Who shall say that illustration did not go with him and help to influence all his future life? At least he was won to like and listen to the new minister, and that was a great point gained.

David had set himself to listen at once. He had liked the minister and he wanted to see now if he was worth listening to. The former preacher he had always considered dry. Perhaps too, the fact that he had never known any other minister in that church since his little boyhood, made his familiar voice uninteresting. The very first words this man spoke caught his attention. "What think ye of Christ?" They were spoken like a question to him and the speaker seemed to be looking directly at him. For some time it did not dawn upon his consciousness that the words were from the Bible. He almost felt that he must arise in his seat and give an answer and he began wondering what his answer would be. Perhaps if the truth must be frankly told he did not think anything of Christ. The speaker had caught his hearer. David had no more time for thought, for he was carried on the swift wings of the earnest, red-hot words that came straight from one soul, charged with an electric current from heaven, into the soul of another living, dying brother. When the end came and he stood with the rest as they sang, some badly, some indifferently, and a few with their hearts, the words,

> "Behold a stranger at the door!
> He gently knocks, has knocked before,
> Has waited long, is waiting still;
> You treat no other friend so ill,"

he felt again that strange force bidding him answer these charges. Was there an unseen choir present which helped on the village voices, and bore the song in angelic strains, straight into his soul? Long years afterward something of this thought came to him, and he did not say it nay.

"It's just as I thought," said Mrs. Deacon Chatterton to herself, looking over her spectacles while the second hymn was being sung; "she's pretty; that kind always are! Humph!" and then she felt thankful in a moral kind of exultation that Eliza Barnes was not out at church to-day; she was saved at least one week of temptation. For some reason Mrs. Chatterton seemed to consider all things pretty a temptation.

The Brower boys went out from the church feeling uncomfortable, they hardly knew why. The sermon had made them feel so. They were too dull to understand the reason and too wicked to heed what had been spoken to them. Perhaps though, the seed fell not all on stony ground in their hearts. But they said on the way home that they did not like the new minister, and what was more, they never would like him.

The benediction was pronounced and David Benedict

was just about to step out into the aisle when the minister placed a detaining hand upon his shoulder.

"One minute, Benedict; I want your sister to teach a class in the Sunday-school and I want you and your brother for my Bible class. Your brother half promised me that he would stay. It won't hinder you to remain, will it? I really need your sister for a teacher very badly."

David gave his consent at once, amazed beyond expression. Joseph had promised to attend Sunday-school! By what power had the minister abstracted that promise, and when had he met Joseph? The millennium must surely be about to dawn. He would not put one hindering stone in the way of either Joseph or his sister. So, although he shrank from going into a class, and tried to get away on pretext of looking after the horses, the minister laughingly held on to him and he went over to the corner and sat down with the Bible class, to the amazement of Deacon Chatterton and the gratification of Deacon Meakins. And there sat Joseph! David could not get over it. The brothers wisely refrained from looking at one another, but sat in their places as if they had been accustomed to coming to Sunday-school from time immemorial. Truth to tell, Joseph had not intended to stay at all, but some strange power in that winning smile of the minister forced him against his will. Besided, Ruth seemed anxious to remain.

The minister escorted her down the aisle to the corner where sat a row of giggling girls, and placed her in front of the delighted and wholly devoted Ellen Amelia. As he went down the aisle he said in a low tone to his new teacher: "You are just the one for that class I am sure. There is one girl who needs you—and probably more—but I am interested in her. She is Deacon Haskins' daughter. You will know her. She is the one who looks as if she had tried to and couldn't."

"And am I supposed to help her try to and can?" asked Ruth, laughing.

"Well, I had not put it that way; I had supposed the proper thing would be to teach her not to try what she cannot accomplish, but perhaps it would be better to show her how to attain to the height of her ambitions."

Then he left her before those girls who were every one of them ready to adore her at once, if they ever got quite over

being a little afraid of her. As soon as the first awe of having
the velvet hat in their immediate midst had disappeared
somewhat, they began to sing very loud and look proudly
over at the other classes of girls who had not a new, stylish
teacher from the city. And so is Christ's work mingled with
the wickedness of this world and the petty sins of the
human heart.

CHAPTER XII

"She was real solemn part of the time," said Ellen Amelia as
she passed her plate for some more cabbage. "I wouldn't
have thought she was that kind. She ain't quite like any girls
I ever read of either, for she don't seem proud one bit,
though she does wear such lovely clothes. She had the
cutest little pin on her collar, a wreath of green leaves with
a little pearl between each one. If I had a pin like that I'd be
just too happy to live. And she had a beautiful ring on. I saw
it when she took off her glove to write in our class book."

"I'm sure I don't know why you shouldn't be proud, if you
want to, without any pin or ring. You've just as good a right
to as she. Your father makes more money than hers ever
did, and because he ain't such a fool as to let you spend it on
gewgaws isn't any reason why you shouldn't be proud of
him, if you want to."

It was practical, anxious little Mrs. Haskins who said this.
But Ellen Amelia did not get her admiration for the
romantic from her mother's side of the family. Her mother
strongly disapproved of the "Fireside Companion," on the
ground that Ellen Amelia might be better employed in
darning stockings for the younger Haskinses than in
dreaming over its columns. She never read it herself and
therefore had no moral grounds of objection. But Deacon
Haskins was weak and yielding where his daughter was

concerned and quietly subscribed for it in response to her earnest pleadings.

"Well, I know one thing," went on Ellen Amelia, with her mouth full of cabbage; "I mean to cut over my brown basque and fix a little jacket to it like hers, and make a front out of that blue and green silk handkerchief Uncle Timothy sent me from New York. I just know I could do it."

"No, you are not!" interjected her mother sharply. "Your brown basque is good enough as it is, and I won't have you wasting your time chopping up good things to make an outlandish copy of a girl you never saw before. If that's the kind of thing you learn in Sunday-school you better stay at home."

Probably the young teacher, who was at that moment kneeling beside her bed and praying that the words she had spoken to those girls that morning might not all have been in vain, would have agreed with the mother could she have listened. But though dress and romance were uppermost in Ellen Amelia's mind, there was an undercurrent of something earnest, some longing she had never felt before, which, strange to say, found its outlet in a desire to dress like her new idol. Miss Benedict was lovely. Why could not she be lovely if she could make herself look like that? She had something higher in her soul that Ellen Amelia had understood, and Ellen Amelia had resolved to have it too if possible. The only way to get it was to try to be like the girl who possessed it. The only way to be like her was to begin with her dress. Ellen Amelia meant well, and would come out right in the end.

She stood at the window of the front room of her father's house one afternoon of that week digging a pin diligently into the window sash and winking back the tears. She and her mother had just been having a rather angry talk about the brown basque. Ellen Ameila was determined to have the little jacket fronts put on in the way Miss Benedict's had been. She had coaxed and reasoned all in vain. Mrs. Haskins was firm. The brown basque should not be cut up nor its fashion altered in any way. Ellen Amelia hated it. It did not fit her. Its plain darts were too flat and the point at the waist in front stuck out. It was a great trial to her. She had resolved to model herself after this lovely stranger, in short to be such a pattern of loveliness in every respect that her mother should be astonished at her. It need not be thought that Ellen Amelia had not recognized the higher something which Ruth Benedict possessed, for she did and longed to possess it herself; but how was she to do so if she could not even attain the outward similitude? The trouble with Ellen Amelia was that she began at the outward instead of the inward to model her likeness. But after all, was she much to blame? She understood better the outward, and who shall say God did not mean the outward adorning sometimes to be the key to the inner one. It is true it might have turned out otherwise had not Ruth's taste in dress been quiet, modest, self-respecting, and lovely. There was nothing of flash or showiness about Ruth Benedict.

Ellen Amelia looked out on the bright autumn world and thought it a dark one. How was she to improve herself and do any of the great things her heroines of the weekly story papers always succeeded in doing in the world, if her mother would persist in throwing hindrances in her path? She sighed discontentedly and wished she could ever have anything she wanted. If only she might have a new dress and make it the way she wanted to! But no, of course her mother would insist on cutting it out in her own way, even if she did have one.

Just then her meditations were interrupted by the wild gesticulations of her little brother Amos, who was waving a large paper package which proved to be an express package, and addressed to her. Ellen Amelia's heart fluttered and she thought of all the possibilities of princes in disguise who might have seen her in some impossible way and fallen in love with her at first sight, found out who she was in an equally improbable way, and sent her some rare gift. Ellen Amelia was always getting up some such sudden picture of ravishing delight for herself only to have it dashed in hard practical bits at her feet by the stern facts of the case. Yet in spite of repeated disappointments and dashing of hopes, her buoyant imagination was always ready for a new possibility of wonder which should "robe her in gown of the finest texture and deck her with jewels so fair." Really there were possibilities of great good or evil in Ellen Amelia, and if some prince of darkness in disguise had happened to appear about this time in her path it would have been worse for her. She was in great danger.

But there was a Wiser than her mother and father watching
over her. Even now some good was coming to her through a
common express package sent by her Uncle Timothy in
New York. He was a policeman there and well to do. He
had no children of his own, and remembered well how he
used to romp with and care for little tow-headed Ellen
Amelia when she was but five years old and he a clerk in his
brother's hardware store. At long intervals, with no seeming reason like a birthday or Christmas as an excuse, he
sent Ellen Amelia something. There had been but two of
these gifts before this one. The first had been a gold dollar,
and the second the aforementioned blue and green silk
handkerchief.

Great excitement prevailed in the Haskins family while
the package was being opened, and Ellen Amelia felt her
importance. Mother Haskins came with her dish towel over
her arm and a teacup she was wiping in her hand.
Grandmother Haskins came with a button between her lips
and little Tommie Haskins' red flannel "Johnny cloths" she
was mending in her hand, while young Amos and Tommie
hung over the paper and gloated over each difficult knot in
the heavy twine in a transport of delight. If you could not
have express packages addressed to yourself, why then
surely it was the next best thing to have your sister get one.

The papers fully unwrapped, disclosed to view soft rich
folds of dark blue serge material, a good full dress pattern of
it. Uncle Timothy certainly had good taste, or else had
asked the advice of the dress-goods clerk. Certainly he
could not have selected anything that would have brought
out better the uncertain complexion of Ellen Amelia, who
would have liked to be beautiful, but alas! knew not how to
make the best of what she had.

After the first excitement was over, Ellen Amelia sat
down to enjoy her present by herself. There was a shadow
over her joy even so early. Her mother had said with grim
satisfaction, "That'll save buyin' you anythin' new this
winter, thank fortune! We must get at makin' it as soon's the
boys' flannels is out of the way," and she had gone back to
her labors in the kitchen, rejoicing truly that her daughter
would have such a beautiful dress, planning the while to cut
it by a pattern which fitted herself, as Ellen Amelia was
growing so large now.

But the daughter took the beautiful goods up to her room and sat down to think. She had visions of the dress as it would look if it were made by her mother,—as her dresses had always been made,—with her own assistance, of course; and she also had another vision of the dress as it would appear if it were modeled after Miss Benedict's. Oh, if she could but attain to a city dressmaker! But, of course, that was out of the question. She had but three dollars and twenty-five cents of her own, and she did not feel like asking her father for more for that purpose. Money was not plentiful in the Haskins family. Ellen Amelia sighed again. A dressmaker was out of the question, and even if she were not she would have to be Miss Dunnet, the Summerton dressmaker, from West Winterton, and Ellen Amelia's soul had aspirations beyond Miss Dunnet. She had secretly compared the hang of Georgiana Brummel's skirt with the graceful sweep of Ruth Benedict's last Sunday, and she longed inexpressibly to be enfolded in such long, graceful folds as Miss Benedict was able to compass. Ellen Amelia was a girl of determination, and when she could not do a thing one way she generally managed to do it another. It was perhaps for this reason that she had impressed the minister as one who "tried to and couldn't." Only he did not know. She tried and accomplished, but by so hard and circuitous a route that the result was utterly different from what she had planned. But this time she determined to do a rather daring thing. She would go to Miss Benedict and see if she could borrow a skirt pattern. She had a secret fear that her errand might all be in vain, and that city ladies did not usually even know that their dresses required a pattern, but she could but fail if she tried. So, making an excuse of some trifling errand, she started out, not without much fear and trembling.

Once on her way, she began to almost repent her hasty action. What would the elegant young city lady think of her, asking for a skirt pattern? Ellen Amelia had walked about a mile and was nearing the border of the Benedict farm, when she determined firmly that she would say nothing whatever about the skirt pattern. Indeed, as she came in sight of the house she began to think maybe it would be better not to go in at all, but to go on up to the Barnes' house and do that errand for her father she had promised to

do some time. It would look presuming in her to call on
Miss Benedict. To be sure Ruth had kindly invited all her
class to come and see her, saying she was lonely and wanted
to get acquainted, but Ellen Amelia could scarcely conceive
of that being exactly true. How could she be lonely and
want common village companionship when she occupied so
novel a position, mistress of a grand home, full of beautiful
things, and two newly made brothers to worship her—for
that Joseph and David thought a great deal of their sister,
she had fully decided, during her brief view of their faces
on Sunday.

When she reached the gate she paused, half turned to go
in, and then quickly looking sidewise at the windows
turned and went rapidly on, a few steps. It was a very hard
thing, however, to come so near this dream of paradise and
not go in. Ellen Amelia looked back again, and saw, oh
wonder of wonders, a window thrown up, and a white hand
with a dainty handkerchief waving at her, and a voice
calling, "Miss Haskins."

It had really never struck Ellen Amelia in the grown-up
sense before, that she was Miss Haskins. It sounded so
dignified and far-away. She expected to be Ellen Amelia to
the ends of her days, unless indeed the wonderful prince
came. She had sometimes thought that he might call her
"Miss Ellen," or "Miss Alène," or "Miss Amélie," as she
variously designated herself after reading some of her
favorite serials.

But to be called "Miss Haskins" by another girl, and such
a girl, putting her on a level with herself, and speaking
the words with such a sweet friendly tone, Ellen Amelia
could scarcely believe her ears. She stopped, of course, and
obeyed the summons, and was almost overpowered by the
splendor and comfort of the room into which she was
ushered, which proved to be the library.

Ruth had been praying for this scholar of hers ever since
Sunday. She had been asking her Heavenly Father to give
her some opportunity of helping her, if it was his will.
Therefore she did not feel that it was all chance that she
should look up from her writing desk by her upper window
and see the figure of the girl for whom she had been
praying. There was something about Ellen Amelia that was
unmistakable even at a distance, if one had once noticed

her carefully. Perhaps it was the "tried-to-and-couldn't-ness" of her. At least Ruth felt sure her opportunity was coming, and when, as she watched, she saw that the girl wanted to come in and hesitated, she helped on the opportunity by opening her window and calling to her.

"I am so glad you were passing," began Ruth when she had seated her bewildered visitor and insisted on removing her wraps, for the day was a cold one. "I was just hoping some one would come, for I am alone this afternoon."

She was very winning and pleasant and she seemed to know exactly how to take away the embarrassment from her visitor. Some fine instinct, or perhaps some higher spiritual guidance, told her that her guest would be more at her ease if she could once have the opportunity to look about the room, and so Ruth made an excuse to leave her alone in that wonderful room for full five minutes on plea of giving a direction to Sally, and when she came back Ellen Amelia, as she had hoped, had regained some of her abundant spirit, and was able to talk. Indeed she even lost her embarrassment so much as to become quite confidential and to admire her hostess.

"You do have the loveliest life!" said Ellen Amelia with an adoring look in her eyes. "My! I just wish I was you!"

"Oh no, you don't!" said Ruth quickly with something of fun, and something sadness too, in her tone. "Why, no one's life would exactly suit any one else. And then think" and her voice saddened, "you have a mother and father; and I, though I had two, have been left without either. You wouldn't change places with me for a minute if you would stop to think. You would not give up your father and mother and your grandmother—didn't you tell me you had a grandmother? Just think what it would be to be without them."

"Oh well," said Ellen Amelia uneasily, "of course I wouldn't want them to die; but if I had never known them and could be you it would be lovely. I think it must be awful nice to have things the way you want them without having to ask a soul, and not have your mother always saying 'No' to everything you want. Ma and I just had a time about something. I must say, I think I'm old enough to do as I please."

Ruth's face grew sad and her heart heavy. How was one to talk to a girl who had such unnatural feelings as this one?

"Oh, you don't know what you are saying, I'm sure, my dear," said Ruth earnestly, placing her pretty white hand on Ellen Amelia's arm. "I can't bear to hear you talk like that. If you were tried once you would feel so differently. Why, I would give all the world just now to have my mother, or some one, tell me what to do. It seems to me I would be willing to do the most disagreeable thing if only I might have them to please once more. And you should not feel so about your mother. A mother is such a wonderful being, almost like God in some of her qualities. A mother has to bear so much. Your mother, I'm sure, does not hinder you from anything that she feels is for your good."

"Oh no, of course not," said Ellen Amelia with a little of the shrug of her shoulders which she used at home when she did not like things; "but her ideas of what is for my good, and mine, are very different. My mother thinks it isn't for my good to ever have my own way in anything. You have your own way all the time."

"That is where you are utterly mistaken, my dear," said Ruth, determining to be bright and not seem to be too severe on the girl the first time. Indeed, her first feeling on hearing her guest speak so of her mother to a stranger, had been one of shocked horror, and she could scarcely forbear a severe rebuke; but further reflection made her feel that probably the mother might be a little hard on her daughter, and if she would help any she must gain the girl's confidence. "Nobody can have his own way in anything in this world without getting into trouble. God is guiding this world, and if we try to take hold and do his work we should get all mixed up. I don't often get my own way and I sometimes have to do things that I don't in the least want to do; but never mind that now. Suppose you tell me the particular thing you want to do, if it is something I may know. I would like to sympathize with you in it at least; or perhaps I can show you it isn't a real trouble after all," and Ruth laughed her happy, contagious laugh.

Ellen Amelia looked down. She suddenly felt shy. She did not like to tell Miss Benedict about her troubles over dress. But the winning voice was saying, "Can you tell me dear, or is it something I must not know? I don't want to pry into things that are not my affairs, of course."

Ellen Amelia flushed. She did not wish to seem to refuse anything that Miss Benedict asked her, and somehow it was all like a story, her asking her in that frank pleasant way, just like "Ethel" when "Mr. Atholind" asked her if—what was it he asked her in last Saturday night's paper?

"My! but you would make a good character for a book now, you look so pretty sitting in that attitude," said Ellen Amelia suddenly, raising her admiring eyes to Ruth's face.

Ruth was disappointed and showed it in her eyes at once. If Ruth wanted to keep a secret ever, she always had to hide her eyes, but they would tell all they knew in spite of her. Ellen Amelia saw the disappointment and knew it had to do with her. She was repentant at once, and with eyes drooping again she said:

"Yes, I'm going to tell you. It's a thing you can know if you want to; only I just know you'll laugh at me."

CHAPTER XIII

After repeated assurances from Ruth that she would not laugh, Ellen Amelia burst out with her confidence:

"Well, then, it's my clo'es. I can't have a thing made the way I want it. Just look at that dress!" and she stood up and surveyed the front of a faded novelty-cloth, which had evidently been purchased more for its style than its durability. "You know it doesn't hang right. I don't know what's the matter with it, so I can't fix it. I've got a new dress to-day, a present from my uncle in New York. It's real pretty and I'd like to have it made nice, like some of yours, but ma will have to make it, and she'll make it the way she did my last year's, only with the sleeves a little bigger, I suppose. I want some jackets and front fixings, but she don't know how

to make them and she thinks it's a waste of time for me to
fuss; and besides, she says I don't know how any more than
she does, so I have to have them the way she makes them. I
started out here this afternoon to ask you if you had a skirt
pattern and would lend it to me, but when I got out here I
got scared; besides, I remembered that probably you never
had a skirt pattern in the house; you most likely sent your
dresses all to some dressmaker and didn't know how they
were made, so I decided to go on. I wouldn't have come in
at all if you hadn't called me. Now don't you think I'm an
awful fool?"

Ellen Amelia's courage was high pitched and failed her
just now, while tears of mortification and embarrassment
filled her eyes. But Ruth soothed her and made her sit
down again.

"I'm very glad you came to me, I am indeed. I think I can
help you. Indeed I have plenty of skirt patterns in the
house, some very pretty simple ones too, and I do not think
I have a single dress that was made by a dressmaker. I made
every one myself. My mother thought every girl ought to
know about that and so she sent me to the finest institution
that could be found in the city for learning dressmaking.
You know the schools of domestic science are very fine now.
I made all my own and my mother's dresses for a year or
two. It isn't so hard when you know how. Suppose you
come up here and spend the day on Thursday and bring
your new dress along and we'll make it. I think we can
finish it in a day or two if we work fast. I have done a dress
in a day with some one to help. Are you a good seamstress?
I'm to be alone all day on Thursday, for my brothers have to
drive over to West Winterton with some sheep. Will your
mother mind? Tell her I know all about dressmaking, for I
went to one of the best schools. Perhaps she'll be glad to be
relieved of it."

Ellen Amelia's eyes shone and her breath came quick.
Could it be true? This young woman with the immaculate
apparel made all her wonderful garments herself! And
could she believe her ears? Was she offering to help her?
Would it be possible that a Haskins could ever look like this
city maiden? And a school for dressmaking! Would the
wonders never cease? She had supposed that dressmaking
was some special gift conferred upon a few maiden ladies

and unfortunate widows, who by patient service had been granted an ability to make things look different from anything any one else could do, and by this earned their living.

She gave her eager and ready consent to spend Thursday, dress and all, with her new friend, if she were not imposing too much upon her. She said she was certain her mother would be pleased, which I fear was a polite little lie she had learned from the "Fireside Companion." In her heart she much feared that her mother would put her foot down most decidedly upon the proposition, but also in her heart she meant to contrive some way to carry out her purpose and have one dress made as she wanted it; for did not this dress belong to herself? and surely she ought to have the right to say how it should be made.

On her return home however, she found to her surprise that her way had been made plain. Her mother looked very tired and a shade of oldness seemed to be upon her face. Ellen Amelia had never before noticed that her mother was growing old, and it came to her with something of a shock. She remembered Miss Benedict's words, "You would not give up your mother." It gave her a strange feeling and she did up the dishes of her own accord after supper without waiting to be asked, which was unusual. She never wanted to leave her reading after supper. The mother seemed to appreciate this unusual mark of daughterliness, for with a gentler tone than she was accustomed to use she said, when Ellen Amelia came back to the sitting room after the kitchen was all in order for the morning:

"Ellen 'Melia, I'm just afraid you'll have to give up havin' that new dress made up till after Thanksgivin', 'tany rate. I've been thinkin' how I could get it in, and I just can't see my way clear, not if I go to nurse at Miss Crampton's them two weeks, and I've give my promise, you know. I feel sort o' done out to-day, and ef 'twan't fer your grandmother I'm sure I don't see how I would've got through the work. As it is, I think I'll go to bed early. I'm sorry you'll have to wait for your dress, but it can't be helped. You can console yourself by thinkin' you wouldn't have hed any at all ef it hadn't been for your Uncle Timothy."

Now was Ellen Amelia's opportunity.

"Now ma, don't you worry about that dress; I'm goin' to

make it myself. I went to call on Miss Benedict this afternoon, and she's invited me to spend the day with her Thursday and she'll help me make it. She's been to a big school where she learned how to make all her clo'es, sacks and hats and everything, and she said she would just like nothin' better'n to show me. I thought it would be a real relief to you, ma, and so I told her I'd come if you didn't need me for anything on Thursday."

Mrs. Haskins did not altogether approve of the plan, but her pride was somewhat pleased to have Miss Benedict, with her pretty clothes, actually willing to help her daughter make a dress, and the weary mother consented, with many a sigh and a misgiving. She told Ellen Amelia she had her doubts about the hang of the skirt, the set of the waist, and was afraid there would be too many new-fangled things on it, but she supposed if Ellen Amelia's heart was set on it, nothing else would do, and as it was a present she had a right to spoil it if she pleased. With which ungracious permission she reflected with satisfaction that her daughter would have a dress and she would not have to worry over it.

Thursday morning dawned bright and clear and found Ellen Amelia on her way to the Benedict farm. Such a gala day had not been before her since she was a little girl and anticipated for months beforehand the yearly May-day all-day picnic. Now she was to have her beloved Miss Benedict all to herself for a whole day in that lovely house. To be sure it would have been no drawback to have had David and Joseph in the background of the setting for an hour or two at mealtimes, and it had been no part of the inducement to her coming when Ruth had mentioned their intended absence. Ellen Amelia had felt the least bit disappointed. But then one could not mind about so small a thing when there was so much in the day besides. She hummed a tune as she hurried along with her face very bright. She met the minister hurrying toward the station and wondered if he was going to meet "his folks" and wondered what they would be like and if she would like them. She wished she could linger to see them, but knew that every moment was precious to the finishing of the blue serge, and hastened on.

Ruth had prepared a large sunny room on the second floor as a sewing room, and all her cutting and sewing appliances were arranged ready. The sewing machine was one of the best and would almost sew of itself. Ellen Amelia admired and wondered over it while she was being shown the difference between it and her mother's lumbering old one. The cutting table, the tracing wheel and bright shears, all had a charm that implements of common every-day work did not usually have for this girl. She was fonder of reading than of work. But she sighed and told herself she would love to sew if she could work with such tools. They studied awhile over some fashion plates Ruth had brought out, and Ellen Amelia supposed she was choosing from them the one she would like her dress made after, but in reality she was being advised as to what would become her and suit her material, and was having her eyes opened with regard to a number of points which had heretofore escaped her notice. It would appear that a style suited to a light, thin evening dress for the lazy beauties who lolled on velvet cushions in the weekly story papers, was not suited to heavy wool material intended for church and street wear, nor indeed for sensible, every-day living. Neither did it appear to be in good taste to put much trimming on even handsome material which was to be worn to church or to any other quiet place in the world where one was in earnest. Ellen Amelia learned, without exactly knowing how, that one's dress always expresses one's self, and that if we do not wish to give false impressions of ourselves we must be careful that the dress shall express what we would have our lives show. She pondered over this fact all day and wondered if religion had anything to do with dress, and tried to forgive herself for thinking a thought so irreverent.

Every moment of that morning was an inexpressible delight and excitement to Ellen Amelia. Fortunately the sewing room held no decorations save the simplest, or the mind of the young girl would certainly have been too upset to do much work. But the rapid, trained fingers of the young teacher were making progress all the time, and she had the rare talent of being able to talk pleasantly and without impatience, the while she worked as rapidly as her fingers could fly.

They had as dainty a lunch together as the lofty Sally could prepare. She sniffed a good deal to herself at having

to waste her fine arts of cookery on a village girl who would
much rather have ham and eggs, she presumed, but she did
her mistress' bidding thoroughly, in spite of her sniffing.
Ruth had tried to have everything as dainty as possible and
yet not so elaborate that it could not be easily remembered
and copied if her guest should choose to do so. She
believed most emphatically in the elevating power of little
things. A girl's manners could not but be made better if she
habitually ate at a dainty table. Also, she tried to have
everything eatable as unlike as possible to that to which she
thought Ellen Amelia was accustomed. And indeed the girl
felt that she was dining on the proverbial nectar and
ambrosia. There was a delicate soup of pale pink color, in
whose rich, creamy deliciousness she would never have
recognized the familiar tomato. There were tiny, shell-like
cups of rich chocolate, foamed with whipped cream, and
there was some strange, new delectable custard in little
molds, and thin, sweet wafer crackers. Ellen Amelia's eyes
were bright and her wits were quick. She was rather afraid
of the array of spoons and forks, but she watched her
hostess and tried to appear at her ease, and really
succeeded remarkably well. Ruth had guessed well that the
ceremony and the strangeness of the dishes would please
her guest more than to have a simple dinner, such as she
had every day at home. Ellen Amelia was one who liked
mystery and newness beyond anything else in life.

After lunch Ruth left her guest in the parlor for a few
minutes to wander about and look as much as she pleased,
and then she came and played and sang a few bright little
songs for her and one tender, sweet one, about a mother
and a home. She had selected these songs with care and
prayer and a view to reaching the different longings she
thought she saw in Ellen Amelia's eyes. Then, arm in arm,
they went back to their work. Said Ellen Amelia:

"Do you think it is wicked to care awfully for pretty
things? I don't suppose you do, because you have so many
around you; but I don't quite understand it. You talked in
Sunday-school as if you were terribly good."

"No," said Ruth, "I don't think it is at all wicked. On the
contrary, I think it is wrong not to have things just as pretty
as you can. If it were wicked to have things pretty God

would not have made the world beautiful. He might just as well have made the sun go down in gray every night, instead of throwing crimson and gold and purple clouds in the west. Just look at the landscape the next sunset hour and see if it isn't beautiful, and then tell me whether you do not think God likes beautiful things, and loves to have us enjoy them too."

"Well," said Ellen Amelia, "I s'pose that's true about the things he made. But it's wicked to like pretty clo'es, ain't it?"

"Well, no; I don't think it is. There is a difference between liking pretty clothes, and being so fond of attracting attention by showy dressing that one thinks of nothing else. I think every one ought to be as careful about having the dress neat and tasteful and becoming as they are about having their faces washed clean every day and their hair neatly combed. It is a duty. Did you ever read 'Ethics of the Dust' or 'Sesame and Lilies'? No? Well, Mr. Ruskin says dressing is a virtue. Here, let me read you a few words while you sew on those hooks. You'll be interested in that book if you never read it. Take it home and enjoy all about the Crystal life and the Crystal sorrows and the Crystal virtues. I'm sure you will like it if you read it carefully."

Ruth left the room a moment and while she was gone her visitor reflected with joy that she should have a book to take home. She wondered who this "Sesame" was, and if the Lilies had to do with another girl, and what the Crystal things were she had spoken of, if they were anything like that story of the lady of the crystal palace and the sleeping knight she read last year.

Then Ruth came back and read:

"LECTURER. I said their (a girl's) second virtue was dressing.

"MARY. Well! what did you mean by that?

"LECTURER. What do you mean by dressing?

"MARY. Wearing fine clothes.

"LECTURER. Ah! there's the mistake. I mean wearing plain ones.

"MARY. Yes, I daresay! but that's not what girls understand by dressing, you know.

"LECTURER. I can't help that. If they understand by dressing, buying dresses, perhaps they also understand by drawing, buying pictures. But when I hear them say they can draw, I understand that they can make a drawing; and when I hear them say they can dress, I understand that they can make a dress and—what is quite as difficult—wear one.

.   .   .   .

"DORA. Then we are all to learn dressmaking, are we?

"LECTURER. Yes; and always to dress yourselves beautifully; not finely, unless on occasion; but then very finely and beautifully too. Also, you are to dress as many other people as you can; and to teach them how to dress, if they don't know; and to consider every ill-dressed woman or child whom you see anywhere, as a personal disgrace; and to get at them somehow, until everybody is as beautifully dressed as birds. . . . Now you needn't say you can't, for you can and it's what you were meant to do, always; and to dress your houses and your gardens too.''

Ruth closed the book and went to work at the blue serge sleeves.

"We shall certainly not get this dress done in a week," she said, laughing, "if I stop to read to you any more, for you don't work while I read." Ellen Amelia laughed and took up another hook, but her mind was on the reading.

"Miss Benedict, do you really mean you think everybody—do you think I could dress well, and—that other thing—how could I dress other people? I don't understand it at all. That book reads something like the Bible, but the Bible says just the other thing. I've had it dinged into my ears ever since I was three, and cried because my apron had a patch of another color right in front. I know it by heart: 'Whose adorning, let it not be of the outward adorning, of the wearing of gold and plaiting the hair.'"

"But, my dear, Mr. Ruskin says nothing opposed to that. He does not say you are to adorn yourself, or wear costly apparel or jewels, nor, in short, to be showy; but simply to make yourself a pleasant object to look upon, so that your presence will soothe others. There is no virtue in an ugly thing. The Bible says, 'He hath made all things beautiful in their season.' Then don't you remember all about Christ's garments? They were not royal, such as an earthly king would have worn, trimmed with ermine and rich gold embroidery, and made of velvets and silks and costly furs. But do you not remember how the seamless coat he wore was so good and fine that the soldiers would not divide it but cast lots for it instead? It has always seemed to me that Jesus would have worn nothing gay or fine to attract attention, but I think the wool was soft and firm and fine, and the color quiet. He was not rich, nor would he have spent his money for princely robes if he had been, for they were not fitting for his work then; but I do not think it is irreverent to think that Jesus selected what he wore with good taste and good sense. The highest ideal of dress that is given in the Bible is the robe of righteousness and the pure white robe that we shall wear in heaven. The Bible seems to hold up simplicity as an ideal of dress and purity. Ellen, may I ask you a question? I am anxious to know its answer. Do you belong to Jesus? Are you trying to follow him in everything?"

The question was a quiet one, spoken in a matter-of-fact tone, and the preceding name "Ellen" sounded sweet to the girl's ears. She had been accustomed to hearing the two names run into one, and, indeed, had been proud of her double name as something high-sounding, but this quiet, dignified "Ellen," had a cultured sound far beyond the high-flown style she had been cultivating all her life. She liked it, and was pleased to be called so. It was the first time Miss Benedict had called her by her first name. But the question itself was embarrassing. She had never been asked this before in her life but once. The old white-haired minister, with his severe countenance, had come up to herself and three other girls as they stood chattering together at the back of the church after service, and said in a kindly, but very grown-up tone, "Little girls, have you entered the ark of safety?" They had been frightened, and had answered "I don't know," and one of them from sheer embarrassment had giggled, because she did not know what else to do, and the old man had sighed and gone on his way, feeling that he had done his duty, and the youthful heart was prone to wickedness. Neither father nor mother

had ever said to her, "Daughter, will you give your heart to
Jesus now?" They had taught her the words of the Bible and
some of the severe side of the meaning, but had not
thought anything more necessary, or else had failed in
courage to do more.

And now, Ellen Amelia, at sixteen, remembered the
scared little group of children huddled together and the old
minister towering above them with his question, and
giggled and made the same answer, "I don't know."

CHAPTER XIV

The dress was not finished that day. There was too much
talking to be done. Ellen Amelia went home at dusk with
her two little books of Ruskin, and a good many new
thoughts. She had developed in some measure, be it ever
so slightly, during that day, for she saw the sunset. For the
first time in her life, really, she saw a sunset and realized
that it was one, and was beautiful, and that God made it,
and that he made it for her as much as for any one else. The
day was cold, and as she started away from Ruth's she could
see the great glowing disk of the sun just slipping down
behind the long stretch of bare young trees which etched
themselves against the sky for a mile or two away upon the
horizon at her right. She watched the sun drop and the fire-
red glory flame up and over the horizon, and then catching
the bits of clouds, turn them from amber to gold, from
violet to purple, from rose to the loveliest blush pink, and
all set out by the fine lines of the delicate fringe of trees.
She saw for the first time the shade of blue on the distant
hills, and wondered that colors had existed before for her
merely in dress goods and ribbons. She felt uplifted and
happier, and then she wondered again how she should

answer that last question of Miss Benedict's, for she had
promised to bring her an answer the next time she came.

Her mother looked at her curiously and asked for the
new dress, and when she found it was not yet completed
said: "Humph! Just as I s'posed. You can't expect two young
girls to get together and bone right down to work. You've
dawdled half your time away, I suppose. I should think two
people with two good pairs of hands and nothin' in the wide
world to do from early mornin' to dusk at night, could have
got one dress done and hung up if they was smart and knew
what they was about. What's that you've got? A book? Well,
you just tell your Miss Benedic' that I don't thank her for
lending you any more books. I'm about crazy now with your
everlastin' readin'. For pity sake, don't set down now to
read! Here, take off your sack and dish up supper. When is
your dress to get done? That's what I should like to know."

The sharp words brought back the disagreeable expression to Ellen Amelia's face, and made her wish to return to
the lovely home where the gate of so many new worlds had
seemed to open to her that day, and to make her feel that
she could almost be willing to try to live an ideal life even in
her own home unchanged. She laid down the new books
with a sigh, and went to do her mother's bidding. And she is
not the first one who has found life, when one descends
from a mountain, rather tame and spiritless. Nevertheless
is it not a good thing, and a thing to be desired, to have
been upon the mountain?

When the work was out of the way Ellen Amelia settled
herself with great zest to the reading her new books, and
for a solid half-hour she applied herself with all her might to
gain an interest in what she was reading. It was all very
wonderful reading, but she seemed not to understand quite
so well as when Miss Benedict had read it aloud to her, and
besides there was so much to be thought about that one
could not go far at once. It did not hold the interest of the
untrained reader half so well as did "Cyril Athol's Grief,"
and in despair she got out her paper and read over a
chapter of that. There seemed, however, to have come a
staleness over this delightful story since she last read it two
days ago. She put it away in disgust and went to bed,
wondering what was worth while in life anyway, and lay

awake a long time to think over that last serious question. Did she belong to Jesus? She had always felt a great reverence and awe for him, but, after serious thinking, she decided that she did not belong to him, nor love him. She was more afraid of him than anything else. Well, if that was so, whom did she belong to? She shuddered at this thought and tried to turn over and go to sleep, but it would not go away. Altogether Ellen Amelia was glad when morning came and she could get up and do something. Thinking was hard work—unless it was dreaming. She was to go that afternoon again to work on the dress, and she had promised to answer that question definitely after thinking it over. It seemed strange now to her that she had not been able to say at once whether she belonged to Christ or not. Now she dreaded to tell Miss Benedict the real answer.

The dress was farther on its way than when she left it the night before, for the head dressmaker had been working. Ruth met her gayly with chat about the dress, and Ellen Amelia's trepidation concerning the solemn talk she expected to have, had almost been forgotten when Ruth finally came around to the question again as sweetly and naturally as if she had been asking if Ellen Amelia wished her sleeves large or small.

"And what about my question, Ellen? Did you find out that you belong to Jesus or not?"

After a long pause came Ellen Amelia's slow, hesitating, "No."

"Well, then, dear, I have one more question to ask: *Will* you?"

The young girl did not answer.

"You would, Ellen, if you once knew him. You could not help it. You love beautiful things and he is most beautiful of all. If I mistake not you are very fond of romance. You could not find more of it than in his life. You are a loving-hearted girl. Look how easily you have given me your love and confidence, me an utter stranger."

"Oh, but," said Ellen Amelia, her face all eagerness, "you are so good and lovely, and you were so good to me right away. You made me feel as if you loved me."

"Well, but Ellen, he loves you more than any earthly being ever could. He has been waiting for you to give him your love for long years. He has called you many times."

Joseph Benedict was in his room just around a little turn in the hallway. He often came to his room now to lie on that couch and read some of the interesting books his sister had placed there. He had fallen into the habit of the house, of leaving his door open. It was such a cheery house now that they could not any of them bear to cut one corner of it off for a time from the rest by a closed door unless it was necessary. He was weary from extra heavy work they had been doing in the morning. He heard his sister's voice, low and clear, and could hear the words she was speaking. He knew that Haskins girl was in the sewing room with Ruth and that she was doing her some good turn, but he had paid little attention to what was going on. Now he heard his sister's pleading tones and he could but listen for the answers which came so softly that he could not tell whether they were of assent or not. It was strange to him that he should care to have Ellen Amelia Haskins say or do anything, but he really felt quite out of patience with her for not consenting to what his sister put before her. It seemed to him a natural thing that she should do so. As to applying the words to himself just then it never occurred to him. He was interested to have Ruth satisfied, and to have that troubled note dropped from her voice. He went off into meditation of what Ruth was, and all that she had done for them since she came into their home. Pretty soon he heard her voice again as clear as before.

"I couldn't live without Jesus Christ, Ellen," she was saying. "He is my very dearest, most intimate friend. He would be just such a friend to you. You can ask him about everything. You can talk to him about everything, and be sure of his sympathy, and sometimes when I come to the hard places in my life it has seemed to me I could almost hear his voice telling me what to do. I wish you would take him for your friend. It is very easy. I want everybody I love to know him."

Joseph did not hear any more that afternoon. Sally came up for some direction and interrupted the conversation, and when she went down she closed the sewing-room door, so he did not know the result of the talk. He lay there wondering, trying to imagine what the Haskins girl would answer, trying vainly to make an answer that he felt would satisfy Ruth. Once he thought of his sister's last sentence, "I want everybody I love to know him," and wondered vaguely if she ever wanted it for him, and felt sure if she asked him some such question he would at least try to frame such an answer as would keep her from being troubled with him. What the answer might involve otherwise than the mere giving of it he did not stop to ask. It was enough that Ruth wanted it.

Several times that evening he found himself almost on the point of asking Ruth how that talk of hers with that stubborn Haskins girl came out, and then he would remember suddenly what had been the subject of the conversation and would stop and look embarrassed. He saw too a troubled look in Ruth's eyes, and rightly guessed she was thinking of the young girl, and was troubled over some unmade decision. Of course Joseph had understood in a vague way that Ruth was trying to persuade Ellen Amelia to become a Christian. He had heard sermons enough to understand the language. But he supposed in a general way that there must be some special need for this urgency in the case of Miss Haskins. She must be under some great temptation or danger and Ruth was trying, as her Sunday-school teacher, to guard her against it. He knew nothing whatever of personal religion himself and cared less, but he was willing to try to help a young girl, especially if his sister's desire was in that direction. He would sooner have bitten off his tongue than speak to Ruth on such a subject; he was not familiar enough with her for it, but he made up his mind that if he ever had a chance to shield that Haskins girl and persuade her to give up any dangerous amusement, or whatever it was that Ruth saw she was in peril from, he would do it.

It was not unlike him then, after such thought, to follow his impulse the next evening when he met her returning from his sister's as it was growing dark, and carrying a large package, to turn and taking the bundle from her, to walk back to the village with her. Ellen Amelia was utterly astonished. Joseph was not the kind of young man who had shown himself fond of offering attentions to young girls, and what little attention he had bestowed had never come in her direction. Her delight at having so unexpected an escort caused her to be a little silly. There were so many stories during last year's serials about young men who had suddenly developed a liking for a lady that it was impossible not to remember some of them now. She proceeded to giggle a good deal and make a few flat remarks about the moon. Perhaps she could not have chosen a topic more suited to disgust Joseph had his mind been wholly occupied with what she was saying. But the evening before he and his brother and sister had been reading together a wonderful poem about the moonlight, and they had discussed it at length. His memory was full of magnificent phrases which his rapidly awakening intellect was beginning to appreciate, and the contrast must have been painful. Perhaps her remarks on the moonlight may have hastened his purpose in what he had to say. Certainly a wiser than himself was guiding his words, for he meditated not on what he said, and he, who knew not Christ, was bearing a message for him that night.

"Miss Ellen," he began; he remembered hearing his sister call her that and it pleased him as being a dignified way to address her. He had no wish to make a comrade of her except in so far as it was necessary in order to accomplish his purpose, which then was to please his sister and help her gain her point with Ellen Amelia. "Miss Ellen, my sister is very much troubled about you. I happened to overhear a few words of what she said to you yesterday, and I can see by her face she feels pretty bad that you won't do as she wants you to." He began to hesitate for words now. Just what was it he was going to ask her to do, and how did people ask such things of others? He tried to remember some of his sister's overheard phrases, but they had nearly all escaped. "She told you it wasn't hard to do," he went on blindly; "and it seems to me you might be willing to do it." He stopped. He wanted to tell her that she ought to be ashamed of herself to make such a girl as his sister feel badly about anything in the world; that she wasn't worth speaking of in the same day with her, and a few like sentences; but they did not sound entirely polite and he was trying to be polite these days to please his sister. Besides, if he said such things he would fail of his purpose.

But Ellen Amelia was struck dumb with amazement.

Could this be Joseph Benedict, talking religion to her? What in the world had come over him? Then her words came to her.

"Why don't you do it yourself, Joe Benedict, if you think it's so easy? She thinks a heap sight more about your being a Christian than she ever did about me. And she is praying and praying for you, I know, for she told me she had some 'very specials' that she prayed for every little while all day. I knew straight-off you and Dave was them. If I was you with her right there in the house with me all the time, I'd do it. You better not talk to me; you don't know how hard it would be for me, nor how bad I want to do it either."

"Me!" said Joseph, stopping short in the moonlit road and looking down at the girl. "Me!"

The new dress in the crackly paper under Joseph Benedict's arm was forgotten. Ellen Amelia's eyes were full of tears, and Ellen Amelia Haskins was not a girl who easily cried "before folks." Joseph saw the tears and felt sorry for her. There was something pleasant as well as astonishing in the message that had been brought to his soul.

"Why of course, you. I guess if it's for me it's for you too. We've both been taught well enough to know that, haven't we? If you heard what she said yesterday you know that it is for you too. He died for you all alone by yourself, just the same as he died for me all alone by myself. You've got a call to answer for as well as I."

Joseph was honest. He did not feel that he could try to persuade any one to do a thing he was not willing to do himself. It wouldn't be fair. He had always been that way. If he wanted to play a prank with a pin on another boy, he would first try it on himself to see if he could bear it; then he would get his fun out of the other boy. Then he felt he had a right to it. He turned to walk on, but he thought of Ruth again, and something too in the miserable little longing face of Ellen Amelia touched him. He looked down at her again.

"I'll tell you what it is, Miss Ellen," he said gravely and slowly, as if he were doing something very hard which he didn't know how to do and yet which he meant to do to the best of his ability, "we'll make a bargain. We won't either of us disappoint her. If you'll do it, I will. I don't know a thing about the business, but I'm willing to learn, if you will. I'll agree to do my best at it."

"All right," said Ellen Amelia after a pause; "I'll do it." And then they went home.

Joseph, as he walked back to the farm and looked up at the clear face of the moon, wondering what he had done and how he was going to keep his promise. And the Lord was preparing ways all about him for his feet that he knew not of.

CHAPTER XV

Louise Clifton stood by the front window of the parsonage, looking out, a discontented curl on her lip. It was plain that she did not like Summerton.

"Mamma, I'm sure I don't see why you ever consented to come here," she said for the fortieth time. "It is the dullest, stupidest old place I ever heard of. You are just burying me. Where shall I have any society I'd like to know? You needn't think I'm going to fall in love with that paragon of a Miss Benedict of Rob's. He is ridiculous. He always was. If we had known he had such an admiration here we needn't have moved heaven and earth and spoiled all our own plans to come to this old hole and make a home for him. If he keeps on like this he will soon have one without our assistance."

"Louise!" said her mother severely. She was a quiet, sad little woman with a white, pensive, refined face. Her daughter Louise had always been too much for her. She had never quite understood her.

"Well, mamma, indeed I can't help it. I wonder what you would have done shut up in such a place as this at my time of life. You were one of the belles of New York society. Why, there won't be a man worth looking at in this place."

"Louise!" said her mother again in distress. "You shock me! Are you reduced to the state that there is nothing worth living for in the world without a young man? It strikes me that that is a very bold and immodest way of talking for a young girl. If your father were here to hear you say such a thing as that I don't know what he would do."

"Well now, mamma, I didn't mean anything so terrible. I only meant that there isn't much fun in the world without a young man, at least for a girl like me. You would lift up your hands in horror at the thought of my going anywhere without an escort. I can't go skating—I suppose they will condescend to have that much like the rest of the world in this horrid place. You know you wouldn't let me go skating alone, or sledding. As for parties and evening entertainments, it isn't likely there will be any of those, so you need not worry in that line. But really, it will be too stupid for anything."

"Daughter, you talk as if you cared for nothing but parties and the like. Have you forgotten your brother? He surely will be all the escort you will need."

Louise laughed a clear, mocking laugh. "Rob! Fancy Rob, the dignified minister that he has become, going skating with his sister! Why, I presume that paragon of his doesn't believe in skating. I really never heard him say, but I suppose she doesn't from some remarks I've heard him make about her. Mother, you don't know it, but Rob has become as stupid as Summerton. He doesn't believe in doing this, and he thinks that is wicked, until I'm sick of talking to him. I tried to coax him to take me in town next Saturday to the *matinée*, and don't you believe he told me he did not go to *matinées* any more, that he felt there was a great deal of harm done to young people by them and he hoped I would give them up; and he furthermore informed me that if I would like to look into the subject he had several books there I might have to study it up and he would help me. He handed one to me, and it was called 'Plain Talks About the Theatre,' and had 'Ruth Benedict' written in a pretty little hand across the top; so you see I am not so far wrong in thinking he got all his ideas from her."

"Louise, I must insist that you do not speak so disrespectfully of your brother. Remember his holy office, if you have no regard for him. He doubtless borrowed the book you speak of from Miss Benedict; but as to his ideas on the subject of theatre-going, he changed them long ago, just about the time of that summer he spent at the seaside, you remember. I know he told me at the time, and I thought it was very fitting for a man who was to be a clergyman to feel as he felt. I was highly gratified and so was your father. Of course it was not necessary for you to be guided by your brother's views so long as you were living in New York and were in your own society and your father's home; but remember that you are under your brother's roof now and a part of his family, and some deference is due to his views. In his position he could not well afford to feel otherwise than he does. I trust that you will not bring your personal views out for the hearing of other people. It might hurt your brother seriously."

"Indeed, mamma, I have no idea of being muzzled. I did not want to come here at all, and did all I could to prevent it. Rob would have it, and now he may take the consequences. I shall not try to make myself agreeable to his churchful of country boors," and Louise made her pretty face into a grotesque twist and pirouetted away from the window, returning just in time to look down and meet the gaze of a very stylish young man who was very evidently a college man visiting his native town on a vacation.

There was something so patronizing in his air, and his very expression said, "You poor benighted people, here, see! I honor you with my benign presence. Be glad that you see me, for I shall soon be gone from this place again. I would not stay here if it could be helped, but as my parents will live here on account of my father's business interests, I cannot help treading your streets for a little time; but I despise you all. You, of course, are proud of me, as you should be." This was Alonzo Brummel. He was loud-voiced, self-assertive, long-haired, walked with the latest English hobble and wore the latest style in baggy overcoat, patent leather shoes, with his trousers turned up, and with stick and tall hat. He stared up at the parsonage window with an undeniably impudent stare, as much as to say, "Well! I declare! A really pretty girl in Summerton, and in the parsonage too! Who in the world can she be?"

And Louise, having much the same feeling concerning Summerton and its inhabitants and being fully as astonished to see a well-dressed young man as he had been to see a pretty girl, I am afraid stared back for a moment. Then she dropped her eyes and a pretty flush spread over her cheek as she turned quickly from the window and began playing the piano furiously that her mother might not ask the occasion of her confusion.

However, it was not long before Alonzo Brummel contrived to be introduced to Louise Clifton. He was at home for his Thanksgiving vacation, and by virtue of some petty excuse had managed to have it begin four days earlier than most of the other students, for he was "lazing" through college with as little trouble to himself as possible, and trying to get away with as much money as he could before the time came for him to earn it. His father was a hardworking man, proud of his children and very generous to them, and he looked upon this son as perfection.

The fact that a young man of fashionable appearance had come upon the scene somewhat reconciled Louise Clifton to her present position, at least until after Thanksgiving. She consented to be quite gracious toward Ruth Benedict, and went with her brother to return Ruth's call, which had been made one day when Louise was out with her brother on a long ride.

But when she saw the lovely home and the sweet girl herself, and found that Ruth was, presumably, rich and certainly charming in every way, her impulsive nature turned straight about and fell in love with her at once. She quite tortured her brother with her expressions of affection all the way home and asked him some pointed questions concerning his friendship for Ruth which he did not care at all to answer.

"Mamma, she's lovely!" she said, bursting into the room where her mother sat, on her return from this visit. "I was entirely mistaken. It was all owing to the blue glasses Rob will look at every one through that I thought her such a poke. She has a beautiful home. It is really just a paradise of good taste and artistic ability. I never saw anything so pretty in my life. She and I will be just cronies. And just fancy, mamma, she rides a wheel! I thought she was too straight-laced to live, from what Rob said. She is to ride with me to-morrow, if the weather continues good. I'm just dying to meet those two brothers of hers. They say she has given up a lovely home and lots of friends where she has always lived just to come here and civilize them. I think I will help her. Rob is always at me to do some missionary work, but I don't fancy dirty-faced little girls with sticky fingers always bringing you bunches of dandelions and expecting you to kiss them and get dandelion milk over your new gray kid gloves. I shall never forget the only Sunday I ever tried at the mission in New York, and I don't want to do anything like it again. But this would be perfectly lovely—two young men. Miss Brummel said they were real nice fellows. I could help her I'm sure. I suppose she wants to get them taught manners and be so that they can go into society. I should enjoy it. They wouldn't be like little mission-school girls."

"No, they would hardly bring you wilted dandelions nor expect you to kiss them," said her brother, who had been listening with increasing disgust and anger to his sister's gushing words. "Mother, I wish you would try to make Louise understand that such talk is offensive in the extreme from a young woman. I fancy there will be no danger of her undertaking a mission with either David or Joseph Benedict when she has once seen them. They will be much more likely to look upon her as a foolish girl than as a helper if she talks in as silly a vein as she has been talking this after-noon." The minister's nerves had been tried to their utmost by his sister's flippancy. "And, by the way, mother," he went on, "young Brummel is no fit companion for Louise. I don't like his look, and wish she would keep away from him."

Then the minister settled to his evening paper, and mother and daughter gave one another a frightened, rather guilty glance, as Louise left the room. The mother spent a sleepless night afterward, wondering if she had done wrong to consent to her daughter's plans, and saying over and over again to herself, "It is too late to change anything now, and there will not be any harm done if he does not know."

The fact about which she was worrying was this: Alonzo Brummel had not been slow in following up his acquain-

tance with Louise Clifton. He was to be at home not much
more than a week, and he meant to have all the fun out of it
he could, in that dull town. His sister Georgiana was bribed
to assist him, and they had called back and forth several
times and planned a walk and a ride. It had also come about
that Miss Louise had mentioned her disappointment with
regard to the *matinée* to be held in the city about forty
miles distant the day before Thanksgiving. Young Brummel
had at once taken up with this and planned a party
consisting of his sister and himself and Miss Clifton to
attend that *matinée*. It fell in exactly with his ideas of a good
time. He said the play was a "jolly" one and "no end of fun."
Louise, however, having been brought up with strict ideas
with regard to chaperones, had insisted that her mother
should be one of the party. After much persuasion Mrs.
Clifton had consented to accompany them. She did it
fearfully and with many compunctions, for she knew her
son would object most seriously; but she insisted that it
should be kept strictly a secret, telling Louise to explain to
the Brummels that her son's position made him feel that he
would rather not have his family attend such places of
amusement. She felt herself very lenient toward such
things. Then too Louise must have some amusement.
Robert could not expect her to give up all her girlhood. So
she had arranged to go with Louise to the city, ostensibly to
do some shopping, and told her son that they would not
return until the late train. Of course the minister had no
suspicions, and would not have pried into his mother's
affairs if he had.

Meantime the friendship between Ruth Benedict and
Louise Clifton was progressing. The minister had said in a
low, troubled tone during one of the few talks he had with
Ruth alone, "My sister needs your help, Miss Benedict.
She is not a Christian. You will understand her, I feel sure,
and see just what she needs," and then he had gone on his
way, and Ruth had studied the bright pretty young girl and
understood.

They took their bicycle ride together. As they passed the
Brummel home Alonzo was lounging in the front window
smoking and reading. He sat up very straight and bowed to
Louise, but stared interestedly at Ruth. He had not seen

her before. He decided that her style was ahead of Miss
Clifton's and he would try to get acquainted with her at
once. She might be more worth while than the minister's
sister. She was well enough for fun, but one liked a variety.
Of course he had heard of Ruth Benedict, but had paid
little attention to the accounts of her till now.

It was also new to him that Miss Clifton rode a wheel. He
would have one for himself sent up from the city immediately, as his own was at college, he not having thought
it worth while to bring it home with him for so short a time.
He would have a ride with Miss Clifton and perhaps with
the other girl as well.

Summerton stared as it rushed to its doors and windows
to behold the minister's sister and the new Benedict girl
flying by. They had supposed that the Benedict girl had had
lesson enough in the spraining of her ankle never to mount
the diabolical machine she called a bicycle again, but here
she was sitting up as straight and smiling and composed as
could be. Mother Haskins, as she looked, sniffed, in spite of
the beautiful new dress which hung upstairs in Ellen
Amelia's closet; yes and in spite of the fact that this strange
benefactress had evolved a dainty little hat of blue serge
with rolled, stitched brim, and soft crown, and no expense
except two cheap black wings. It not only was the most
becoming and plainest, neatest hat Ellen Amelia ever had,
besides being exceedingly stylish (which latter point
Mother Haskins did not know), but also saved the expense
and trouble of getting Ellen Amelia something new for her
head, or arguing her into wearing the old last winter's one.
Mother Haskins was very much afraid that Ellen Amelia's
next ambition would be a bicycle. As for the minister's
sister, Mrs. Haskins was scandalized. The minister ought to
be told at once, and she would surely make it her business
to do so were it not for the darning that must be finished
that afternoon. Besides, she dreaded making the first call
on the minister's grand little mother. So she retired to her
darning, predicting dire trouble for the two innocent riders
before the afternoon was over, and was surprised and truly
sorry to see them return perhaps two hours later with
smiling rosy faces, looking as if they had but just started
out.

It was that very evening that Alonzo Brummel, upon pretext of a very rusty acquaintance with Joseph Benedict and some business of questionable importance with David, called at the Benedict farm. He received his introduction to Ruth and before the evening was over endeavored to make her acquaintance more intimately, but found it was not an easy thing to do. Ruth, though she was usually sunny and bright and always on the lookout for winning people for the sake of the good it might do, had a great dislike for a certain class of young men with a bold stare and an ease before strangers which sat upon their youthful shoulders all too easily. Alonzo Brummel was one of these. He made her feel uncomfortable, as if in the presence of something ugly, she did not exactly know why. She was not wise enough in the world to understand that the bold stare he gave at a pretty girl told more than she could read of his knowledge of the world and its evils. She only knew she felt uncomfortable and wished to get away from him. Therefore she declined rather frigidly when he proposed a bicycle ride in her company, saying she had other duties at the time he named, and when he proposed another time she said firmly that he must excuse her.

David was exceedingly glad of his sister's discernment. He did not like young Brummel. Though he had been shut up in this small town all his life, with only occasional visits to the neighboring city, still he knew the signs of the hard young face better than some who have been among wickedness always. Besides, the city is not the only place where wickedness lurks in hidden corners, and a young man with eyes and a pure heart cannot go through any corner of the world without seeing the signs of sin.

Alonzo Brummel went home trying to make up his mind whether it would be worth his while to pretend to be very religious during the few days left him of his vacation, in order to please this rather extraordinary Benedict girl, and finally decided it would be much easier just to have a good time with merry little Louise Clifton. She was much more to his mind after all.

Ruth at that moment on her knees was adding Louise Clifton to her list of those she prayed for more earnestly. As she prayed she remembered the bow between the girl and the young man that afternoon and the few words the gay young girl had said about him, and she added a petition that Louise might be delivered from any danger that might come to her through Alonzo Brummel.

CHAPTER XVI

Louise Clifton was taking lunch with Ruth Benedict. It had been no part of Ruth's plan to have her brothers come in contact with her new friend any more than necessary, for she did not think that Louise would be a help in influencing them for good. There were girls she could think of who would help wonderfully and whom she felt sure they would like, but Louise was like a dangerous bit of some combustible material. Ruth never knew what she would do next. There was a bright side, and a sweet, lovable side, as well as a gay one, to her character. To Ruth she had shown this principally, though there had been a glimmer now and then of daring; but it remained for David Benedict to bring out a new phase of her disposition.

David and Joseph were to be away all day, as was often the case when they had some business connected with the sale of cattle in some village not far away. Ruth usually arranged to have some one with her on these days to lunch, for she did not wish to bring her outside missionary work in to spoil their home life unless she felt the guests were such as would be pleasant to her brothers. So Louise had been invited for Tuesday. The young men had both started away from the house early, as they had expected to do, David to West Winterton and Joseph in the opposite direction. Louise arrived at the hour appointed and the two girls took a ride together returning home about lunch time, where to her surprise Ruth found her brother David. He had been disappointed in seeing the man with whom he was to transact his business, he having been called away suddenly by the illness of a relative, and thus David came home earlier. Ruth felt a little troubled. She feared lest her brother might not enjoy having this gay, rather frivolous, and certainly very stylish young woman sitting opposite to him at the table. If David should freeze up and be stiff and Louise should take a turn of trying to shock him, Ruth felt that there would be more harm done than any good her endeavors to help Louise might have done. Indeed she had felt rather discouraged about the minister's sister since their morning spent together. Louise, with her impulsive girl-nature had fallen very much in love with Ruth, and gushed a great deal over her, but still she laughed at anything grave she might try to say, and persisted in making herself out to be shockingly wicked, in a bright interesting kind of way. She would talk of her brother in a mocking strain, laughing at his country church and making merry over the people. Ruth dreaded to have David hear her talk so. What would he think of the minister's religion if it could touch his own sister no further than to provoke fun? She flew to her refuge and sent up a petition for help and then remembered that the Lord was guiding and that no harm could come where he was and tried not to worry any more about it. So David was introduced to Louise Clifton and sat down in the library for a few minutes talk before lunch, and behold!

Louise shone forth in a new light. Her face was as full of expression as a kaleidoscope. In spite of her silly talk about helping those Benedict boys she had meant what she said, and was truly interested in doing anything to elevate them. It became doubly interesting also when she found this one so tall and really handsome. He could talk so well too, and when he smiled, that grave face of his and those great deep blue eyes lit up as if a hidden lamp were suddenly lighted behind them and shone through his whole face. He was a new kind of young man to Louise, and she could not help liking him. And when Louise Clifton liked any one she could always win a liking for herself. It was not deceit, nor theatricals which caused her to so change her behavior. It was perhaps an instinctive consciousness of what would please the one with whom she was talking, and the natural impulse of kindness. She did not mean to act a part.

Perhaps, if the truth might be known, David appealed to the highest and best that there was in her nature and she immediately brought it forth. Certainly no girl could have been sweeter and shyer or more modest than was Louise Clifton. She did not throw herself at the young man and make him take notice of her, neither did she patronize him and try to make talk. She simply and pleasantly asked him questions about Summerton and answered his. She told one or two incidents that had occurred during their ride, and when she looked up and caught his eye her face flushed a pretty shy pink and she looked down again as though she had been making herself too prominent. David thought her truly the brightest, prettiest, sweetest bit of humanity, always barring his sister, he had ever looked upon, and Louise found herself wondering in what way she could possibly help this young man. He seemed to be at ease in talking with a stranger, and not to murder the English language when he spoke. He certainly could not be very wicked, for his mouth had too clean a cut and firm a look for that—though it must be confessed Louise was hardly as yet a good judge of morality in a man; if he wore faultless clothes and could dance and wait upon her gracefully, it was all she asked as yet.

Her own moral and intellectual judgment had hardly been as well developed as her brother's, nor as much so as it would have been had her father lived. But there was something new to her, an independent dignity, in David, and she was interested. She would certainly do all in her power to help him if there was anything she could do, she told herself; and meantime she apparently could not seem other than simple and sweet and childlike in his presence, perhaps because David himself was so simply natural and frank and in earnest in all he did and said. After lunch he lingered in the house for nearly an hour and let Miss Clifton show him about a laughable little game she had brought over with her, and Ruth watched her brother in surprise mingled with a wonder as to what the outcome was to be of this new acquaintance. Could it be possible that these two, whom she had thought so opposite to one another in everything, were meant to help each other? Truly the ways of God were past finding out, but she would wait and trust him, for he knew the way he took and she was walking with him.

Louise liked to provoke that grave face to a smile. It was something new to watch the play of light that came across David's face, and when he at last got up and said he must go to his work, she turned to Ruth with her old, saucy smile again and said: "Your brother is just as nice in his way as you are in yours. Now let's have that music." And Ruth could never guess from her actions whether her guest regretted her brother's going or not. So much had Louise Clifton's home training been worth. Ruth could but admire her for the frank, pleasant way in which she spoke about her brother, and then dropped the subject. There was nothing of the foolishness in her speech now that there had been concerning Alonzo Brummel. Nevertheless Ruth decided that she would not take the responsibility yet of actually planning to bring these two together again. If the Lord, who was guiding, saw this best he would do it, and he might not want them together again. Ruth could not see the way clear before her, and therefore she did not have to act. It was not long however before her trust was rewarded with being allowed to see something of God's plan and understand a little of the various influences that had been at work.

Louise Clifton leaned back in the car and breathed a sigh of relief. She and her mother were off to the city for their day of shopping, and nothing had been discovered by her brother. She had been almost certain something would turn up to spoil her pleasure. Young Mr. Brummel and his sister were to come on the noon train and meet them at an appointed place. Louise reflected with joy that she was to have one day of doing as she pleased, and she chattered pleasantly to her mother and tried to smooth the anxious look from her face. Mrs. Clifton was not quite sure that she was doing altogether as her dead husband would have liked her to do. She did not rouse easily from her worried little thoughts, and Louise at last began to study the passengers. There was a man sitting two seats up the aisle across from her with his face turned to the window. The back of his head was handsome, and she could not help admiring it as her eyes came back several times to his broad shoulders and heavy head of hair that looked like a sealskin coat, she told herself. By and by he turned his face a little, and then she saw that it was David Benedict. She was pleasantly surprised, and wished he would come and occupy the seat in front of them, and as they left the car at the city station she tried to catch his eye and bow, but David was intent on his own business and apparently did not see them.

Louise was disappointed that Mr. Benedict had not seen her. He had somehow given her a feeling that he looked up to her as a being far superior to himself, for whom he felt a sort of reverence. This feeling was pleasant to Louise. Other men had admired her and told her so; but none had ever given her the impression that they thought of her as spiritually above them. She had been more a merry companion to others, and was as willing to join in any wild prank as they had been. Mr. Benedict had taken it for granted that a woman who was beautiful, was good and above anything wrong or untruthful or impure. Louise thought she would always like to have him keep this feeling for her. It gave her a respect for herself which she had never felt before, and she felt she would try a little, just a little, to live up to this ideal that she seemed to understand David Benedict had for women. His sister had been so, and of course he saw no reason why she should not prove so also. Louise was pleased.

There was another Summerton traveler that morning in the car. He sat directly behind Mrs. Clifton and her daughter, and he had a set, protruding chin and heavy, uncomfortable eyebrows of grizzled gray. He looked the minister's mother and sister over carefully and severely, shaking his head once and gazing gloomily out of the window. Deacon Chatterton did not feel particularly pleasant this morning. Some investments out West were in doubtful condition, and he was going to town to get a lawyer to look them up. He did not approve of a minister having a mother and sister who looked so gay and fashionable. It showed a spiritual lack in the minister somewhere.

Meantime at home various things were going on.

When Ellen Amelia Haskins had entered church the first

Sunday after her new blue serge was completed, she created more of a sensation than any stranger that had yet visited Summerton. To have strangers come to church dressed finely and looking pretty was of course an interesting thing and one to be look at and remarked upon; but to have one of their own number, who had grown up from babyhood in their midst, and who had not even been away for a visit of a few weeks,—nor what was more astounding, even been to the dressmaker, in the knowledge of any one present,—suddenly appear before their astonished eyes in gown and bonnet of faultless style and becomingness undreamed of, and with her hair arranged in a way unknown to Summerton maidens save as they had occasionally observed it in their shopping visits to the city, was a thing not to be gotten over easily. She seemed to move in a more graceful way, and her whole face took on a really pretty look.

"My land!" whispered Eliza Barnes to Mrs. Deacon Chatterton, with whom she happened to be sitting; "who ever dreamed she could be so pretty!"

"Humph!" said Mrs. Chatterton, as she observed the advent of Ellen Amelia with disapproval; "beauty that can be put on and took off ain't much beauty to my mind," and she severely studied the hymn book the remainder of the morning, and rigidly refrained from encouraging Ellen Amelia in her pride by looking once more in the direction of the Haskins pew.

The two young men with lowering brows and thick protruding lips back by the door, who came to church now because there was nothing better to do, looked up with interest. Ellen Amelia had not been an admiration of theirs heretofore, but dressed in this way she seemed to have suddenly grown up and to be worth while. The Brower boys were always looking out for a new girl, and when they found her she usually regretted it if she allowed their coarse charms to attract her attention. Heretofore Ellen Amelia had never been in danger through them. They preferred pretty girls, and there were plenty of them throughout the country who were glad of their acquaintance, for were they not heirs of a great farm and an estate of dimensions that varied according to the imagination of the speaker? Ed nudged Bill, and Bill glowered back at Ed, and nodded and whispered, "She's great! How'd she do it?" and after church, when they lingered as was their wont, by the door and watched the outcomers, they sauntered along toward her home by her side, and the poor, silly girl's heart beat high with wild excitement. She had never had the like happen to her before. She knew they were rather wild, to be sure, but they also had the name of being worldly wise, and they were young men and well-built, and when they tried to please, not altogether bad-looking. Remember, Ellen Amelia's head was full of stories and her mind was used to idealizing everybody—except perhaps her own immediate home circle, with whom she was forced by circumstances to come in constant contact. Ellen Amelia minced along between Bill and Ed Brower and cast sidelong glances to see if the other girls saw her, and wondered trembling what her mother would think if she knew, and whether father would disapprove. And then they almost took her breath by a proposition. She was feeling herself a Cinderella enough already with her new gown and two princes, but with a ball added her head was completely turned, and so at her father's gate she giggled out a sort of promise, as much of a promise as she dared make, and went in blindly to sit down and think what kind of wild delightful whirl the world had gotten into. And she forgot completely that she had promised but three days before to try to love and serve the Lord Jesus Christ with all her heart and soul and strength and to make him the first consideration of her life.

When Christians go to sleep then the devil thinks he may sleep also, or go awhile to other more important places perhaps; but when some Christian gets awake and goes to praying, and one and another and another are stirred by this one's prayers to kneel, then does the devil hasten back and send a good force of his emissaries to the front. There is no time so easy as a young Christian's start to turn him in another direction. If you can spoil everything for him then you have him with no more trouble. And so the devil, seeing that some good live Christian workers had come to Summerton, and that things in the sleepy old church were waking up, and some souls were asking the way to light,

concluded to have a ball. A ball was an extraordinary thing
in Summerton. People could not remember when there
had been such a thing before. It happened that Thanksgiving Day was the tenth or fiftieth or hundredth anniversary—it matters little which—of something or other of mild
importance in the town, and what more fitting than at such
a season there should be a celebration, and what better for
a celebration than a ball? And because it was such a strange,
new thing for Summerton, and because it was in commem-
oration of some sacred little event, people who in general
utterly disapproved of dancing and frowned upon worldly
amusements with more than usual vigor, condoned the
offense of the committee of arrangements, and even
consented to lend their presence for a time. It was more to
them as if they were playing at having a ball than as if they
were to have a real one. Of course everybody in the town
did not feel in this way, and the whole matter was kept as
quiet as possible so that not until two or three days before
Thanksgiving did the story leak out and get itself talked
about. The invitations had been in the hands of a few, and
had been given quietly, at first to those they were sure of,
and afterward where they had occasioned much discussion
and some bitter words and bitterer tears on the part of strict
parents and greatly longing children. It is needless to say
that the Brower boys had it in their power to invite whom
they would. And thus poor Ellen Amelia met her first great
temptation.

The ball was to be held in a public hall. It had not even
the excuse of being strictly private, but then it was to be
only village people, no strangers, and what was the harm?

Ellen Amelia Haskins, on the first Sabbath afternoon
after she had promised to give her life to the Lord Jesus
Christ, sat herself down to look over her wardrobe, and see
what it was possible to construct out of the accumulations of
her few years that would answer for a ball dress, and wished
for the hundredth time that her good fairy would waft a
wand over her beautiful blue serge and change it into a
nile-green silk with real point lace trimming and *Maréchal
Neil* roses.

CHAPTER XVII

It was not until the day before Thanksgiving that the minister heard about it and knew that some of the principal members of his church were involved in the arrangements. He sat in troubled silence after the messenger who brought this unpleasant news had departed, and wondered if he should do anything and what he could do. He half wished his mother were at home that he might consult her, and then remembered that his mother would not understand and would have no help to offer. A faint color stole into his cheek as he realized who was the only helper he felt he could find in true sympathy with his feelings in all his church; for while there were many good and true members who would frown upon the ball, they would one and all censure the ones who had gotten it up and those who would attend it so severely that there would be no use in asking them to help in any way.

Later in the afternoon he found his way to Ruth Benedict's home and inquired for her. She was in the little music room back of the parlor. Joseph had thrown himself down on the easy couch by the piano after lunch and begged for a song, and she had given him not only one but many, bright, funny ones, and gay and sad; and at last as he lay still she ventured others in a tenderer tone, some old hymns she loved, one or two which gave the invitation to Christ in pleading words, "O prodigal child, come home, come home."

There were tears in Joseph's eyes under those closely closed lashes, and he dared not open them lest the tears would show themselves. He did not understand the feelings that were moving him these days, new manliness and courage. He knew that he had accepted that invitation

to come home, and yet he did not feel that he was farther
than on the threshold of the gateway. He would have liked
to ask Ruth something about the way, and what he should
do with his new resolutions, but he could not think how to
put it, and the courage was utterly lacking to speak a word
of the matter.

When the knocker sounded through the house Ruth
turned softly, and seeing her brother as she supposed
asleep, she quietly drew the heavy *portière* behind the
lighter one of beads, and went to meet the visitor. Joseph
lay there, not asleep, but thinking over his life, and trying
to form some idea of the future out of the chaos he stood in
at present. He heard the minister's low, troubled tones, and
knew that he was asking advice of his sister, and felt that it
was fitting he should do so. Almost unnoticed the thought
passed through his mind that the minister and his sister
were very much alike in a good many ways, and ought to
enjoy one another's company; and he was glad that Robert
Clifton had come there to live to make a pleasant friend for
Ruth, as well as for the rest of them. But suddenly his
wandering thoughts stopped, and he listened intently to
what the minister was saying.

"Yes, Miss Benedict, I'm afraid it will reach a good many
of our young people, and hurt them the more because it
seems it is an unusual thing. You know a new thing always
has more influence than an old one. If they were accustomed to having dances here we might hope that one more
might not do any especial harm, but some of the young
people who have never tasted the charms of it before are to
have an opportunity now. I understand that several of our
best families have promised to allow their young people to
attend, and that some have gone so far as to take a few
lessons in dancing in the city in order that they may appear
to advantage on this occasion. There is one young woman in
particular about whom I feel very anxious. She promised
me two weeks ago to think carefully over the matter of
personal religion. I had hoped she might soon unite with
the church. But now she is to be allowed to attend this ball,
and I fear much that it may turn her thoughts in other
directions. She is very young and so easily influenced. It is
Miss Haskins of whom I speak; and by the way, she is in

your Sunday-school class I remember. Perhaps you can do something. I am told that her father cannot say no to any request of hers—he is rather weak in a good many ways I should judge—and that her mother, though strict in such matters usually, has for once been overruled and the girl is to go. Just the mere fact of her going might not be so bad, perhaps, if she were not to be escorted by a low-lived scoundrel who is not fit to be in decent society. Those Brower boys are really much beneath her in every way. I cannot understand what her father can be about to allow it. The poor girl is too young to understand how dangerous they are."

The minister and Ruth said a good deal more and made some plans for future work, and possible help for some of the young ball-goers, but Joseph heard no more. He was making some plans of his own. Then as the minister took his departure he thanked the earnest hostess gravely and told her, his face illumined with a kind of spiritual light, that he always had occasion to thank God for her words whenever he met her. And then their eyes met and these words which he had intended should sound so commonplace took on an added meaning, because his eyes could not keep it secret that they meant a great deal to him, and Ruth's eyes went down and her cheeks flushed a little as she tried to take them in the commonplace way in which he had spoken, and then after he had gone she went to her room to think it all over, and make up her mind why it was that she seemed to feel so happy over what Mr. Clifton had said more than over ordinary praise. But she remembered her brother Joseph soon, and going softly to the closed *portière* to see if he had awakened, found him gone. Joseph was in his room making a toilet for his first call upon a young lady. When he made up his mind a thing had to be done he did it right away.

Louise Clifton's plans had progressed very well. She found all the things at the stores that she had come in search of, and her mother had consented to her buying several things she had set her heart upon. Mr. and Miss Brummel had met them at the appointed hour, and gone with them to the appointed high-class restaurant where they had indulged themselves in all the indigestibles that

Summerton did not produce. They were now on their way
to the opera house. Georgiana and Mrs. Clifton were
ahead. Alonzo Brummel and Louise lingered behind chat-
ting and stopping to look at a fine display of orchids in a
florist's window. Mrs. Clifton walked rather rapidly. She felt
uncomfortable about this part of the journey, and she
wanted to have it over as soon as possible. Georgiana
wished she would not go quite so fast, and suggested once
or twice that the others were far behind, but Mrs. Clifton
said she wanted to get there and sit down, she was tired. So
they had stood for several minutes waiting in the entrance
way when Louise and her escort finally came up the many
stone steps.

It was nearly time for the early train to Summerton, and
David Benedict was hurrying along the street. He noticed
young Brummel's perculiar jaunty hat ahead of him, and as
he rapidly drew nearer he recognized Louise Clifton
walking with him. It gave him an unpleasant sensation as it
always did when he saw something pure and white in close
proximity to something filthy, but he thought nothing of it
except to wonder mildly how they happened both to be
here; but then he was here himself, and it was no great
wonder if they had happened to meet upon the street in a
city so near their homes. However, just as he was passing
them they turned across his path and mounted the stone
steps. He bowed and looked up quickly to see where it was
they were going, and then with a shade of something like
disappointment crossing his face his eyes met Louise's
smiling face, and she felt almost imperceptibly that she was
in danger of falling from the high eminence where he had
seemed to place her in his esteem. She bowed and smiled
and the color mounted into her cheek and David was gone.
But though she laughed and talked freely she felt uncomfortable, and could not forget the look in David's eyes.

Young Brummel had seen her bow, and from force of
habit had lifted his hand to his hat, and then, looking to see
who was the recipient of her favor, he gave a coarse,
familiar nod, and laughed, asking her how she came to be
so intimate with that clodhopper. Louise's face grew
suddenly pink with indignation. She never could bear to
see injustice done, and she knew in her heart that David

was far superior in every way—unless it might be in the cut of his clothes, which indeed were not bad—to the young man who was making fun of him. With a touch of the *hauteur* she could sometimes employ to advantage, she told him icily that Mr. Benedict was the brother of her dearest friend, the loveliest girl in the world. And then young Brummel thought it wise to change the subject. But somehow Louise's pleasure in the afternoon's performance was clouded. She criticised the scenery and the dresses, and did not like the soprano's voice, and curled her lip over some of the jokes which Alonzo thought exceedingly funny and laughed uncontrollably over. She wondered how he could enjoy it. Indeed the play itself seemed vapid and uninteresting. She did not know that she was defiantly trying to look at it all through David Benedict's eyes, and prove to herself that if he were here he could not possibly see anything out of the way in it, while she saw a great deal that did not please even herself, now that her eyes were somewhat opened.

Then she began wondering how it was that David had any ideas about theatre-going at all, living as he did in the country where there were no theatres. Why should he have opinions on the subject? It was absurd. Surely Ruth could not have had reason or opportunity to speak to him on the subject. She must have been mistaken in thinking she saw disapproval in his eyes, and what right had he to disapprove of her actions, anyway? But indignation with him did not suit her mood. She was anxious to help him in some way. She truly wanted to be a missionary, and had an indistinct idea that while she was not a Christian herself, nor had any personal interest in the matter, she supposed it was a very good thing for a young man, and if she could help him to procure some religion of the right sort to help him well through the world and keep him from being wild—which term in her mind had a very dim and misty meaning—she would like to do so. It was certainly annoying to be blocked in her influence at the outset by some notion of his concerning theatre-going. It was also provoking when one had once tasted the joy of being an angel of light to a young man to suddenly see him discover a flaw in his angel. Altogether Louise was cross and a little unreasonable, and

when on the journey home, Alonzo Brummel contrived it
so that his sister and Mrs. Clifton should sit together and he
should be with Louise again, she was very quiet and
unresponsive. He had been getting ready all the afternoon
and making this opportunity to tell her of the Summerton
ball, and ask if she would not like to go just for fun, and "to
laugh at the rest," for he had taken it for granted that she
felt as superior to the village as he did.

However, when Alonzo Brummel broached the subject
of the ball Louise was all attention. It sounded even more
like what she was wont to call a "lark" than this trip to the
city. Of course her brother would object, but what of that?
He might as well learn soon as late that he could not control
her movements and that she was not going to walk in a
straitlaced fashion just because he was a minister and she
had been forced to come and live with him. She felt a little
uncertain about her mother's consent however, for Mrs.
Clifton had shown decided signs of wavering concerning
this city trip, and it would be better not to endanger the
ball by mentioning it to her so soon after the other
escapade. Better let her have time to recover from her
worry and see that no harm came from it. Besides, Mr.
Brummel suggested that she should spend the evening at
their house and they would all go from there. He represented that his sister would be going. Poor Georgiana
served her brother many a turn that she never knew of
during this short vacation. He forgot perhaps to state that
Georgiana could not tread a measure to music to save her
life, and that his mother was so bitterly opposed to the
grand affair getting up at the hall that Georgiana would no
more be allowed to enter its precincts than she would to
take a walk down the broad road to destruction. Mrs.
Brummel had a few stanch principles which she had
inherited with the "Lives of the Martyrs," and from which
she in nowise allowed herself or her daughter to depart.
She supposed that her son reverenced them also, and he
took care that she should not find out otherwise.

And so Louise Clifton arranged to spend the evening
with the Brummels, and did not notice that Georgiana
looked rather surprised when, as they parted, she said:
"Well, I shall see you to-morrow evening," and Alonzo had

difficulty during the remainder of their walk home to invent a suitable reason for her having said this which should not interfere with his plans.

And while these plans were going on, those who had been set to watch the walls of Zion were continuing in prayer, and planning for warfare with the evil one. Ruth in her own quiet chamber was trying to remember once again that the work was God's and not hers, and that he could make right come from even what seemed all wrong. She turned over plan after plan. Should she try, for instance, to have a little impromptu Thanksgiving party of her own?— have her Sabbath-school class and any others who were in peculiar danger from the next evening's entertainment, and invite the minister and have a delightful time that would outshine the other's attraction? No, there were objections to that. It was too late. The young people who were going had all gotten ready by this time and could not be detained now by a quiet evening of popcorn and conundrums. Besides, she could not hope to prolong such an entertainment late enough to save them all from going to the hall afterward, for that entertainment was likely to last till the small hours of the morning. She saw ideas in this thought for future use, but none that would do to carry out now, for the simple reason that none of her guests who needed it would be willing to come to anything she might offer them that night. But Summerton wanted entertaining, it was plain, and if the good of life would not give it them then they were ready to take it from the evil.

David was wondering in his heart why he was so certain that his sister Ruth would not go to that ball nor have anything to do with it. His first intimation of it had been some days before. He had heard the Brower boys talking in the grocery, and he thought he heard his sister's name mentioned, but when he came in sight of them there was no more said. He ground his teeth to think that his sister might be mentioned by such lips as theirs and was thankful that breath of theirs need never reach her ears.

The minister was praying and lingering in prayer for his church. He was young and these were his first people, and he fairly agonized over them, as a mother will with her first child, whenever they were in danger or doing wrong. It hurt his sensitive nature to have them grieve their Saviour. His high-strung temperament was constantly feeling the slights put upon his Master and theirs. Would they never come to Christ and live for him? Must Satan ever have the mastery? He would not give up the work though he could not see his way clear before him; but he felt sorely discouraged now at the outset. It was the old weary problems so often quoted from Lowell:

Truth forever on the scaffold, Wrong forever on the throne,—
Yet that scaffold sways the future, and behind the dim
    unknown
Standeth God within the shadow, keeping watch above his
    own.

CHAPTER XVIII

Joseph Benedict stood before the Haskins door and knocked as an evening caller knocks. He had never stood there in such capacity before. He had never gone to call upon a young woman before, but all the strangeness of his position was overcome by the solemn errand which he felt he had to perform. He had taken vows upon himself with this girl that they would both try to live a Christian life. Without any instruction in the matter, Joseph understood that a public ball was no place in which to keep such a contract. It is a strange fact that the untutored, un-Christian mind almost always puts down theatre-going, dancing, card-playing, and the like as things unfit for a follower of Jesus. You will find this is especially the case among young men who have been brought up in the country and are familiar with only the crudest kinds of these amusements. Whether they would be refined into thinking differently by coming into constant contact with worldly Christians is a question. But these are by no means all found in the cities. It is true that sometimes such persons, when they become Christians themselves, will be found indulging in and condoning such amusements; but usually before they come to Christ they will criticise them in one who professes Christianity. Such people as Joseph will often have higher ideals for Christians than they have for themselves.

"Is Miss Ellen in?" he asked of the youngest Haskins, who opened the door and his own mouth at the same time and at about the same width. The boy seemed not to understand, and the question had to be asked again. Then the boy retreated, leaving the door wide open and revealing the Haskins sitting room with the family just gathering after supper. "Ma!" called the boy, "ma, come 'ere!"

"Who is it, and what does he want?" answered a woman's voice.

"It's Joe Ben'dict! He said 'Mi'zellen'!" said the boy incoherently.

Mother Haskins went curiously to the door to see what might be the matter.

"Is Miss Ellen in?" asked Joseph with a bow, as he had seen the minister do when he came to call on his sister.

"Miss Ellen?" repeated the mother dazedly; "oh, you mean Ellenmelya. Yes. She's here. Did you want to see her?" Mother Haskins did not quite like the idea of so many young men coming around her daughter all at once. She was suspicious, but she supposed he had some message from his sister, and as he did not seem disposed to subject it first to her judgment, she went in search of her daughter.

Ellen Amelia came, looking tired and surprised. She had been working hard all day on a ball dress which was not nile-green silk, but which nevertheless did credit both in fashion and taste to her few recent lessons in dressmaking. She had caught the style from one of Ruth's papers, which she wished with all her heart she dared borrow; but something uneasy in her heart told her it was wiser not to let her teacher know of her intention to go to that ball, and so she had plodded on by herself, and had been disappointed even to tears many times, but had still persevered.

She invited Joseph into the grim and silent parlor, which was as stiff and unwholesome as the Benedict parlor had been before the advent of Ruth, and Joseph looked about and pitied the girl from the depths of his heart because she had no lovely home like his. It was his way to go straight to business, and so without waiting to be seated he began.

"Miss Ellen," he said with the manner an older brother might have used, "I heard you were about on the point of breaking your promise, or leastways of putting yourself in the way of breaking it, and I came around to see about it. You know there's two of us in it, and I take it that it is the duty of each to see that the other does his part."

"What in the world are you gettin' at, Joe Benedict?" asked Ellen Amelia sharply, a troubled feeling beginning to steal over her as she remembered how little thought she had given to the solemn promise made so short a time ago.

"Are you going to that ball in the town hall?"

"Well, what if I am?" said Ellen, her cheeks getting red and her eyes defying him. "I don't see what that's got to do with what you were talking about. What's the harm? All the church folks are going. Why don't you go yourself?"

"I don't go because I don't want to," answered Joseph honestly; "but if I did, I wouldn't after that promise I made. I don't count that as one of the ways to keep such a promise. I don't pretend to know much about this new kind of living we've agreed to try and do, you've had more teaching on the subject than I; but if I know anything, I know that hall to-morrow night won't be a fit place for any young girl, let alone a Christian, and I wish you wouldn't."

There was a little change in Joseph's voice now, a note of anxiety lest he might fail, the smallest trifle of a pleading inflection. It touched the girl's pride and her coquetry at once. She was pleased and would see how far he would go, and how much he cared. Not that she meant to give up the ball now, with that pink tarletan dress almost done on her bed upstairs, and that dollar and a quarter paid to the city dancing-master to teach her a few forbidden steps.

"But I can't help it now, it's too late. I've promised, Joe, and besides it'll be heaps of fun."

"Then it's true you're goin' with one of those fellows? I didn't believe that. Ellen Amelia Haskins, don't you know better than to trust yourself for one hour with either of those fellows? If you knew half what I know about them you'd never let them speak to you again."

"Now, Joe Benedict, I never thought you'd go to slandering other fellows just out of jealousy"; it certainly was very silly and conceited and unwise and really unpardonable in Ellen Amelia to so forget herself, but she did say it. She spent many hours of repentance over those few words afterward and remembered them through her life with shame, but she said them, and Joseph stood towering above her, wrath and disgust and pity mingled on his face. he felt that the girl needed a thorough lesson. He wished it was not his duty to give it, for that moment he felt a contempt rising in his heart for the poor silly girl. He jealous! But she saw what she had said, and shame began to rise in her face at sight of his. Then pity came for her and he suppressed his anger by a mighty effort.

"Now, look here, Miss Ellen," he said, his voice kind but firm; "you know you didn't mean to say that. You know that I never asked you to go to that ball, and wouldn't have, and that if I had wanted your company there were other ways to get it than talking about the man you were going with. That all goes without saying. You wouldn't have said that if you hadn't been put out. I suppose you want to go, and you'll be disappointed about it, and all that, but it really can't be helped. It isn't a proper place for any good woman to go. I wouldn't let my sister go there, no, nor go near those two men either, and isn't it my duty to do all I can to take care of my sister's friend? You know I don't care, except for her sake and for the sake of the promise we both made. If you meant anything by that you must give up this ball. Can't you believe me when I tell you it isn't a fit place for you?"

Something in his masterful tone touched Ellen Amelia. Something shamed, and something frightened her too. She could not trust her womanhood in a place of which a man spoke in this way. She had innate refinement enough in her nature for that. It may have been something the same feeling that came to Louise Clifton when she found that she was in danger of falling from her spiritual supremacy over David Benedict. Ellen Amelia said nothing and the tears came to her eyes. For a few minutes words were impossible. She choked and tried to gain control over herself. All thought of the pink dress had vanished now. She felt as if God had sent her a condemning message and she could but yield before it.

"What shall I do? I promised," she said helplessly, looking up at Joseph, who still stood quietly watching her, hardly knowing what to say now that her tears had come and his errand had been told.

"Tell them you can't go. Write a note. Put it in the post office."

"But," said Ellen Amelia, the blood rolling in rich waves over her temples and forehead, "they don't take 'no' easy. I did tell them first I couldn't, 'cause I knew ma wouldn't like it, and I didn't think it was any use tryin' to get pa to say so, he a deacon in the church; but they said, Oh yes, I could, they would come for me and get me off somehow. And now I've promised, they'll be mad. And Bill, he was comin' for me; he'll come anyhow. I just know he will; he's awful set in his way and he said he'd chosen me for his partner to-morrow night, and you see he won't have any other. If he should come after me I don't know what I'd do. I'm afraid I'd have to go anyhow, now. I couldn't do anything. He wouldn't understand if I'd tell him all day why I couldn't go."

Joseph set his lips firmly and stopped to consider a moment. As he had come in he made up his mind that Bill Brower should be frustrated in some way. How? He looked down at the melting flakes on his sleeve and on the tops of his boots. It had begun to snow quite hard before he came in. Ah! There was an idea. If it kept on all night there would be sleighing. He looked up with a quick decision.

"I will come for you. I will come to take you sleigh-riding. We will go up to our house. You are to take dinner with my sister. Will you be ready? I will come early; it will be dark at six oclock, and even if they were lingering about they could not know."

Half an hour later Ellen Amelia stood in her own little room and looked in the seven-by-nine looking-glass watching the color roll over her face and neck as she thought again of the words she had spoken, taunting this young man and telling him he was jealous of another's having her company. Then she grew redder as she remembered his

words which had come with the immediate frankness which
utter indifference toward her would prompt, "You know I
don't care except for my sister's sake."

She tried to flash her eyes in indignation at herself for
having submitted to his talk after that, and called herself a
fool for giving up a pleasant companion who admired her,
and a whole evening full of untold delights, to go with this
man who had said he cared nothing about her, to take a
sleigh ride which neither cared to take, and like as not be a
burden at a Thanksgiving dinner where she was not
planned for nor wanted. But only tears would come instead
of flashes, and she turned out her light, and hung away the
pink tarletan without noticing how she crushed it, and cried
herself to sleep without trying to pray. Poor miserable
child! Had God forsaken her at the outset of her trying to
walk with him? How tenderly did the watching Father look
down upon his child that night! He saw just how he was to
lead her feet to pleasant paths and beside still waters by and
by.

Downstairs Ellen Amelia had been obliged to answer
numerous questions as best she could, and she had tried to
keep her own counsel, but had failed. What her mother and
grandmother could not divine they could draw out of any
one. Before the note was written declining to go to the
town ball in company with Bill Brower, Mrs. Haskins senior
and junior were in possession of such of the facts as they
thought were worth while. They did not count Joseph in
the case except so far as the sleigh-ride was concerned,
though Mrs. Haskins addressed the deacon after their
daughter had retired, as follows:

"Deacon Haskins, I think it's time your daughter was
attended to. She ought to be sent away to school or
somethin', unless you want her carried right off before your
face and eyes. Since that Benedic' girl has come and rigged
her up in those new-fangled things, here's been three
young men to see her, and she ain't more'n a babe yet in her
understandin' of things. If she can't be made to understand
housework, or care for it, maybe she could learn a little
more and get ready to teach somethin', for the land knows,
if she should be left to keep herself now she'd have to
starve! And I'll miss my guess if she wouldn't do it gladly in

company with them story papers of hers. I will say in justice
to that Benedic' girl, that she has done one good thing in
gettin' Ellen 'Melia to give up that ball, but I shouldn't be
surprised to hear that there's somethin' a good deal worse
gettin' up to match it, or she'd never have give it up. It
seems to me it's a pretty state of things, anyway, when a chit
of a girl can come in town and get my daughter to do a thing
with a few words, that I've failed in with hours and hours of
lectures."

Deacon Haskins was not the man to reply that if she had
lectured less she might have accomplished more. He only
replied that "Perhaps it might be a good plan to send the
gearl to schule awhile longer," and then he turned over his
paper and was absorbed in its columns.

Joseph strode home through the fast-thickening snowflakes wondering why on earth he had done all this and
brought so much extra trouble on himself, and what he
should do now, with a sleigh-ride and a dinner party on his
own untrained hands. Could it be possible that he was
trying to do something in this way for his new Master, or
was it merely to get ahead of Bill Brower? He decided that
it was a little of both. Then he went to his sister.

It was rather hard explaining, but he managed to do it.
He tried to make it out that he had done it all for Ruth, and
explained carefully that he heard her and the minister
talking about it the day before as he was dozing on the sofa.
According to his account the whole thing had been a most
commonplace happening. He had "seen" Ellen Amelia and
the subject of the ball had "come up," and he had "found
she was going," and had told her it was not going to be a fit
place for girls to go to and she had better come to their
house, Ruth wanted her.

Ruth's eyes brightened and her heart grew glad. This
brother was joining with her in her plans to help others,
and also he was showing his confidence in her by inviting a
dinner party for her before he told her. She was pleased
beyond expression. Entering heartily into the plan she
wrote a graceful note to Ellen Amelia saying that she was so
glad she could come, that they wanted to have a pleasant
little frolic on Thanksgiving evening. This she dispatched
the next morning by the willing Joseph, together with a

little note to the minister in which she asked his presence at
her impromptu dinner and desired that he should tell her if
there were any others whom he would like her to invite.
David to her surprise quite entered into the affair, offering
several helpful suggestions. She had feared he might wish
to withdraw from the party altogether, but instead he
seemed to be planning things on a much larger scale than
she had thought of. When Ruth wondered what she should
do for extra help in the kitchen, so that Sally might be able
to attend to the waiting at the table, it was David who
thought of a woman, went to see if she would come, and
promised to take her back before nine o'clock to put her
little children to bed. So though the party was hastily
gotten up, things were in fine trim for the evening before
the high-noon had come. And then Ruth had time to go to
her room and pray with trembling and with hope for the
success of her evening. For there were others to come
besides Ellen Amelia, suggested by the minister and
Joseph, who suddenly developed into an excellent enemy
to the town-hall ball.

Could Ruth have known as she knelt for those few
moments by her bed in prayer before she went to finish her
other arrangements, that her brother Joseph was just then
standing soberly by the couch in his room, looking out at
the window, thinking that some higher power than theirs
must be asked to help their plans, and wondering how
people prayed, and finally kneeling solemnly down and
closing his eyes—how would her heart have throbbed with
joy! No words came. His thoughts took no expression.
Common words that he had heard other people pray in
meeting did not fit his thought, besides he felt awkward and
afraid of blundering in such a grave matter. But he knelt
there for several minutes in reverent waiting, and then
arose and went to carry out a commission of his sister's. And
that was Joseph Benedict's first real prayer; and it was not
for himself.

CHAPTER XIX

☆

It was near six o'clock. The last tardy member of the decorating committee had left the hall and the janitor had thankfully locked the door and hurried home to his supper, feeling glad that the affair would be over before many more hours, and his responsibility and attendance would cease. He had scarce ever had such arduous labor connected with his duties, except the time when those city people had taken possession and tried to raise some money to found a Home for Aged and Decrepit Canines, by a fancy bazar and amateur theatricals, and had made three dollars and seventy-five cents over expenses, which they had given to the janitor for his five days of extra labor, and then having had their fun, departed for more fertile pastures, leaving the Summerton cats and dogs to live and die unblessed and uncared-for.

The members of the committee of arrangements were eating hasty suppers, and scolding their husbands for forgetting to send certain last things to the hall. Some few had even begun to dress, or were exhibiting hastily constructed dresses to admiring grandmothers, who were to remain at home with the small children, and who must get their pleasure in some way.

Ellen Amelia, not having to eat any supper, stood before her small looking-glass arrayed in coarse pink tarletan. She had bought it in the village drygoods store, and it cost very little because it had been on hand for several years, Summerton not being given to pink tarletan except by the eighth of a yard to dress an occasional doll, or make popcorn bags for the Christmas tree. Mrs. Haskins had set her lips firmly when she discovered what had been bought, but the money had been Ellen Amelia's own, saved for a long time, and it was spent, so what was the use in scolding? She only said, "I'd like to know what earthly use you'll ever make of that thing afterward! It ain't strong enough for mosquito bars," and shut Ellen Amelia's bedroom door hard and went downstairs, and the daughter had sighed and thought how very hard it was to be like other people with such a mother. It is true she had her doubts about the propriety of wearing it to a dinner at the Benedicts', but they were largely overbalanced by her desire to wear the gown now that she had sacrificed her money and her time to get it ready. Besides, a dinner, according to her literary experience, was a grand affair, at which Miss Benedict would probably be arrayed in "black velvet, with a necklace of large solitaire diamonds encircling her lily white throat, whose whiteness far outshone the gems in brilliancy." She wondered if Ruth would have her brothers adopt full evening dress. She was not quite sure what that was, but she was full of anxiety to see it.

The dress certainly was pretty and becoming; although, had she but known it, she would have looked better in blue. But her cheeks were red with excitement and her eyes shone like two stars. She was not going to the ball, but she was going to something, and with a young man, and that was a great deal, even if he had told her he cared nothing for her except for his sister's sake. The pink dress had large puffed sleeves to the elbow, below which her plump arms were bare. She looked regretfully at them with a sort of apologetic feeling because she had no gorgeous bracelets to deck them with. She had cut the neck as *décolleté* as she dared, her father being a deacon and her mother a little behind the times as to fashion, and being frightened with the rather undressed effect, had shirred a full ruffle of soft, very old muslin in to help piece out the way to her throat. The muslin had been a dainty little fancy apron that had been a treasure and delight in days gone by, but she had ruthlessly cut it up without a sigh for this grand occasion. An old summer hat contained three very pink, very crushed roses and some buds. These she renovated and placed on her left shoulder where they drooped as gracefully among the cheap pink and white ruches as if they had been real flowers amid costly silk and chiffon. She

surveyed the effect awhile and longed for a necklace of
pearls or something of that sort, even if it were but a gold
chain; gold chains were not plentiful in the Haskins family,
and she finally contented herself with a rusty bit of black
velvet ribbon tied about her throat, which added much to
the effect and really helped to bring out the color in her
cheeks. Altogether she made a pretty picture as she came
down the stairs into the dining room where the young
Haskinses were gathered, prepared to get what comfort
they could from the remains of the dinner's turkey. Tommy
stopped chewing, with one end of the wishbone in his
mouth, and Amos dropped his under jaw in mild amaze.
Deacon Haskins looked and saw before him his young wife
as she was years ago in a pretty pink calico, and wondered,
and was delighted that his daughter could look so like
an angel, and the heart of the New York grandmother
throbbed with pleased exultation that a grandchild of hers
should appear in such good style. But practical Mother
Haskins, who had yet good common sense among her
virtues, stood in the kitchen door with the coffee pot and
spoke out in indignation:

"Ellen Amelia Haskins, you little fool! Are you actually
thinkin' of wearin' that tawdry rag to Farmer Benedict's
house to supper? Now you can turn right round and go back
upstairs and dress yourself decent. Bare neck an' arms in
the middle o' winter, and you a deacon's daughter too. Pa,
why don't you speak up an' tell her she's a disgrace to her
bringin'-up. This is some more o'them trashy papers! Now I
shall clean them out o' this house. Deacon, I hope you see
now what you've done by humorin' her in them story-
readin' notions."

But Ellen Amelia, with a graceful sweep of the gown,
long practised before her nine-inch mirror in imitation of
that given by the Countess Luclarion, swept out of the door
into the hall leading to the front room, only saying
impressively and in tones that should not reach the ears of
the waiting young man, "Certainly, ma, I shall wear it. Did
you s'pose I paid my money out and made it for nothin'?"

Then did Ellen Amelia appear before Joseph Benedict,
and in the smoky light made by the kerosene lamp which
Amos had hastily brought when he opened the door for

Joseph, she looked like some delicate pink angel floating before him. He did not know that the tarletan was coarse and cheap, nor the velvet ribbon rusty and creased, nor the flowers soiled and crumpled. He only saw the artistic whole, with all the defects hidden by the kindly shadows of the room. He looked and dropped his eyes, for it seemed that it was some beautiful vision which almost ought not to be looked upon by common, disinterested eyes. Neither was he used to *décolleté* dressing and he felt a little startled by it. He had an innate instinct that made him drop his eyes from the plump round neck. But there was no denying that Ellen Amelia had been suddenly transformed into a beautiful being, the like of which he had never seen before. At last he gained his senses and his voice. He spoke gravely. It seemed that he could not be otherwise with this girl. She was to him like the visible presence of his promise to God. She was the paper on which his promise was written and must be guarded and reverenced, not for the paper's sake but for the promise it held. Ellen Amelia felt this, and although she did not understand it, she resented it. She wanted to be reverenced for her own sake and not for the promise, however sacredly she might regard the promise.

"You are very beautiful," he said, slowly brushing his hand across his eyes as if to clear them from the blinding vision; "but isn't that rather thin?" and he reached out a rough finger and awkwardly felt of the material in the enormous puff that surrounded her arm. "You'll catch an awful cold such a night as this. It isn't safe. I'll just sit down and wait while you go get a good warm flannel dress on," and he suited the word to the deed and sat down.

Poor Ellen Amelia! Her humiliation was complete. She turned without a word and fairly flew through the hall and dining room and up the stairs and threw herself upon her bed and cried. It was some twenty minutes later that she appeared in the front room arrayed in her dark blue serge, with her coat and hat and a thick veil over her face. She had washed the tear stains away as much as possible, and she trusted to the cold air and snowflakes to do the rest. As for Mother Haskins, there never was a more surprised mother in her life. She had no more expected that Ellen Amelia would go upstairs and change her dress than she had expected the gray cat to change his fur for white. What had happened to the girl?

That ride was a peculiar one. Ellen Amelia scarcely spoke a word from the time she was carefully tucked into the sleigh until she was handed out on the doorstep at the Benedict home. There was something in her silence which embarrassed Joseph, and made him endeavor to get up a conversation. However, he was not encouraged much and he soon gave it up.

Early in the evening young Brummel called at the parsonage for Miss Clifton. He had a horse and cutter and asked her if she would mind taking a short turn in the snow before going to the hall. It was not until they had taken quite a ride and were turned toward the village once more that Mr. Brummel casually mentioned that his sister was suffering from a severe headache and would not be able to go with them that evening, and, "How about it?" Should he stop at the hall at once? It was later than he supposed, and fully time to go if they meant to have any fun before the rather early hour when Louise's mother would expect her to return. Louise consented to go at once to the hall, though she felt just the least bit uncomfortable about going without even Georgiana as *chaperon*. At the door he left her, pointing out the dressing room and telling her he would return in just a moment, as soon as he could find a man to take the horse to a neighboring stable.

David Benedict had slipped away from the table as soon as dinner was over. He had promised Mrs. Stevens to get her home as soon as possible after the dinner was out of the way, and David never neglected a promise. He went and harnessed the horses to the sleigh, the same one in which Joseph and Ellen Haskins had taken their silent ride, and in a few minutes Mrs. Stevens was flying through the snow to her children with a basket of good things under the seat for their delectation.

David deposited Mrs. Stevens and her basket at her own door, and then, bethinking himself that possibly the post office might be open thus late in the evening, even though it was a holiday, and there might be a letter for Ruth, he drove over to the stores. The town hall was the next door but one to the post office, and as David hitched his horses he naturally looked over toward the hall and wondered who would go there. He saw another cutter standing before the door and a lady being helped out. As the lady parted from the gentleman at the door the full light of the entrance-way fell on her face and he saw it for just an instant before she passed in. It was Louise Clifton. One glance at the retreating form in the cutter and he felt certain that her escort was Alonzo Brummel. Hot indignation burned in David's veins. Here was this girl's brother at his home, doing his best to save some of the young people from going to the hall, and here was his sister entering as if it were a matter of course. But no thought that it was her fault crossed his mind. She did not know of course, where she was going. It was all the fault of young Brummel. He was capable of any sort of misrepresentation, David believed, if he was at all like what he had been in their old days in the village school. With a sudden impulse that was unusual for him, for he was a cool-headed man, David flung the reins into the sleigh and strode across the intervening space between himself and the open hall door. Louise had disappeared within. The two Brower boys were lounging in the doorway, evidently just preparing to go in. He heard their coarse laugh and more. He heard a sentence about the lady who had just passed in, that sent his blood racing at fever heat to his brain. Then these men were exulting over the thought that the minister's sister was to be a guest with themselves this evening, and were even boasting of the number of times they would put their vile arms about her, and take her pure white fingers in their polluted ones. David could scarcely keep his hands off them as they entered the door with him. He set his teeth hard and clenched his fists unconsciously. One thing he meant to do. Louise must be rescued from this open door to the pit even if he had to carry her away by main force. He would not have it rest upon his soul that a pure girl should be allowed to suffer the touch of hands like those that had just gone in, and he knew many others who were in all probability in the hall now, who were no better. If he did anything, it must be done at once before Alonzo Brummel returned. With desperate haste he turned to the door labeled, "ladies' dressing room," and knocked.

"Is Miss Clifton here?" he asked of the frightened girl with a curling-iron in her hand and several hairpins in her mouth who opened the door a very small crack. "Please tell her someone is waiting for her at the door, and wishes her to make haste. It is very important."

David did not stop to think what he should say. He spoke with authority, and his face looked white and drawn. He turned and went outside. He did not wish to meet her in the glare of the light before every one. He did not yet know what he should say to her.

The girl with the curling iron conveyed her message and added by way of explanation as Louise turned with a scornful surprise toward the messenger, "I suppose it is the minister waiting outside perhaps. I guess something's happened. He looked awful scared when he give me the word." This was spoken in a cheerful tone and intended to excite her interest, but it struck terror to Louise's heart. What had happened? Her mother? Her brother? Was some one sick or was Robert merely angry? No, Robert had gone out to dinner, she did not know where. He could not have found out possibly, so soon, for not a soul knew yet except herself and Mr. Brummel that she had come here. It must be sudden illness, or the house on fire, or something dreadful—a telegram from New York perhaps. A hundred awful possibilities rushed through Louise's excited brain as she struggled with her wraps and hurried out to the steps.

She wondered a little and was still more frightened when she found it was David Benedict who was waiting for her.

"What is it?" she asked excitedly. "Oh, what is the matter, and where is my brother? or Mr. Brummel?"

"Come this way and I'll tell you," said David gravely, hurrying her across the snowy pavement to his own cutter, putting her in with haste, and tucking the robes scientifically about her. She saw that he was hurrying with all his might and she kept quite still, her heart throbbing painfully, until he jumped in beside her and started the horses off at a furious rate. He felt that he must get her far away from the vicinity of those two vile creatures who had dared to speak of her in the way he had heard, as fast as he possibly could."

"Now tell me quick," she pleaded, laying her hand

earnestly on his arm, "what is it? My mother—is she sick? Don't be afraid tell me the worst at once. I can bear it. I can bear anything but suspense!" Poor child, she thought she could bear anything, and yet when she found out what was the matter she could not bear it at all.

David looked at her in surprise. "Don't be frightened," he said almost tenderly. "It is not your mother. There is nothing to be frightened at now. You are safe. I will take care of you."

"What is it then? What do you mean? I was not in any danger was I? How could I be?"

And then David Benedict perceived that he was not going to have an easy task to explain to the kidnapped young woman his strange and summary action.

CHAPTER XX

"I do not understand," said Louise. "What possible peril could I be in, and how did you come to find it out?"

"Did you know what kind of a place you were going into just now?" asked David.

"Certainly," answered she with some asperity; "I was in the town hall, was I not? I understood that was the name of the place. I was going to a ball, just to see what it was like. I wish you would tell me at once what is the matter. I do not in the least understand." Her tone was quite determined. She was prepared to give her rescuer a hearing, but it must be no trivial matter for which he had thus meddled with her affairs. He saw that he must explain fully, and that he had but one chance to save himself in her eyes. That chance was to tell her the truth—the whole truth. He never stopped, however, to think how she might regard him. His only care was for her. She must not be allowed to go back to that place even if he was obliged to resort to using force, or in other words, his advantage of the sleigh and two good horses over her. He would take her to her brother and let him manage the affair if she would not be persuaded. David set his lips, for his task was made the harder by the sudden dull disappointment that settled upon him when he found that the young woman did not regard a public ball with any degree of shrinking at all.

"Miss Clifton, did you know when you went to that place that you would be expected to dance, and to dance with every one present? Did you know that some of the dancing and the dancers would be unpleasantly familiar, and that some of the men with whom you would be thrown would not be fit companions for you?"

Louise's cheeks fairly blazed.

"Do you mean to say that you have undertaken to manage me?" she asked indignantly. "I do not understand what all this means. I knew, of course, what sort of an entertainment I was going to attend and, of course, I expected to have a little fun in dancing. As for the young men, I think I could take care of myself, and I am bound by no village laws to dance with all of them. Indeed, I suppose there are very few with whom I should have cared to do so. If that is what you have made all this fuss about, please turn about this moment and take me back. Mr. Brummel will think it unpardonable in me to have gone off in this unexplained fashion. I thought at least that some one was dead by the way you acted. Did my brother send you after me? I demand to know that! He had no right whatever to keep me from any entertainment I wish to attend. I cannot help it that he has silly notions. I am not a minister, if he is. I insist upon being taken back at once, Mr. Benedict." She lifted her head imperiously, but David only answered quietly:

"That I decline to do, Miss Clifton."

"What do you mean?" asked Louise, her voice fairly shaking with her anger.

"I mean to protect you," said her driver again quietly.

"From what, pray? I shall need to claim protection from you if you keep on like this."

"From yourself," said David, "and from the devil," he added fiercely under his breath.

"From myself! What do you mean? I can attend to myself. And you need not insult me by swearing in my presence."

"Yes, from yourself," answered the quiet voice again. "I must protect you so that you will do nothing that you would regret if you knew all about it. And I was not swearing. I meant those other words. If the devil was ever anywhere you would have found him in that hall to-night."

"Again I demand to know what all this mystery is about. You have hinted darkly at awful things. Now if there is anything awful you must tell me."

"I will try," said David his voice almost pained in its tensity. "Though I'm afraid you will wish you had taken my word for it. If you will let me I will take you to my sister and she will explain."

But Louise was high-wrought by this time. She had a strong suspicion that some notions of either Ruth Benedict or her own brother had been at the bottom of all this and she was in no mood to wish to see Ruth.

"I demand to know, and to know at once! If there was anything the matter you can certainly tell me. Had some one threatened to kill me?" with an ill-concealed smile.

David took a firm hold on the reins and turned his eyes full upon her, and even in the starlight she felt the steady, calm gaze. There was a quieting effect in his tone which seemed almost masterful and he said clearly and with no hesitation now: "Then I will tell you, Miss Clifton, as well as I can. In the first place I do not know what dancing is in the city, but I have an idea that it is very different here. For instance, you would not have been allowed to choose your partners sometimes, but would have been forced, in a wild, frolicsome way, to dance with whoever chose to seize you about the waist. Your attempt at a refusal would only have put them—these young gentlemen—on their mettle and rendered it certain that you would be subjected to further liberties. If a girl does not wish to dance with any particular person then that particular person is supposed to attempt to make her dance with him, if not by fair means then by foul ones; and you might, you probably would, have found yourself whirling about in the arms of young men, whom if you knew, you would not speak to, to say nothing of touching, and utterly unable to leave the place or even get your footing till you had been carried twice or thrice around the room. I have been to these places; you have not. I am not a Christian, I am sorry to say. I hope I am a gentleman. At any rate I was so disgusted that I never go myself any more, and I could not bear to think of my sister or any one for whom I cared being found there. Have I said enough, Miss Clifton?"

"I was not aware that you were a crank as well as the rest," broke in the girl in an icy tone. "I think this has gone far enough. If you do not take me back at once I shall scream for help when we pass the next house."

"Ah," said David with a heavy sigh, "I see I have not said enough. Wait one moment, Miss Clifton, let me tell you the rest; I had hoped not to have had to say this, but you force me to do so." In his unconscious absorption he stopped the horses and looked her full in the face again.

"You said you could take care of yourself. The two young men who are the vilest of all that would have been there to-night, and who would have appeared to the best advantage because they have money and dress well, were standing by the door as you went in. I happened to be within hearing at the moment. *They were betting which would have the privilege of holding you in his arms the greater number of times to-night;* and wait; they were exulting over the thought of—they spoke of—they said—heaven help me! I cannot repeat to you the words they spoke! You would never look me in the face again. But believe me, on my honor as a gentleman, it was such a thing that only the fear of dragging your name in the filth prevented me from knocking them down then and there. Though they are young their lives are vile, their words are vile, their very thought is vile; and these would have been your partners in the dance by this time." David suddenly ceased, shut his lips hard, picked up the reins, and struck the horse a cut that sent them flying. He felt a dreadful fear that in his excitement he had forgotten himself and gone too far, saying things that were unpardonable if said to a young lady, yet somehow he did not care, either. He had risked a great deal, but it was to win, and he had won.

Louise sat suddenly stunned. She too had a dim idea that

David was saying something which was improper to hear, and that she ought to stop him, but had she not brought it upon herself? and could it be true, this awful thing he was saying? She shuddered to think what the coarse mouths might have been saying, or rather she could not dream what it was, but some instinct told her that it was bad enough and made her loathe herself for giving them any chance to speak of her at all. As David went on, his earnest, manly tones, and the way in which he bravely spoke out, although his voice quivered with feeling, those words not usually spoken so plainly by a young man to a young woman, and which were evidently so hard for him to speak, gave her a new respect for him. There was something grand after all in his telling her this, though she was so ashamed of herself for making him do it that she could scarcely hold up her head. There suddenly came over her a wonderful change. She was frightened meekness itself. The tears had come to her eyes, a strange thing for Louise Clifton, for crying was a thing as utterly alien to her nature as frowning to a rose. They sat in silence for some minutes and then David as they skimmed along slowly reined in the horses until they came down to a more moderate pace. At last Louise gained voice to ask meekly in a choked tone:

"Where are we going?"

David stopped the horses as suddenly as before and answered with a deference which was quite a contrast to his manner a few moments before:

"Wherever you say, Miss Clifton. Will you go to my sister?"

"Oh, I guess so," answered the poor girl. She felt utterly crushed by the terrible thing which had been told her. She had been one of those girls who had always said in answer to any argument against promiscuous dancing, "Nonsense! Men are not all so bad as they make them out, nor girls either. I would never dance with a man who was as bad as that. Don't you think I'd like to hear of any man daring to talk in that way about me?" and her eyes would flash and she would hold her head high, and walk indignantly away; while her satisfied, ignorant little mother would look pleased, and smile and murmur, "No one would ever dare breathe an evil word in connection with my daughter. To

the pure all things are pure," and the matter would be
dropped.

Louise remembered several occasions when a maiden
aunt had undertaken to make her mother believe that
dancing schools were terrible places, and the mother had
indignantly repudiated the idea and sent her daughter from
the room, saying that her aunt's talks and the selections she
read from her various tracts were more contaminating for a
young girl's purity than if she danced all her life through.

Now these things came back to her. It was true then that
men talked about girls. Oh, it was awful to think that
another man, and surely a good one, had heard them. Here
Louise turned and stole a look at the outline of the face near
her, clear-cut against the cold starry sky. There were purity,
tenderness, and pity in his face. She could see that he
wished all his heart to atone in some way for the severity he
had been obliged to use. But he kept a kindly silence for
the most part, only once or twice saying a word about the
snow, and once calling her attention to the view as they
came in full sight of a lovely bit of landscape, the new moon
hanging, starred about, above a little tree-fringed hill, a
tiny dark house below with a speck of light in the window,
and dark, bare poplars lifting their brown arms piteously
against the luminous sky.

As they neared the Benedict house Louise roused
suddenly from her painful thoughts. She saw the many
lights and knew there must be guests.

"Oh, who is there?" she asked suddenly, putting out her
hand to the reins to stop him, and quickly he obeyed her
wish and stopped in the gateway. "Have you strangers?" she
asked.

"No, only a few friends from the village," he answered
reassuringly. "Your brother is there. They will be glad to see
you. I shall say nothing to them."

"Oh, no, I can't go in," said Louise shrinking back, "not if
my brother is there. I would not have him know for
anything. I went to Brummels' to spend the evening with
Georgiana. He will think it strange and ask me questions. I
cannot tell him now. Take me home, please. Or no! Mother
does not know. Oh, what shall I do?" She covered her face
with her hands and cried outright. David sat only a moment

regarding her, and then suddenly taking up the reins he turned the cutter about and gave a word to his horses which made them fairly fly over the frozen snow. Louise looked up pretty soon and saw that they were not going home, and she did not know the direction.

"We are just taking a sleigh-ride," answered David cheerily. "Are you warm enough?" and he tucked the robes carefully about her again. "It is a beautiful night and perhaps this will be as pleasant a way as any for you to pass your time. At what hour does your mother expect you to return? You can go home then and simply say you had a ride. If I had a mother I think I would tell her all about this, but I don't suppose I am competent to advise, and I'll fix it all right for you so that you can do as you please."

Louise looked timidly up at him. He was very kind to her. Somehow she seemed to have grown very young and ignorant all at once and felt that he was some one to look up to. He seemed so strong and good and kind.

"It would frighten my mother terribly," she said after a few minutes of thought. "She doesn't know the world much. My father shielded her from all knowledge of such things. She would think I had done some dreadful thing and could never be trusted again, and I am sure I don't know that I can."

"You must not feel in that way," said David earnestly. "You will be all the more careful now. You were taken care of. Some strange power that I did not understand made me go to the post office against my better judgment to-night, for I knew there was scarcely a possibility of there being anything in the office on a holiday evening." Then a sudden flash illumined his face and he said solemnly and reverently and wonderingly, "Maybe it was God. Miss Clifton, do you know God? Are you what they call a Christian?"

Louise sat in wonder. The question, the very question that she had sat in her room two days before and pondered whether she could ask of him. For she had actually considered whether she might not try a little real missionary work by finding out if religion was what he was supposed to need to make him a success in the world. It may seem strange that one who did not belong to Christ would care to try to bring another, but it is nevertheless

true that some do. They see that religion is a good thing—
or would be for another—and while they get along in the
world very well themselves without it, they have kind-
heartedness enough to make a little effort to help some one
else get it. Louise decided that it would be a very novel and
a very interesting thing to do, besides being a thing which
would surprise and please her mother and brother and
Ruth, and perhaps make them treat her with a little more
respect.

And now she found her heathen actually asking the very
question of his would-be missionary which she had half
planned to ask of him if the opportunity ever offered.

Altogether it was a strange ride and a strange talk those
two had out under the starlight that Thanksgiving evening,
but there will never come an anniversary of that day when
they will cease to be thankful for the ride and the talk and
the decisions that resulted therefrom.

Louise found herself set down at her brother's door at ten
o'clock a crushed and meek little being whose main desire
was to get to her room and cry, and whose heart was
burdened with the thought of the searching questions
which had been asked her by one who did not know Christ
himself yet, but was seeking to find him.

When Alonzo Brummel returned from attending to his
horse and after making himself presentable in the gentlemen's dressing room went to the appointed spot to meet his
young lady, and found her not, he concluded that she had
grown tried of waiting and had probably gone into the main
hall with some of the girls, as it was a very informal affair.
He made his way slowly through the hall speaking in his
patronizing way to this pretty girl and that whom he had
known in his younger and less pompous days. He was
puzzled as to what could have become of Louise. Just then
Eliza Barnes, the girl of the hair curler in the dressing
room, who had opened the door for David, accosted him.

"Hello! there's Lonnie Brummel, girls. Wait a minute; I
want to speak to him. Say, Lon, Miss Clifton's gone. I
thought you might be lookin' fer her. I guess 'twas her
brother come after her in a mighty big hurry, and she
looked scared enough. Dave Benedict brought the word in

for her to come right out. I s'pose the minister didn't want to come into the hall. He hustled her into a sleigh and drove off quick and slick. I peeped through the curtains and seen 'em myself."

Alonzo Brummel uttered a word under his breath that he would scarcely have liked to speak before the minister's sister; but finding that he was hopelessly left to his own resources he set about finding the prettiest and silliest girls in the room and having as good a time as possible, going home somewhat later than he had planned to take Miss Clifton away, it must be confessed, and letting himself quietly into his father's house by a way known to his younger days when his mother kept a more strict watch over his bedroom door than could have been desired. He received, however, the next morning, a stiff, violet-scented note informing him that Miss Clifton begged his pardon for having left him so abruptly the evening before, and desired to explain that she had been called for in great haste and had not had time to leave any word for him. It was so altogether cutting and summary in its tone that Alonzo Brummel decided to spend the remainder of his vacation with a friend in New York, and he departed that day for a more genial atmosphere. He did not just care to be at home when his mother should discover where he had been spending his time the evening before.

When David reached home at last he found that the guests were preparing to take their departure. Indeed, Joseph had been much worried to know how he was to get Ellen Amelia home without the horses and the cutter.

When the last one had gone and David had helped to put Miss Haskins into the cutter and watched them drive away, he turned back and stood by his sister Ruth, his face deeply serious.

"Ruth," said he, and she knew by his tone that he had something to tell her which meant more to him than anything he had ever said to her before. "Ruth, you pray, I know. I want you to pray for a—for some one who needs help very much, some one who doesn't know how to pray."

Ruth looked up quickly, her face lighting with glad surprise.

"O David," said she, "do you love Jesus? And is it

yourself you mean? I will gladly, but why don't you pray too?"

"No, I don't think I know Jesus yet," he answered simply, as a little child might; "but I want to. I mean to," he added with emphasis, "and I'd like you to pray for me to, if you will. But this other one is a woman, and she hasn't anything to stay her life on. I shall try to pray for her myself, but I wanted you to help. You know how better than I. She needs it very much. And Ruth, you thought it was queer, I suppose, that I stayed away so long to-night; but I want you to know I had to. No, I didn't go to that ball," he said as he caught a shade of anxiety across her face. "I was afraid you'd think I did, but I'm not that kind. I had to keep some one else away. If God ever sent any one anywhere he certainly sent me downtown this evening."

He took his sister's hand and stooped and kissed her on the forehead, and then went upstairs to his room.

And as Ruth went to her room to pray as she had promised, she carried a worry in her heart. What village girl had gotten a hold upon David? Was there some one then who would be a drag upon him? Had his heart already been entangled? She had grown to love her brother David very deeply. She sighed and wondered and wished, and then she prayed, and as she prayed the weight passed away from her heart and she rejoiced; for was not David seeking for Jesus? And a voice had whispered behind her:

> Fearest sometimes that thy Father
>   Hath forgot?
> When the clouds around thee gather,
>   Doubt him not!
> Always hath the daylight broken—
> Always hath he comfort spoken—
> Better hath he been for years,
>   Than thy fears.

CHAPTER XXI

Ellen Amelia had been very quiet during the entire evening spent at the Benedict Thanksgiving party. She did not seem to recover from the successive humiliations which had brought her here in quiet and accustomed clothing. Her usually gay and voluble tongue was so still that the other girls asked her if she was sick, and Ruth looked at her in a troubled way many times fearing that Ellen was disappointed because she had not gone to the ball instead of coming to her.

Joseph too watched her in a kind of maze. He had not been at church the Sunday preceding and therefore the effect of the new dark blue dress was particularly bewildering. He was hardly sure he knew Ellen Amelia. She certainly did not look like the same girl he had known all his life and gone to school with, and, it must be confessed, at whose follies he had laughed many times.

What had she done? He was not well enough versed in the art of dress to lay it all to that. The pink tarletan had dazzled him, but the whole question of apparel appeared in a new light when he had noted the marked change in Ellen Amelia wrought, as he had presently to acknowledge to himself, by the donning of a new gown and, most mysterious of all, one not at all extraordinary either in fashion or in material. He could not understand why one dress rather than another should make a person's appearance so different. He did not know that there was all the difference in the world between a dress that fitted the form and one that did not. Neither did he reckon on graceful folds and lines that curved just right, nor—and perhaps this made the most difference of all—upon the soft waves of hair about her face and the low coil behind, which just fitted her face, in place

161

of the hard unbecoming knot and tight frizzes which she had hitherto supposed to be the height of fashion. Ruth had somehow managed to get in a lesson in hair-dressing with all the rest, and the result was a much more pleasing Ellen Amelia. Joseph looked at her as she sat in the big chair in the corner and thought she was not unpleasing. Indeed, on second thought he was not sure that she was not pretty. If she was not so awfully silly he did not know but she would be interesting, but as it was he did not understand how Ruth could waste her time on her. He wondered for the hundredth time why Ruth did it, and then the thought came and softened his expression, "She does it for Christ's sake," and he thought perhaps he would like to help her, or some one, for that reason.

The minister had interrupted his thoughts just then, sitting down beside him and gradually drawing him out with stories of his own life. He asked Joseph about his school days and drew from him the wish that he could have kept on with his studies. "Father always meant I should," he said suddenly with an impulse of confidence in the man who seemed to be so interested in him. "And my brother was anxious for it too. He had two years at the academy in the city, you know. But we both agreed that I ought not to do it till the farm was clear of the mortgage, and now that it's out of the way I've grown too old." He heaved a little sigh of regret, like the winding sheet to his desire, and seemed to lay the subject away. Not so the minister:

"Not a bit of it. One is never too old to learn. Why, man, you have so much to learn, and if you don't do it here you'll have to waste a great many years of eternity learning it. Learn what you can now." There followed a quick succession of questions on the part of the minister and answers by Joseph.

"Well," said the minister straightening up at last, an eager light in his eyes, "there is no reason why you shouldn't catch up soon if you want to, and go on to college. I had no idea the schools in Summerton carried one so far. Now, if you would really like to go on with your studies I should be delighted to help you. You know I'm not long from college and I love to teach. You'll have plenty of time these long winter evenings, and if you make good use of them who knows but you might be ready to enter college by next fall? I'm not saying you could, you know, for I haven't examined you yet; but you might. Stranger things have happened. Will you do it?"

"Do you mean," said Joseph his eyes burning with excitement and his hands clenched in his earnestness, "do you really mean you think I could make something of myself in the world?"

"I certainly do," answered the minister.

Joseph was so occupied with the wonderful new thoughts that the minister had awakened in him and the stirring of old ambitions, that he scarcely noticed Ellen Amelia till they were half-way home. Then she aroused from her silence and made a remark.

"I wish I could get away from Summerton, and learn something and be somebody!"

It was said half fiercely, and not in the least as if she expected an answer, but more as if she were thinking aloud. But there was a note in her words which appealed to Joseph. He had had these very same feelings before Ruth had come to them to make home something worth while, and even now his sister's sweetness and brightness made him long to do something to make himself more on a plane with her intellectually. Now this evening a way had been opened, a hope that after all he might possibly be something more than he was, and in his exultation he felt a sympathy for this girl beside him who had the same desires and no hope of their fulfillment, for of course Ellen Amelia had no possibility before her but to live and die in Summerton. He tried to arouse himself from his own pleasant thoughts and say something to comfort her, even as the minister had brought hope to him, but what could he say? He could not promise to help her, for she had been through the same schools in which he had been graduated. She was as far advanced as he. "Couldn't you get some book to read?" he offered lamely as an alternative in place of going away.

"Where would I get books, and how would I know what to read? I've read all my life, and it only seems to make me more unhappy. Ma don't like me to read, anyway. Sometimes I think I'll just give up and never touch a book again, if that's what she wants, and go into the kitchen and never do another thing but bake and scrub and wash dishes the rest of my life. I don't see how I'm a-going to keep that promise I made to you, anyway. There isn't any chance at home. I s'pose, to be good, one ought to be willing to do all sorts of ugly things and not care, and not ever want anything else; but I can't help wanting other things. I'd like to do something big and grand. I s'pose I ain't fit; but I'd be willing to go through most anything to make me fit, if there was a chance for anything better than just what all the Summerton girls live for."

"I s'pose," said Joseph, speaking slowly, as if he were treading on unfamiliar ground and must choose his words carefully, "that if you do the best you can, God will see to the rest. The Bible talks like that, and most all sermons say so, and it seems as if the Christians professed to believe that, though to be sure there don't many of them act as though they remembered it. But look here, Miss Ellen, let us be different from that sort of Christians. If the thing's worth doing at all, let us do it as well as it can be done by us. It seems to me, it isn't fair to God not to do our best. Then, if he's anything, he's to be trusted to bring it out straight, somehow. I s'pose if he wants you to do some grand work in the world, he could fix it out so you could manage to do it; but if I was you, I'd do first the little things at home he's given you. I tried to find a place last night I used to hear father read at prayers sometimes when I was a little chap, about being faithful in little things and then you'd get to be a ruler over a good deal more, perhaps, sometime. Anyhow, if I was you I'd try it."

"I will," said Ellen Amelia, with her usual prompt decision. "I'll begin to-morrow morning and darn every stocking in mother's basket before I touch my paper that comes in the morning mail."

They were at her father's door by this time, and as Joseph helped her out and turned his horses homeward once more, he felt a sense of exultation that the little work he had tried to do for Ellen Amelia had not been wholly without effect. There was a new kind of joy in doing this sort of thing, which is given to souls who labor to help others, and which made him long to do more for his new

Master. He mused over what the girl had said as he put the
horses up and wondered what kind of a paper she took, and
thought he would ask her sometime. She might be more
advanced than he knew. He had never dreamed that she
took a paper all herself. But he decided that in all
probability it was a fashion paper.

With much excitement and eagerness he went on the
appointed evening to meet the minister and take his first
lesson in Latin. He had not told Ruth nor David yet. He
wished to see whether he could really do anything at it first.
He was charmed with the lesson. And indeed he might well
have been had he possessed a mind even less eager for
knowledge than his really was, for Robert Clifton was a
teacher of no mean ability. He had considered seriously at
one time whether he would not let his passion for teaching
have the mastery over his life, but the Lord had called in
the direction of the ministry, and he had obeyed. Ruth
would have been astonished to know that a little word of
hers, spoken unwittingly at a time when he was unsettled
about the matter in that summer of their meeting long ago,
had sent the final conviction to his heart that his Master
wished him to work as a minister.

The hour of the lesson was long drawn out, and neither
teacher nor pupil was willing to stop when the clock struck
a warning hour. Mrs. Clifton wondered what in the world
Robert could be doing with that young man in the study so
long, and wished that—if it was true, as he said, that the
fellow was worth anything at all—he would have thoughtfulness enough to bring him downstairs to talk a little while
to his sister. Louise was very restless and unhappy. She
tried to read and to play and to embroider, and finally, after
sitting for a few moments in every chair in the room, had
retired. Mrs. Clifton sighed and wondered how long she
was going to be able to keep Louise in this little town, and
half wished Robert would get married, that she might take
Louise where she would not feel hampered by her brother's
profession.

But the young man was allowed to depart finally without
having even been brought into the parlor, and Mrs. Clifton
retired, with her curiosity unsatisfied.

As Joseph walked homeward that night, his busy

thoughts went far ahead of the present, and he pictured to himself many things he would do in the world with the knowledge he should acquire. Summerton was asleep, for the hour was late. As he passed Deacon Haskins' house, a sudden thought struck him. He stopped short and looked up at the house. "Maybe I might," he soliloquized aloud. "If I thought He wanted me to I would." He walked on after that, looking up at the clear starlit sky and letting his soul reach out behind that "dim unknown." He had read Lowell's great poem not many days before, and admired it, and certain lines of it came to him now. He wondered if God was really there behind the dim unknown, standing within the shadow, keeping watch above his own. He wished, as many another has wished, that he could see him once, and be sure—sure beyond the possibility of a doubt—that God did care for little things that people did and said. And there came to him through the still midnight a conviction that God did care.

It was the very next evening that Joseph Benedict presented himself at Deacon Haskins' door and asked for the daughter of the house. Her mother called her, and herself gave her the sitting-room lamp to carry into the parlor; but when an hour had passed and there seemed to be no sign of the visitor taking his leave, she thought it high time to do something. She cautiously opened the parlor door, and to her horror saw Joseph and Ellen Amelia bending their heads together over a book. They did not see her, nor apparently hear her, as she opened the door, and went on with earnest talk about some jargon she did not in the least understand. She stood contemplating them for a moment, and then as softly shut the door and turned away. She sat down at her sewing again, but there was a compressed look about her mouth, as if she knew some-thing and had surmised a good deal more, though she said nothing. When Joseph went away, which he did in a few minutes, for he was in a hurry to get back to his own study, Ellen Amelia lingered in the chilly haircloth parlor, and her mother, going in search of her, found her poring over a paper, upon which were carefully written rows of words.

"Ellen 'Melya, what on earth has possession of you? I should like to know what that Benedic' girl has on hand now? I do wish you'd come out here and finish up that job of mending you begun. I've got to have them things right away."

The daughter came and sewed quietly for the remainder of the evening, only answering abstractedly, "It's Latin, mother. I'm studying Latin." But from time to time as she sewed she glanced at the paper in her lap and her lips moved constantly. Mrs. Haskins looked at her eldest child with trouble in her eyes.

"I'm just that troubled about her I can't sleep," she remarked to her mother the next day. "She goes around mumbling all the time, 'A mo, a mass, a mat.' I'm sure I don't know what high-flown notion'll take her next. If she wanted to study she could have done it some other way than getting a young know-nothing of a fellow to teach what he don't know himself. I don't know but I'd rather she'd have even gone to that ball with the Brower boy. He at least looks decent. And after she got her dress made and all!"

But Ellen Amelia was engrossed in Latin and saw nothing else that went on, though she did honestly try to do her best in everything that came to her hand. This Latin was something that came nearly up to the measure of her heart's desire. Joseph had promised to give her every lesson he took himself, and while she knew very well that he was not doing it on her account at all, but only for the sake of doing his best to keep his part of the promise, she meekly accepted the help she got and began to look up to and admire her teacher with a kind of awe mingled with deep respect.

Things went on at this rate for about six or eight weeks, and at last Mother Haskins got the deacon sufficiently aroused to the danger of his daughter's present amusements to send her to West Winterton to the academy. Ellen Amelia was perhaps a little disappointed to give up her Latin lessons, but she was told that Latin was taught there and that by real teachers, and was bidden look upon the added advantages of the other studies she would have. So she stifled the wish she felt to have things to go on as they were, and managed to feel a degree of the gratitude that would have been hers a half-year before, and took her departure, leaving Joseph free to use all his time in study.

He felt relieved at first to find that the task he had set himself was no longer required of him, but after a few days he began to miss the pleasure he had had in imparting knowledge to this eager learner, and to think it might even be an advantage to him to teach some one else, for in teaching he learned so much himself, and so he looked about for another pupil. Ellen Amelia came home every Friday now and saw Joseph across the church every Sunday, and once he bowed and asked her how she was getting on in her studies. She remembered that bow with pleasure, for there seemed to be a touch of the courteous respect in it which he gave to his own sister.

The communion occurred soon after she had begun to attend the West Winterton Academy, and Ellen Amelia, David and Joseph Benedict, were among those who, having publicly professed their faith in the Lord Jesus, were welcomed to membership. This first accession to the church since the coming of the new pastor created a stir of astonishment in the community. It was long since there had been any one to unite with their church save an occasional person by letter from the city. The young people had almost without exception remained outside the church. Now to see them coming in so willingly, nay eagerly, made their elders ask, "What is it?" There had been no special services as yet, only the earnest preaching of the conscientious young pastor. They did not know of the quiet, heart-to-heart talks he had taken time for, with this one and that. They only saw the results. Men who had heretofore stayed at home on Sunday now were uniting with God's church. David Benedict was generally supposed to be somewhat indifferent, if not slightly infidel in his tendencies; but yet he had been the first to offer himself; even before the meeting at which the invitation had been given, and his brother had not been far behind. The deacons shook their heads and said they did not know about taking in people in such a wholesale way, to be put out perhaps in a year or two, or else be a dead weight to the church; and Deacon Chatterton allowed that in his opinion the examination ought to be a very rigid one. He certainly did his part to make it as much of an ordeal as possible. Poor Ellen Amelia Haskins felt that there were no more trials left in life for her worth mentioning when she came out of that lecture room. She trembled from head to foot and her face was almost as white as her handkerchief. Mrs. Chatterton never quite understood how it was that all her prophecies concerning the harm that Benedict girl would do in Summerton and in her own home never came to anything. She looked with doubt on the three young people as they stood together in the front of the church. She would not believe that there would not come retribution of some sort upon them all, just for what, she did not state even to herself.

Ruth was very happy. She had longed and prayed that her brothers might find Jesus and yet she had hardly hoped that they would come so soon. After that Thanksgiving night when David had asked her to pray for some one, she had been able to talk with him about being a Christian. They had had many long talks together and David had ended by becoming a simple-hearted, earnest Christian, giving himself to God as a little child might do, and having the glad heart-rejoicing just as a child rejoices over his sins forgiven. He was so happy he went about singing and whistling all the time. There seemed to be a bond warm and deep between the brother and sister now which never could be broken. They had begun at once to pray for Joseph, claiming the promise "If two of you shall agree on earth as touching anything that they shall ask, it shall be done for them," never knowing that their prayer was already answered and that Joseph was trying every day to walk in the straight and narrow way. David and Ruth had been sitting together in the twilight of the Sunday afternoon talking about their brother. They were worried about him lately. He spent a great many evenings away from the house and never explained where he went. He seemed much absorbed in something too. Ruth wondered if it could be one of the village girls. She was always a little troubled about those village girls. Just as they were saying that they must tell Joseph about their intention to unite with the church next Sabbath, he entered the room and, sitting down beside Ruth, began in his straightforward way to say what he had come to tell them.

"I wanted you to know beforehand," he said, "that I am going to unite with the church. I've been thinking about it a long time and I'm going to do it now."

Before he had finished speaking, David had grasped him by the hand and there was a pleasant surprise for Joseph to find that his elder brother was already a Christian. "Before they call, I will answer; and while they are yet speaking, I will hear," repeated Ruth solemnly.

And that night there was a family altar set up in the Benedict home, and from it went up prayers of thanksgiving and praise. There must have been joy around the throne of God and among the angels in heaven and among the saved ones there, for the father and mother surely were permitted to look down to earth and know that their two boys would meet them by and by, and that it was through the agency of their dear daughter.

CHAPTER XXII

Ellen Amelia Haskins was certainly changing greatly. Her mother noticed that she was quieter and more willing to help when she came home Friday nights. She really began to have hope that her daughter would settle down and be like other girls. She still read books to be sure, but they were solid-looking study books. There came no more illustrated story papers into the house. They had ceased suddenly, shortly after Ellen Amelia began the study of Latin. Mrs. Haskins supposed that the deacon had "braced up" at last, and heeded her many injunctions to stop the paper; but the truth was that Joseph Benedict had asked her what paper it was she took that she had mentioned to him the other night, and she had triumphantly displayed the latest arrival to him, whereupon his decided face took on a decided frown, and he tore the paper in half and told her it was not fit for her to read. Ellen Amelia was dismayed, but by this time Latin and her teacher had such a hold upon her that she did not say him nay, and after a good cry by herself, and a good deal of faltering resolution, she wrote a letter and stopped her paper nine weeks before its subscription ran out. And when in due course of time her father had asked her if it wasn't about time she needed to fix up that paper business for another year, and secretly handed out the money with a confidential nod, she surprised him by saying that she wouldn't take the paper any more, but if he would just as soon she would take the money for a study book she needed very much.

Her father and mother had been much surprised and pleased when she united with the church, though her mother's expression of it to her was that she was "sure Ellen Amelia hadn't acted much like a Christian durin' the past year, but she hoped they'd see a change now." And Ellen had made up her mind that not only they but God should see a change in her. And they did, although it did not come all at once. She was still Ellen Amelia. She still showed much silliness. It was not to be expected that her habits of thought could change all at once. But God and his workers were molding her for her place in the world, and although she did not see it, wonderful things were in preparation for her.

Out of the Thanksgiving party had grown a permanent source of culture and growth, not only to Ellen Amelia, but to many other of the young girls in Summerton, beginning with Ruth Benedict's Sunday-school class. Something had been said about Ellen Amelia's new dress, and it had been admired openly by the other girls. Ruth answered brightly, "Yes, isn't it pretty? And she made it herself too." The girls exclaimed over this, and would have been almost inclined to doubt it had any other than Miss Benedict made the statement. But Ellen Amelia with her native honesty came to the front at once:

"Yes; I made it myself after I was taught. Girls, you don't know what a teacher we've got. She can do anything. She showed me how to cut and fit this dress, and helped sew it. I think it would be a good deal honester myself to say she made it and I helped a little, but she insists that I did it."

The other girls admired more, and wistfully wished they could have something as nice, and before the evening was over Miss Benedict had an eager class in dressmaking, all ready to begin work whenever she should set the day. Ruth sighed when she went to her room that night, to think how much more eager they were to learn dressmaking than they had been to take up some extra Bible study she had suggested. She wondered if maybe she was doing right to go on and get them interested in things of the world? Might it not take their thoughts from higher things? These things were important, of course, but were they worth while if they took the entire attention? She pondered long over the question, but at last decided that it was worth while, and that she felt she might be able to make the class profitable in other ways, as well as to teach the girls how to make pretty dresses well and economically.

And so the class began in a large upper room which Ruth had decided should be used for any Christian work the Lord sent to her. It had been used as an attic, and had never been entirely finished off, for the rafters and beams were uncovered. But the ceiling was high, and the windows large and many. Ruth saw possibilities for a gymnasium and many other things as well as dressmaking classes. David, her helper now in all good schemes—for it is a great thing to have one person who believes in you, when you have a plan to carry out—made several long, strong tables, rough but serviceable, and one bright Saturday morning the girls, including Ellen Amelia, gathered there with scissors and thimble and cloth and thread, prepared to do as they were bidden. The first lesson proved a success. The girls were wild over their work, and would have been delighted to meet oftener. They were given a certain amount of sewing each to have finished before the next lesson. While they sewed they talked, and the talk ran on various themes, all suggested by the girls, but guided by Ruth.

"Miss Ruth," said Effie Haines, a pretty butterfly sort of girl who hummed from one thing to another, like a bee among the flowers, and who was very fond of brightness and fun, "Miss Ruth, you didn't go to the ball the other night, and you didn't want any of us to go; we know that, but would you please tell us just all the reasons why? I know some people say dancing is wicked, but I never knew why. Do you think it is?"

"Not in the least," answered Ruth smiling, at which

every girl in the room stopped sewing, and opened her eyes wide in amazement.

"You don't!" ejaculated Ellen Amelia. "Why, I thought—Joe sa——" then she stopped unnoticed, but the red blood stole up in her cheeks, and she said no more.

"Why, no; of course not," answered Ruth innocently. "What possible harm could there be in getting up on the floor and hopping around?"

They all laughed uneasily, feeling certain that there was a catch somewhere.

"They danced in the Bible, you know," said Ruth, "and danced unto the Lord. There were a great many times when dancing was used as praise to God in the old days. It's a pity it wasn't used more nowadays that way." Ruth went quietly on with her sewing, as if she had said the most commonplace thing.

The girls could not see whither she was leading them and Effie Haines protested. "But, Miss Ruth, that isn't real dancing; they just danced around with timbrels all alone."

"Well, we use a piano. What's the difference? A piano isn't wicked, is it?"

The girls laughed embarrassedly now. Ruth saw that they did not know what to answer her.

"Dear girls," she said, "you asked me an honest question and I answered it honestly. I do think that dancing as it is carried on to-day is wrong, and not only wrong, but exceedingly dangerous. I do not believe that dancing just of itself is wicked, and by that I mean whirling around to music just from pure joy in life. But I know that you meant more than that by your question. You meant to ask me whether I would dance myself, and whether I would advise you to dance, and I say no to that, most decidedly. The dangers that lurk in dancing are so great that it seems to me one is only safe to let it entirely alone in every form. You see dancing nowadays isn't merely hopping about alone as Effie has said. It means hopping around with some one else, and that some one else is sometimes a man. Now tell me honestly girls, would you, any of you, allow a man under any other circumstances, unless you were engaged or married to him of course, to take such liberties with you as are allowed in dancing?" The girls looked down at their

work and their cheeks grew a shade redder. All of them had
not had such careful teaching as had their teacher, but they
knew what she meant, and if some few of them had
occasionally allowed a young man to hold their hands in the
dark on their way home from meeting, and to kiss them at
the gate just for fun occasionally, they were ashamed of it
now, and hoped Miss Ruth would never find it out, and
resolved never to allow such a liberty again.

And then Ruth entered into a serious talk which would
have done credit to a wiser head than her own. She told
them solemnly what a wonderful, awful power was this gift
of God, this influence of woman over man, and man over
woman. She reminded them that when they came to give
their earthly lives into the keeping of some man who was all
the world to them, they would want to bring hands
unsoiled by the touch of other men, and lips unkissed by
any other half-love or play love. The girls sat back and
neglected their work while they watched her earnest face
and drank in her words. They had never heard such talk
before and it appealed to the best that was in their natures.

Ellen Amelia, watching her, made up her mind that here
was a higher ideal of manhood and womanhood than any
which she had ever found in the columns of her weekly
story paper.

"My goodness!" said Effie Haines thoughtfully as she
wended her way home with the rest of the girls. "It must be
an awful lot of trouble to live with all those ideas; but
they're lovely though, aren't they, girls? Isn't she good! My!
I wish I was like her."

That was the first talk they had. Thereafter it became a
regular thing after the special lesson in cutting or fitting had
been given for the day, to ask questions. Sometimes the
questions were written, and the themes discussed were as
various as the characters of the girls. The mysteries of love,
the sacredness of marriage, were themes which interested
these girls, who discovered that they truly wanted to find
out the right about everything. Not that Ruth laid down her
way of thinking as law to them. She only talked over things
and suggested reasons to them. Sometimes she read a
selection from some good writer bearing on their topic.
Sometimes she was ready with clippings from the newspa-

pers and quotations from the encyclopædia to prove certain facts which they had never heard of before. She was teaching these girls to think, and to reason out right and wrong for themselves, and above all she had the Bible to refer to constantly. Sometimes the girls had dainty cards given them containing a single verse which answered a question they had asked at the last Saturday class. The class grew larger and the members were quite regular. When Ruth found that they all loved dancing so, and that the mere motion to music was pleasure to them, she suggested some gymnastics, and at a certain hour the various gowns and other garments upon which they had been working were laid aside and they all stood up in the great attic room and went through some most delightful exercises which were utterly new to them. Ruth was an adept in all sorts of gymnastics, and made the little work she gave them intensely interesting as well as profitable physically to them. This last feature of the class took like wildfire in Summerton. The girls told their friends of course, and every girl in town was crazy to join. Ruth was flooded with petitions from interested mothers and eager girls, and at last a class was formed in the town hall, and a piano and an accompanist hired. "I can do some good and gain some influence by it perhaps, and certainly I can give them something delightful which may take the place of dancing," she said to herself, and she went to her class feeling that her Master had called her to it.

Deacon Chatterton shook his head of course and declared it was all wrong and just as bad as dancing—frivolous, wicked to waste time in such useless ways—and no good would come of it.

But many and many a time Ruth had opportunity before or after her class, when she was helping some girl in a particularly difficult turn with the Indian clubs, or the dumb-bells, to get in a little word about her longing to have the girl give herself to Jesus, and many a one first found Jesus Christ in the old town hall, sitting in a darkened corner late in the afternoon after the rest of the class had gone, and talking in low tones with the earnest-faced little teacher.

The dressmaking-class was confined, however, to Ruth's

own Sunday-school class, and the earnest talks over the
sewing were long to be remembered by all of them. There
came a day too when Ruth ventured a new plan. Just before
they were folding their work to go home she said:

"Girls, I wish you would kneel down with me here and
let us have a little prayer meeting together. I know I am
asking something unusual, but I would like it so much. You
know I've been praying for you all ever since I took the
class, and isn't it about time you helped me? Some of you
don't belong to Jesus. I do want you to know him right
away. Can't we just kneel down here together and will you
try to think God is here and you could see him if you looked
up, and then will you ask of him what you most want? I
don't want to force any of you to pray, of course, if you are
not willing, and I don't want any of you to do it just because
I ask. If you have nothing in your heart to say, then never
mind; but I think you all could say, 'Dear Jesus, I want to be
saved,' or 'Dear Lord, show me the way to thee." Ellen,
dear, will you pray first and will the others follow right
around the room, please?" And then as quietly as if she had
been asking them to cut a skirt lining this peculiar girl knelt
down and waited.

Her tone had been so every-day and matter-of-course
that not one of them had thought to demur. Indeed they
were too frightened to do so, had she given them a chance.
They knelt quickly to get away from their own embarrassment.

Poor Ellen Amelia Haskins knelt, her heart beating faster
than she had ever known it to do before, and wondered
what she should say. There was an element of the dramatic
and noble which would have struck her in this strange
scene if she had not been a part of it, but as it was there
suddenly came to her a sense of her utter inadequateness to
fill the position required of her. And yet she was a professed
Christian. She knelt and waited, and Ruth's words came to
her: "Try to think God is here and you could see him if you
looked up." Then she was ashamed that she had no words
for the great God, and she choked and the tears came, and
at last in desperation she stumbled out the words, "O God,
forgive me!" There were pauses, and then the others, all
but two, asked something—some humble, frightened peti-

tion. And after Ruth had prayed a few words which seemed to bring the realization of Christ's presence plainly to their minds they rose with tears on their cheeks.

"I think that was the first time I ever really prayed," whispered Effie Haines as she took her leave, pressing her tear-wet face on Ruth's shoulder; "I am glad I did it. Maybe I'll try again."

And that was not the last little prayer meeting that ended a day of dressmaking at the Benedict farm, for that was where Ellen Haskins learned to pray.

But Louise Clifton had gone to New York on a visit shortly after Thanksgiving, to get rid of her troublesome thoughts, and indulge some of her worldly longings, and she was not a part of all this. It seemed a pity to David, looking on, that the one for whom he was praying with strong, deep desire, earnest purpose, and firm belief, should have been allowed to go away just now when she might have been drawn into this tide of helpfulness that was sweeping through the village. He thought a good deal about it sometimes, and when he came to pray he was troubled to find a questioning note of the wisdom of God's planning in this particular case, and then he pulled himself up short and said: "See here, David Benedict, are you running this, or is God? Don't you suppose God knew and loved this bright, sweet girl before ever you found out what danger there was surrounding her? Now you just let things alone and God will manage. If you do your part God will surely do his."

But always he prayed night and morning that God's angels would surround her and guard her feet from temptation. And his prayer was answered. Louise had sought to do this and that thing to amuse and distract her, and was constantly foiled in her attempts. There was something strange about it. Accident or weather or the sudden illness of a friend would keep her away from places she most desired to attend. When she did succeed in going, troublesome thoughts would seize upon her and destroy all pleasure in what she heard or saw. She began to feel like a child and to wish for her mother. Her nerves seemed all unstrung. In truth she was not well, and constantly her mind would go back with shame to that uncomfortable night when David Benedict had been obliged to kidnap her and carry her off like a little child to save her from a terrible danger into which she had foolishly thrown herself in her ignorance.

Once at a concert she saw Alonzo Brummel in the distance, and he came over to her and tried to appear upon very intimate terms with her until her friend Fannie Gleason, whom she was visiting, said:

"What is the matter with the poor little man, Lou dear? You were very hard on him. I quite liked him. He was real bright and handsome, and was elegantly dressed. Who is he?"

And that night Louise Clifton wrote to her mother that she would like to come home at once.

CHAPTER XXIII

☆

There was a large religious gathering in session for two days in the city near Summerton, and thither Robert Clifton and David Benedict had gone. They had arranged to spend the night that they might attend the evening and early morning meetings, which were important. It was the first gathering of the kind David had ever attended and it was a treat indeed to him. Joseph would have liked to go too, but they could not both be away and he declared that it was more important for David to attend, as it had to do with Sunday-school work, and David, having just taken a class, was eager to learn all he could about it. Ruth rejoiced in the thought that her brother had gone to a Sunday-school convention in company with the minister. Her brothers were a great source of happiness to her in these days.

The second day of the meetings was drawing to a close. The afternoon session was over and the minister was preparing to take the train home that he might be in time for a special meeting, while David was to stay for the evening closing session to hear an especially fine speaker whom Robert Clifton was anxious that he should not miss. They were walking slowly up the steps to the hotel when one of the messenger boys of the house stepped up to the minister and asked, "Ain't you Mr. Robert Clifton? Well, here's a telegram been waitin' fer you an hour. I went down to the church, but couldn't find no trace of you."

The minister tore the yellow envelope open hastily, a shade of anxious anticipation on his face, and as he read, the expression changed to one of annoyance and perplexity.

"I'm sure I don't know what I'm to do," he said, looking up at David in a troubled way. "My mother has telegraphed me to take the midnight train for New York and bring my sister home. I cannot possibly go unless it is a question of life and death. She does not say Louise is ill, merely that she wants to come home. I can't leave the temperance meeting at home this evening, after being so prominent in getting it up and after promising to speak. And there is Judge Tanner's funeral to-morrow morning, which will last all day, as they are to bury away over at East Ivy Hill. And it is getting toward Sunday. I could not possibly go until Monday. I don't understand mother's sending me this special word just now. She must have forgotten the funeral."

In his heart the minister knew that to his mother the funeral would make no difference. She deemed that his duty toward her and his sister was far above any duty he had to the church or to any outsider, dead or alive. He had tried many times to explain such things to her, but she had cried and told him that his father had not so looked upon duty, and that he would be ashamed of his son if he could know how utterly bereft of a care-taker she and her daughter were. But he did not so far forget himself as to mention these things to David Benedict.

David had listened courteously and when the trouble was made known he instantly said:

"Could not I be of assistance to you? I will gladly go to New York if you will trust me with the care of your sister. I could not well take the meeting and the funeral or I would be as willing to do that."

The cloud lifted from Robert Clifton's face at once.

"The very thing," he said in a relieved tone. "Wouldn't you mind a bit? I'd gladly pay your fare twice over to get rid of the journey, and just now especially."

"I should enjoy it immensely. You needn't think of paying my fare. I have thought for some time of taking a trip to New York and there is no reason why I cannot as well take it now as at any time, if you will tell my sister what has become of me and ask Joseph to attend to one or two matters for me. Do you think your sister will object?"

"Certainly not," answered the minister decidedly. "Why should she? I know of no one with whom I would sooner trust her."

Robert Clifton had but a few minutes in which to make his train, so they had not much time to talk. He wrote a hasty telegram to his sister, "Be ready to start home to-morrow," signing his own name, and giving careful directions to David how to find the house where his sister was visiting, he hastened away to his sermons and his meeting and funeral, feeling relieved beyond measure that he need not stop all his work just at this busy season, to take the long trip to New York.

David Benedict, the evening meetings of the convention over, sat him down in the railroad station to await the train to New York. He was exultantly happy. He had not yet stopped to examine himself to see why he was so deeply glad. There was time enough for that. To his sister Ruth he had sent a single message, "Please pray that I may be led of the Lord," and Ruth, as she read it a few hours later, smiled to herself, and was glad that her brother was so changed as to make this a natural message for him to send her, and yet it sounded very like the David he had been during the past few weeks. Then she read it again, and remembered the first night he had ever asked her to pray for some one, and thought a moment and said aloud, "I wonder if it can be she."

David was interested in all that went on about him. He watched an elegant young man who came in with immaculate overcoat, umbrella, and dress-suit case. He observed the accustomed air with which he bought his ticket, and the matter-of-fact way in which he asked a few pertinent questions concerning his train. There was something about the young man that David liked. He looked down at himself and was dissatisfied for the first time with his own Summerton ready-made clothes. Not that they were not fine and good, but there was a finish about the city young man that pleased David. He felt that he would move with more ease if he were dressed in that way. He began to reflect that it might be a good plan for him to look after a few minor details of dress himself if he was to escort a young woman on a journey. She must not be made to be ashamed of him. He wondered if there were little things about traveling which he ought to know in order to make the journey a pleasant one for her. He would watch this young man and see. And presently, as if to help him, there entered a young woman with an elderly gentleman, who seemed to be the sister of the young man and who was apparently going in company with him. David made up his mind that he would let nothing escape him, and see if he could profit by their conduct for the homeward trip. Accordingly, when the train was called he followed them out and attempted to enter the same car, but a uniformed porter forbade him saying, "Sleeper ticket, sir. This is the sleeper for New York." Ah! David had forgotten that. He was willing enough to sit up all night if need be, for the journey was a pleasant novelty to him; but if he would keep near these two he must do as they did, so he hastened back to the station and managed to secure the last berth left. Luckily it proved to be in the same car with the two, and he watched the numerous little attentions of this young man for his sister with increasing interest, noting carefully the orders to the porter and the mysteries of electric bells. He would know all he needed to know without having the humiliation of asking the young woman he was to escort.

David did not sleep that night. It was too novel a position for him to care to sleep much, but he rested and thought. Alone in the darkness of his berth there came to him a realization of the wonderous care of God. He thought of the train and how it was plunging along in darkness, and how he lay there as quietly and safely as in his own home. God was caring for him. He rejoiced that he knew the wonderful God. He was a Christian who really and truly, "rejoiced in

the Lord." Life seemed to be opening before him so rich
and full.

Then he began to examine himself. What was this other
feeling, a sort of elation, which seemed to belong especially
to this journey? It was something very sweet and beautiful.
He had not stopped before to ask himself what it was. Was
it?—yes, it surely was because of the fact that he was going
after Louise Clifton, and that it was to be his precious task
to bring her safely home, and that now she was to remain at
home and would be among them again. Was that a wrong
feeling for him to have? No, he could not feel that it was.
She was one of God's creations. Had he not been praying for
her with his whole soul for weeks and months? He could
not tell why he had felt the burden of her salvation so
strongly upon him, but it had been there, and he had fully
obeyed all commands it had laid upon him, and fairly
poured out his soul before the throne for her. It had been
given him to realize her danger and her need so fully that
night of their Thanksgiving ride, that he had felt God must
and would answer and show her the light. He had not
doubted but that the answer would come. She was so sweet
and bright and beautiful. His own feeling about her he had
never questioned. His anxiety had been for her, and so he
had prayed. Now it suddenly came to him, "I love her," and
he rejoiced in that love as he would rejoice in any other
great gift. He felt at the first that his love did not necessarily
include the return of it by her, neither did it include his
possession of even her friendship; but he and she were in
the world and he could love her, and he was glad that he
could. It was a new joy he had not thought of before with
relation to himself, and it was all the more pure and holy in
that it was as yet utterly unconnected with any doubt of the
future or of possession. He guarded this newly discovered
treasure in his heart as sacred. He would not even think
about it too much lest it should be tarnished by constant
handling. A beautiful hope began to come to him. Perhaps,
oh, perhaps, the Master would accept his humble service
and let him be the messenger through whom the message
of life and salvation should be brought to her soul. And all
that night long David Benedict, the new-made follower of
the blessed Jesus, lay in his berth and prayed, and in the

morning he arose peaceful and refreshed notwithstanding his vigil.

Meantime the minister had been passing through less calm seas. His train was late for one thing. A freight wreck ahead of them had kept them almost an hour on a side track. When they finally reached Summerton he had but forty-five minutes in which to go home, eat some supper, dress, and prepare to present himself at the town hall temperance mass-meeting.

His trouble began as he took his latchkey from the parsonage door. His mother appeared on the upper stair-landing in as much consternation as her small body could express.

"Robert! My dear boy! What has happened? Didn't you get my telegram? Where is your sister?"

The minister was tired and worried. He had been trying all the way up from the station to remember whether he had left his notes for that evening's address on his study table. If he had he feared much for their present existence, for one of the things which he could not persuade his over-scrupulous mother to do was to let his desk, with its multitudinous papers, alone. She would clear it off every time he went out, explaining carefully, "No one has touched it, Robert, but myself, and of course I would not throw away anything of value," and she could not be made to understand that the scraps of scribbled paper were some-times of more value than all else the minister had on his table. He was too loyal and courteous a son to scold after such occurrences, and merely made his request that it should not be touched again, but always with the same result. He was growing now so that he carefully put under lock and key all papers before he went out; but he had a strong suspicion that he had not gone back to the study to do so before he left for the convention, on account of a sudden call to the parlor to see a man just before train time. It was this worry which perhaps made his tone seem a little annoyed and sharp to his mother. He had forgotten completely about Louise and the telegram until his mother brought it to his mind, and now for the first time it dawned upon his inner consciousness that in all probability she would not think he had done the best he might have done in sending David Benedict in his place.

"Yes, I received your telegram, mother; but you surely knew I could not go the New York this week. You were well aware that I had to speak at a meeting in the town hall this evening, and that I had a funeral to-morrow morning which would keep me all day, and that Sunday is almost here with its two sermons which are scarcely touched as yet."

There were times when Mrs. Clifton could grow exceedingly indignant, and at such times she waxed quite eloquent. This was such an occasion. She had worked herself into a fretful state over Louise's letter lest the girl were sick which might perhaps excuse her seeming unreasonableness.

"Robert, you cannot mean that you ignored it! You do not intend to tell me that you count any duty in the world above that you hold to your mother and sister? I should not have telegraphed you if there had not been a sufficient reason. There is something the matter with Louise, and she needs to come home to her mother at once. Certainly, I remembered the temperance meeting to-night, but I also remembered that it was only a temperance meeting. There won't be half a dozen people out, and Deacon Chatterton can talk well enough for them. As for the funeral, the minister of the other church could go. The living are of more account than the dead, always. And your sermons don't need to be fussed over so long. You can get up and talk well enough for these people for once. You always put a great deal more work on your sermons than they appreciate, anyway. I insist, I command, as your mother, Robert, that you leave to-night to bring your sister home."

Mrs. Clifton's cheeks were red and her eyes were bright. There were signs of recent tears on her face which her son did not see. She had been worrying about her daughter and crying for her departed husband all day long.

"Mother, you forget yourself. I shall have to remind you that you do not know all about my duties or you would not speak so. It would be utterly impossible for me to go to-night unless it were a matter of life and death. But you need not get so excited. I have sent for Louise. What does she say is the reason for her sudden desire to come home?"

Mrs. Clifton ignored the question.

"Sent for her!" she fairly screamed. "Do you expect Louise to travel alone? Oh, if your father could see you now and know!" and she ended with a groan.

Her son put his hand upon her shoulder and tried to quiet her.

"No, mother dear; listen. I have sent a suitable escort for her. Do not worry like this. Please order some supper, for I have but a few moments before I must be at the hall."

Mrs. Clifton straightened up.

"Whom have you sent for your sister? I wish to know at once."

"Mother, I have sent a suitable, safe person."

"Tell me at once who the person is. When you get so far as to turn your family duties over to the hands of strangers I wish to be consulted."

"Mother, I have sent a person whom I would trust with the most precious possession I have in the world. I have sent David Benedict. He offered to go when he saw my perplexity." The minister stopped. Somehow he felt as he had when he had done a naughty thing as a little boy and stood before his mother to account for his conduct. This sending of a young man for his sister seemed suddenly to appear before him as a heinous offense.

Mrs. Clifton's consternation silenced her for a moment. "David Benedict, indeed! Well, thank fortune, she is well enough trained to refuse to come with him! The impertinence of his suggesting such a thing! Well, it appears that I shall have to go after my child myself." Whereupon she swept into her room and closed the door to dissolve in tears of bewilderment and grief, while her puzzled, worried son recovered from his shock and rummaged wildly through his papers for some suitable notes—his intended address being gone beyond recovery—and finally rushed supperless and addressless to the meeting to search his mind in vain for any trace of what he had so carefully prepared. He wondered vaguely in the meantime why it had been so dreadful to send a good Christian young man to escort his sister home. There was just one little ray of comfort in the whole troubled evening, and that was that he had promised to let Ruth Benedict know what had become of her brother, and he knew that her smile or some words of hers would pour oil into his wounds and make him glad. He had known this certainly for some time now, and it gave him deep joy. But he felt very uncertain whether she even quite approved of him yet. He dared not hope it. Once he found a little scrap of a poem which seemed as if it were written to give him help. He cut it out and pasted it in the fly leaf of his memoranda book:

God's plans for thee are graciously unfolding,
    And leaf by leaf they blossom perfectly,
As yon fair rose, from its soft enfolding,
    In marvelous beauty opens fragrantly.
Oh, wait in patience for thy dear Lord's coming,
    For sure deliverance he'll bring to thee;
Then, how thou shalt rejoice at the fair dawning
    Of what sweet morn which ends thy long captivity.

CHAPTER XXIV

It was rather early in the morning for New York high life when David Benedict presented himself at the house where Louise Clifton was staying and asked to see her at once. He had done a good deal of sightseeing. He had purchased a dress-suit case like the one he had seen on the way, for it had struck as a very useful article. He had stowed it with various gifts for Ruth and Joseph and a few articles for himself, which it had occurred to him would be good things to have, and which he had not hitherto considered necessaries. The young man on the train had made a difference in David Benedict's ideas of cultured life and refinement. He had left his old overcoat at a coffee and mission house, where he had stepped in for a few minutes to join in the singing and rejoice in the number of reformed

men who were testifying to the power of Jesus to save, and
he had bought a new one, the counterpart as nearly as he
could find it, of the one his admiration of the night before
had worn. The new overcoat had necessitated a new hat
also, and he had added gloves. Altogether, 'had he but
known it, he looked a great deal better than the young man
he had so admired, for David was a handsome man, with a
rugged, unconscious, homely beauty that had much ster-
ling character behind it.

Louise, and Fannie Gleason were attired in becoming
wrappers, sipping chocolate and eating delicately toasted
bread. Each had a book beside her, and they were having a
delightfully late breakfast in their room, having just arisen,
and not having anything particular in view for the morning's
occupation. Louise's long golden hair was hanging down her
back over her rich creamy cashmere wrapper. She liked
occasionally to be lazy and pretend that she was a damsel of
an Oriental court, who lolled and lived in defiance of the
stern laws of work-a-day life. Besides, she meant to try a
new way of arranging her hair soon, and she wished to take
plenty of time to it.

The servant brought her a telegram which proved to be
from her brother. Louise tossed it on the table, and felt a
little disappointed now that she knew she was actually to
return to the stupid little town. She had not thought her
mother would be so summary. She had hoped she would
come on and make a visit or go somewhere else with her.
Besides, there was a delightful invitation for next week,
which had arrived just after she mailed her last letter to her
mother. She did not want to go home nearly so much as she
had done two days before. She told Fannie about it, and
they talked it over and decided to keep Robert over the
next week if possible. Fannie was only too eager for an
interesting young man to add to their pleasant circle. He
needed a change and rest. All young ministers were worked
to death; that was a matter of course. Louise was not so
certain that she could keep him; but she decided she would
at least let him return alone if he would not wait a few days,
and then, while they were talking, the servant came again
announcing a young man who did not give his name, but
had said,

"Please tell Miss Clifton I have come for her."

"It's Robert, of course," said Louise, getting up annoyed, "and he will be in a hurry, of course, and here I am in this rig. I can't go in this way, and my hair all down too. He'll just have to wait till I'm dressed. I shall not have an easy task, Fannie, I assure you, for Rob is awfully set in his way and as devoted to his seven-by-nine church as a mother to her child. I wish I was ready, for by the time I get down he will be so worked up over having to wait that I sha'n't have nearly so easy a task."

"What do you wait to dress for? Go along, now, and I'll fix it all up. Maggie, tell the gentleman to go to the morning sitting room and his sister will come at once. There, go along. There isn't a soul about now. Mamma went to her executive meeting half an hour ago, and nobody will see you but the servants. You look as sweet as a picture. My! I only wish I had such hair."

The morning sitting room was on the second floor, and was furnished all in soft, dull yellows and browns with luxurious couches and deep easy-chairs and pillows. David was ushered into it, and not many minutes later he heard a soft step on carpeted stairs, and Louise stood in the doorway, coming to meet him with a smile of welcome on her face intended for her brother. She paused in the center of the room, taken aback by the presence of a stranger. She stood just where a patch of morning sunshine caught her hair and made a glory of it, and the soft tones of golden brown and yellow in the draperies of a door and couch behind her made a fitting background for the creamy folds of her morning gown, which was all soft and white, with a touch of lace, filmy and rich, at throat and wrists, and a clasp of gold filigree at her waist. Louise dearly loved the artistic in her toilets, and it was perhaps for this reason that she had fallen so quickly in love with Ruth, for she felt they had an artistic bond in common.

David had risen when he heard her step, and now he stood spellbound gazing upon her. He had never seen any one so lovely. She looked like some bright celestial spirit as she stood there with her halo of golden hair. He could not speak, he could only gaze, and his earnest, truth-telling face must have almost frightened the girl with its intensity of admiration if she had not been bewildered by his unexpected appearance. She stood dazed a moment, fully realizing her position and her costume, and unable to collect her faculties sufficiently to know what to do. But the quietness and deep reverence of David's gaze suddenly brought her to herself, and she turned and fled. Had he been almost any other young man of her acquaintance, Louise would have blushed and laughed, and though she would have been embarrassed, she would have quickly twisted up the flowing hair which gave her so much trouble and sat down with a comical explanation; but being David, she fled. She did not know why she felt so about this young man, but she did. She flew up the stairs to her room, only pausing to give a passing servant a stiff message for the waiting gentleman in the morning room that she would be down by and by, and then locking her door she made a more leisurely and careful toilet than even she was accustomed to do. The young man might wait now as long as he chose. When next he saw her she would be as dignified and distant as it was possible for apparel to make her. She even meditated putting on a hat, but decided that that would be absurd. Her cheeks grew redder and redder as she progressed with her toilet. She was beginning to grow indignant with David for having gotten her into such a ridiculous plight. She would not be reasonable and see that it was all her own fault. She was thankful that Fannie had gone into her mother's room and was not there to witness her excitement.

And David, his vision vanished, stood staring at the spot where she had stood, almost blinded with the sight. When the servant entered the room with the message, he bowed quietly and sat down; but when he was alone he looked again at the place where she had stood, and said in a reverent tone and with an almost holy light upon his face, "I love her," and then putting up his hand as if to cover his eyes, he added in an audible voice, as if he were registering a vow, "But it shall not make any difference."

Then he sat back and leaned his head against the soft upholstery and looked like a man who had been privileged above many. There was a rapt look upon his face. You would have believed it if you had been told that he was praying.

And the time did not seem long to him before Louise returned. He understood it all. He did not need her dignified explanation and apology. He greeted her with a gentle, deferential tone, and he forestalled all she had to say by apologizing for causing her any trouble. Then he told her simply that he had come for her, and asked when she could be ready.

"But where is my brother?" asked the astonished young woman. "He was to come for me."

"He could not come, Miss Clifton; there was a meeting and a funeral, and he feared you would not like to wait until next week, so he sent me. I am sorry you are not to have a more desirable companion, but I will do my best."

"Well, I'm sorry if you have been to any trouble," began Louise, determining at once not to go home in David Benedict's company under the present circumstances. "But I had decided not to return until next week or the week after. I shall write my mother so at once. I hope you did not make a special trip on my account. I supposed you were here on business. My brother will doubtless be able to come for me soon, or—I could go alone. It is not a difficult journey." Louise realized that she was being almost rude by the way she was talking to her visitor, but she stumbled ahead blindly, making it worse with every sentence.

With just a shadow on his quiet face and a note of something different in his voice, did David express the sudden pain she gave him by her words, as he said, "Have you then not forgiven me yet?" Then his tone changed to the old masterful one, and Louise was at once reminded of her compulsory sleigh-ride on Thanksgiving night. "Miss Clifton, I have no right, of course, to insist; but I have been charged to bring you home, and I wish you would come. Indeed, I think it would be better. Your mother is expecting you and I should not like to return without you."

In spite of herself Louise had to give in, for she was ashamed of herself. She talked haughtily a few moments more, but she knew in her heart from that first masterful sentence he had spoken that she would consent to go.

Fannie, in her room again, was growing impatient to know the result of the conference. She had made a hasty toilet after Louise left and sat waiting for her return.

"You don't mean to say you're really going, and going to-day! Why, Lou! You can't possibly get ready; the train leaves in two hours. And who is he? Is he a special friend of the family? Maggie says he's awfully handsome. Is he fond of you? My, I envy you! You'll have a grand time on the way— a whole young man to yourself for so many hours! I predict all sorts of interesting episodes. He must be awfully nice or your mother would never let you go alone with him. She is so particular about chaperons and such things. Do take me down, Lou, and introduce me, quick. I won't be left out altogether."

So Fannie rattled on, while Louise opened bureau drawers and without seeming to care or know what she did, unceremoniously dumped their contents into her trunk. Having made up her mind to go, Louise seemed to be in a fever of impatience to get ready lest they might miss the train. And all the time she kept wondering to herself why it was she did as David told her.

Fannie was taken down and introduced, and came back to help her friend with the last little preparations, going into raptures over David.

"Why Lou, he's just magnificent! I think you are the slyest girl I ever saw; you never once mentioned his name all the time you were here. Oh, I know there's a good deal more to this than you will admit. Wasn't he at home when you left? I can't think what made you come away. Had you been quarreling? I just believe you had; and I'll tell you, Louie dear, it doesn't do to quarrel with men that have such firm chins, for they always get the better of one. Tell me the truth, Lou, did you get clear into the room so that he saw you with your hair down before you discovered it wasn't your brother? Oh, I just know you did by your face; and I would have given anything to have seen his face when he first looked at you. You were a perfect angel in that white and gold gown."

Louise was very much annoyed by this talk. It seemed as if all sorts of sacred things were being tumbled about and torn open by Fannie's curious tongue. She got away from her at last, though she had to spend a very tiresome hour with her while David went away for his lunch and to order a carriage. He had watched that morning as the young man of the sleeper ordered a carriage and put his sister in and then sat down beside her. David made up his mind that he would do likewise with the lady of his care.

Fannie went with them to the station and chattered with David all the way, and he was grave and pleasant and respectful. He was wondering what Louise found in her to like. But she was Louise's friend and he treated her accordingly.

It was a relief when at last the train moved out from the station. David had secured two chairs in the parlor car. As there was no sleeper on the day train he discovered that the chair car took its place. He seated Louise and waited upon her in all the ways he had seen that other young man use, and then he set himself for an hour to be as agreeable as it was in him to be. He had read much and could talk well. He was not all gravity, as Louise discovered. He could make witty remarks and tell bright stories; and while he knew nothing at all about the "small talk" which was common parlance with most of her young men acquaintances, he succeeded in making her forget herself and her unusual position. Then he bought one or two of the latest and best magazines, and with a delicacy born of innate refinement decided that he would not bore her with too much of his company, so murmuring some excuse of hunting up the porter and giving orders for supper at the best point he went away. He really seated himself in the common car for an hour and closed his eyes and prayed.

When he returned to the parlor car he found that the young lady had finished looking at the papers and was gazing out of the window looking tired and somewhat cross. She looked up as he sat down beside her, and asked:

"Mr. Benedict, do you smoke?"

She asked the question as if she wanted to find out for a definite purpose, not as if she objected to it particularly. David looked at her in astonishment, and then a sudden light broke over his face and he smiled.

"No, I do not smoke. You thought that was why I went away for so long? It was not. I wanted to give you a rest from my company. Do you like smoking?"

"You need not do that again, Mr. Benedict; I would rather have you stay here. I am ashamed for the way in

which I treated you about coming home to-day. I was—
well, I——" Louise found she could not quite explain what
had been the matter without saying more than she cared to,
so she stopped in confusion.

"I understand," said David; "Never mind that; and thank
you for saying you would rather I would stay."

He was looking at her so earnestly now that it confused
her, and struggling to find a topic for conversation she
seized his last unanswered question.

"No, Mr. Benedict, I don't really like smoking; but I don't
know any reason why I should object. Nearly all my friends
do smoke, except my brother; but—I was a little surprised
that you should, you seem so—so—well, so different——"

"Thank you. I'm glad I don't seem like a smoker; but I
must be honest and tell you I used to smoke until I found
my sister, and she made me see how disagreeable a thing it
is. I'm sorry I ever smoked. I never will again. But, Miss
Clifton, I want to presume very much on what you said a
moment ago. You said you would rather I would stay here,
and I am going to ask you to be kind enough to let me tell
you what I have wanted to say to you for a long time. It may
seem unfair to you that I should take this time, when you
are so situated that you cannot get away from me if you
would; but I think you will bear with me. It is very
important. I don't think I can promise to stop, even if you
ask me, till I have told you all I wish. Will you bear with
me?"

Louise looked up with frightened eyes. She had seen
David's grave, steady gaze at her during the few hours they
had been together that day, and it had made her heart throb
with wonder and a strange new kind of joy she did not
understand, but she dreaded anything that he might say. It
was so new she did not want to have it brought out and
looked at till she had time to think and understand herself.
Instinctively she knew that his look had been of something
deeper than friendship. Was he going to speak of it now?
She could not utter a syllable, and her silence seemed to
give him the permission he asked. Yes, it was a story of love
he had to tell—of wonderful love—but not of his own.
Louise, as she listened—and she could not but listen,
because the words came from a heart which had communed

much with God, and knew exactly what it was speaking about—felt that she was a little child being shown Jesus for the first time. So simply, so gently did David put the whole matter of being a Christian before her, that she felt as if it would be the most natural thing in the world to give herself entirely to Christ right away that minute, and not stop to think how it would affect this or that question. David had thought about this talk for weeks and even months. He had not even fixed it in his mind that he was to have the opportunity for it; but still he felt that sometime the chance might come, and he kept asking himself just what would reach him if he were a young girl like this one. He had thought about it so much and prayed about it so much that when the Master gave the opportunity he was ready for the work, and the Spirit gave the words. He spoke, Louise afterward many a time thought, as if he were inspired for the time. If his words were written here, which they cannot be, because there is no record of them except in Louise's heart, they might not be understood. It was partly the earnestness and fire with which he spoke, the high, exalted look on his face, the firm conviction of his listener that he knew and had proved what he said to be true, the great longing in his whole expression, his own great love for Jesus—that won her first to listen, then to long, and then to love this Saviour whom he would fain bring to her knowledge.

It was growing dark. The train rushed along through the blurr of indistinguishable objects. Their chairs were turned together toward the darkened window, and they did not notice that the porter coming through had lighted all the lamps. For a full hour David had leaned forward eagerly and talked in low impassioned tones, of reason, pleading, explanation. Louise had answered very little. Her face was turned away toward the window and her eyes were drooping to hide the tears which gathered fast. To her it was as if the Saviour in very presence stood there between them pleading for her soul, and she was longing to give her heart to him but could not do it, and the ache of resistance was very great. At last David seemed to have said all that he had to say. His purpose was almost accomplished. He placed his hand reverently on one of her little trembling, cold, gloved hands and said in tones that almost pierced her with the longing they expressed,

"Won't you, oh, won't you come to him now?"

They sat for a full minute thus. David hardly dared breathe, and Louise could not speak or get control of her voice. An undiscerning observer on the other side of the car curiously wondered what kind of a quarrel that handsome bride and groom were having which kept them busy so long, and then retired behind his paper, concluding it was not worth while to watch, and never knew that a decision was being made which would affect two worlds. And then Louise turned her head toward David with a quick motion, and looking him straight in his earnest, longing eyes, with her own brimming over with tears, answered him tremblingly:

"Yes, I will. Show me how, please."

The rest of that evening's ride flew swiftly by for the two. The supper which the porter presently served to them seemed nectar and ambrosia, and might have been chips for all they knew about it. Louise said little, but she felt much. It may be because she had so joyful a leader in her first steps in the new life that she felt so very happy. Her heart seemed lighter than the air. She felt that everything was new, and Jesus had been made to her a reality. That was the secret of it all. He loved her and she loved him. She looked up with a new reverence at the young man who had shown her the way, and whose face was shining with the joy of an angel and a man together. Henceforth he would to her stand out from and above all other men on the earth. He was more like Jesus Christ than any one she had ever seen, and Jesus Christ he had made to become her ideal.

CHAPTER XXV

It was late that evening when Louise Clifton finally arrived in Summerton. Her anxious brother had paced the platform for an hour trying to escape his mother's reproaches. He was afraid that his sister would come and afraid that she would not come. He was not sure which would be the worse for his mother was in a terrible state about the impropriety of her traveling so far in company with a young man. However, he was relieved to see her. As she kissed her brother, she wondered shyly if he would care for the decision she had made this evening, and she drew a sigh of almost dismay a few moments later when she realized that David, who had been such a strong tower of help to her, was to leave her now, and she would have to walk alone. No, not alone either, for Jesus would be with her; but that thought was so new that she did not always remember it at first.

She wondered what David would do, in her place, a few minutes later when she saw her mother. Mrs. Clifton met her daughter with open arms and tears.

"You poor, dear child! To think you had to come with that man! It was dreadful! I could not help it. I suppose you did not dare to stay there when Robert had sent him. I was so sorry for you."

"Why, mamma dear, what do you mean?" said Louise, her happy face puzzled for a moment. "Mr. Benedict was very kind and good. I could not have had a more considerate traveling companion; he did everything that a mortal could do to make it pleasant for me. And, mamma dear, I've something I want to tell you, something I think you will be glad about. I have given my heart to Christ, and I'm going to try to be a Christian. I haven't been the kind of daughter I ought to have been in lots of ways, and I wanted to tell you the first thing, that I'm going to try to be different now."

But the mother looked at her with dismay. She did not understand such talk.

"My darling child!" she exclaimed; "don't talk in that way, I beg of you. You have always been a dear, good daughter, and as for being a Christian, of course you are. You have been well brought up and taught to believe. You have never known anything else. Come now, my dear, and get to your room. You are utterly tired out. You will not feel so melancholy in the morning."

In vain did Louise urge that she was not in the least melancholy. She was very happy. The mother only looked the more frightened, and smiled and tried to get her to rest, and at last with a sinking heart she gave up the attempt and let her mother go. David had been so heartfelt in his joy over her salvation that she had unconsciously felt that her own loved ones would be also. It rather chilled her to have her mother take it in this way. Was the new life going to begin so hard at once?

The mother, poor bewildered soul, went to her long-suffering son for comfort.

"Robert," she said in excited tones, when she had closed his study door, "Louise is ill. She is not herself. She is talking religion, and you know how utterly foreign to her nature anything sad or melancholy is. I am afraid she is going to die or have a fit of sickness or something. I have heard of people talking in this way before dying. I knew something terrible would come of all this—putting meetings before your own family. Oh, if you or I had only gone for her instead of letting her be brought in this way!"

"What do you mean, mother?" demanded the thoroughly aroused and much-berated young minister. His nerves were quivering with the strain of the past two days. But the mother turned away, and he walked out of the study and went at once in alarm to his sister's door.

"Louie, may I come in?" he called anxiously. "Mother says you are sick. What is it? Tell me all about it. Didn't David take good care of you?"

She opened the door, laughing and crying all at once, and

burying her face in his coat had a good cry, which was what she needed after the excitement of the day and the nerve tension she had been under for weeks. In a minute, when she could get control of herself, she told him shyly and sweetly how David had helped her, and how she had given herself to Jesus. "And mother doesn't understand me," she added wistfully.

"But I do," said her brother, a ring in his voice she had never heard him use for her before. And he stooped and kissed her in such a way that she felt comforted.

Coming back to his mother in the study later the minister said in joyful voice: "Mother, you are mistaken about Louie. She is not going to die; she had only just begun to live."

During these days Ellen Amelia Haskins had been steadily improving in mind and spirit. She was much under Ruth's influence, which could not be other than a blessing to her. Some things were happening too which helped to change the current of her life and give her a purpose. The minister's wife in West Winterton had a sister, a missionary, and it chanced this winter that she came home on a visit and spent a week with her sister. The minister availed himself to this opportunity to hold a missionary meeting, and as it came on a week night when Ellen was in West Winterton, and was held in the academy hall, she attended the meeting. Then a new influence reached her. She listened spellbound to the woman's story of the trials, the joys, the triumphs, of the missionary's life, and her soul was filled with longing to go. She recognized that here was something great in life that she could do which would please her Master, and she formed a settled purpose in her heart that she would do all she could toward getting ready, and then if the Lord willed it she would go. "I'll just get as far ready as I can," she said to herself, "and then he can do as he pleases about sending me." She said it with a humble, willing spirit and she set her energies to learn all she could in every way she could. Her mother began to be proud of her and to take heart of hope and predict a marriage with a thrifty farmer, and ask her if she didn't intend to try to secure a school to teach in a good district for the next winter, but Ellen said she didn't known and worked steadily on.

And then something wonderful happened to her. The Lord was opening her way step by step. It was almost time for the summer vacation when the word came that Uncle Timothy had died very suddenly, and that he had left to Ellen Amelia the sum of three thousand dollars to do with as she pleased.

"If I was you I'd quit school at once," said her mother, a pleased, proud look on her face; "you'll not have any need for any more schoolin' now; you won't have to teach, and anybody'll be glad to get you, now you're well off. It makes a difference, in spite of all they say, and you can be more independent when you marry, if you have money of your own (Mrs. Haskins had been possessed of eight hundred dollars when she married the deacon, which she had willingly and humbly put into his business to help him along, but she often used the remembrance of her dowry as a rod with which to rule her husband). I wouldn't stay on at the 'cademy another day 'f I was you. You don't need to care whether you pass or not now."

But Ellen Amelia closed her lips which were becoming refined with gentleness and following her Saviour and went to pray about the matter. Having laid the subject before her all-wise Leader she went quietly to her father and put her plan before him.

The deacon sat on the back porch whittling and waiting for his dinner. He put down his knife and the front legs of his chair and listened carefully to his daughter's story, a film of mist gathering over his eyes as she talked. He answered her slowly at last and with a choke in his voice.

"Wal, Ellen, you couldn't do anythin' that would be greater honor to yer ancestors 'n to be a missionary. I mus' say I am pleased to have a child of mine willin' to make such sacrifizes. I mightly hate to lose my little girl, but if yer heart's set on goin' I sha'n't say the word that'll stop you. Go ahead to your college or whatever you like. The money's yours an' it might be worse spent. I'll help you all I can," and then he sat and chewed the end of his stick and remembered how Ellen Amelia had looked when she was two years old in a pink calico pinafore and her face all bread and molasses.

But when Mother Haskins heard of the proposed plan,

her first practical objection was: "Wal, I should like to know
what you need of more schoolin' ef you're goin' to bury
yourself out in some outlandish place in the-land-knows-
where, with little naked heathens. I guess, if you've got
enough knowledge to teach here in this Christian land,
you've got enough to teach sinners that don't know their a-
b-c's."

Mother Haskins, it must be explained, was disappointed.
Missionaries were well enough, she felt, for a cousin once
or twice removed, but she had looked to see her daughter
marry a rich farmer and settle down where she might
superintended the new home and manage Ellen Amelia's
children. However, she found that her talk was of no avail
as she could not immediately produce the rich, thrifty
farmer to help her out, and so she settled down to console
herself with what glory reflected upon her for having
brought up a daughter who was to go to college with the life
of a missionary as a halo in the future. And she found it not
empty of honor, but rather one upon which she reflected
with increasing satisfaction.

One afternoon in the sewing circle she remarked with
pardonable pride and a pin in her mouth:

"Yes, it will be hard to give her up, but then it's a great
blessing to have one's children turn to the ways of
righteousness; and they do say that 'out there' (which term
applied to some far-away mission field and represented her
daughter's future home veiled in the mist of somewhere or
nowhere to her mother) they don't have sech hard times,
with plenty of servants to do everythin' for one and not a
livin' thing to do but preach the gospel. No, I don't suppose
she'll have much trouble learnin' the langwidge; she's so up
on her Latin an' Greek that these uncivilized langwidges
can't be much mor'n a-b-c's to her."

Mrs. Deacon Chatterton, on the other side of the room,
felt that Deacon Haskins' wife was getting too puffed up and
needed her pride taken down, and so she remarked with
one of her characteristic "Humphs!" that she would "just
like to see Ellen'melia when she got real seasick on the
ocean, and if she wouldn't be ready to cry for Summerton
and her ma then she'd miss her guess"; and then she shut
her lips firmly, feeling that she had done her duty, and

experienced a pang of something like envy for the woman
who had a daughter who was to go as a missionary; for Mrs.
Chatterton really loved the Lord and was zealous for his
work, and enjoyed what glory reflected upon her as being a
member of a church whence should go out a messenger
who should help to bring in the Kingdom.

But Ellen Amelia went about her work from day to day
with a growing expression of sweetness and content. The
way in which the Lord was leading her was so wonderful to
her that she had been awed into perfect trust.

'Tis so sweet to trust in Jesus,
    Just to take him at his word,
Just to rest upon his promise,
    Just to know, "Thus saith the Lord."

She had heard those words sung in that missionary
meeting in West Winterton and had asked for the book that
she might copy and learn them. There was another hymn
that went over and over in her mind and she hummed it at
her work in these days. It was this:

I would not have the restless will
    That hurries to and fro,
Seeking for some great thing to do,
    Or secret thing to know:
I would be treated as a child,
    And guided where I go,
I ask Thee for the daily strength,
    To none that ask denied,
A mind to blend with outward life,
    While keeping at thy side;
Content to fill a little space,
    If thou be glorified.

She was learning to make these words truly her own and
as she sang them she sometimes thought of the time when
Joseph Benedict had told her that if she would try to be
faithful in the little things there might be a chance some
day that she would rule over many. She wondered if he ever
thought about her and her Christian life and if he knew how

she thanked him in her heart for the words he had spoken before he knew the Lord, and of the promise he had made her give. She resolved that if, in the future years, the Lord ever opened the way for her to go to a foreign land and teach others the way to Christ, she would, before she went, if there was any opportunity, tell him how much he had done for her, and thank him for it all under God. She felt that it would be fitting time when she was leaving her home perhaps forever.

Then in the fall Ellen went away to college. Ruth had a hand in planning where she should go, and helped her with her outfit and sent messages to some of the teachers and pupils who were friends of her own, to be kind to this friend whom she loved, and finally took a short trip just to see her safely established and be sure that she would be happy and under the right influences. Then began a new life for Ellen Haskins, and for a time she drifted out of Summerton life entirely and began to be looked upon by the Sunday-school children as a wonderful being with an unworldly spirit, who was willing to give up everything that life held good to go and preach dry sermons to wicked people who were a great deal more interesting to them unsaved and uncultured.

Joseph Benedict had gone away too, and for him the minister and David had prayed and rejoiced and labored much. Robert Clifton had made sure that he was in just the best college that could be found and himself made many arrangements which opened the way for Joseph's broader, better life, and Joseph went with a heart full of high ambitions and holy thoughts to see what the world contained for him. And lo, and behold! the first thing that he came across which fascinated him was the student's volunteer missionary movement, which he joined forthwith, and there were two from the Summerton church, albeit Summerton did not know it yet.

Just at this time Summerton was occupied with the lovely ways of the minister's sister and the marked attention which was openly paid her by David Benedict. Summerton of course could not keep still about that, it was not to be expected; but the strangest part of it all was that neither David nor Louise seemed to care to try to hide it, as a good many others would have done.

Mrs. Clifton had not understood her daughter's new character at all at first; she was so sweet and willing to do what was asked of her, and seemed to have lost all her old dissatisfaction with life. Her mother worried and even cried about her, but gradually her worry changed to a new alarm and she made plans to take her daughter away at once. What was all this that was come upon her? A young farmer, a common, ordinary man with no polish and no manners to speak of, nothing in fact—and who knew how much or how little money behind it?—was constantly with her cherished daughter and that daughter smiled upon him and watched and obeyed his least wish as if it were law, and seemed living in a maze of happiness. Mrs. Clifton became peremptory at once. She decreed that Louise should never see him again, that he should not enter the house and ordered Robert to prohibit him the grounds. She also told her daughter to prepare at once to leave with her for New York on a trip whose time limit should not be set at present. Louise in dismay went to her brother, and together they tried to dissuade their mother from her purpose, for David had already told the minister how his sister had become the love of his life. But it was all to no purpose. Louise tried to be submissive, but she could not keep the tears from coming, and she suddenly discovered to herself what a world of desolation it would be to her without David.

And then, just as they thought there was nothing else they could do to persuade their mother to remain quietly in Summerton during the winter with her son and daughter, there stepped in a new influence, and it was no other than David. Robert had thought of Ruth and had talked with his sister about asking her to try her persuasive powers on their mother, but neither would have thought of asking David. Indeed they would have considered his appearance as disastrous to their wishes beyond anything that could have been done. Louise called upon Ruth and mentioned that she was feeling sad that her mother wished her to go away and could not be persuaded to give it up, and that this was to be a farewell call for the winter perhaps instead of a pleasant hour of converse about their various plans of work. Wise Ruth guessed at some thing which Louise did not tell, and, troubled over the sorrow this would bring her brother, went to her Heavenly Father with it, and then told David.

Then David went out into the starlight and walked to the parsonage and ringing the bell asked to see Mrs. Clifton. She came down, and stranger than all the rest, she was gracious and was conquered. In truth, no one could see David without liking him—I had almost said loving him. Mrs. Clifton was struck by his unusual appearance and character. He told her so frankly that he loved her daughter, and he asked her blessing on his suit so engagingly that she surprised even herself by giving it. Somehow it was given to David in a remarkable way to win hearts, and he won Mrs. Clifton's at once. So courteously did he treat her, so tenderly did he calm her fears about certain little foibles of her own, that fifteen minutes later she went back to her room and Louise, who was sorrowfully packing handkerchiefs by the open trunk, and with a smile on her face and a real motherly tear of mingled joy and sorrow said: "Louie, dear, you may stop packing and go downstairs. Somebody wants to see you in the parlor; and I guess you may as well tell Morton on the way to come and help me put these things away. I suppose I may as well give up this trip now, for I should have to take it alone if I went."

CHAPTER XXVI

There was to be a great missionary meeting in Summerton. It was a sort of missionary conference. West Winterton, North Springville, and several surrounding towns were to attend in full force. There was an all-day conference and an evening mass-meeting. Robert Clifton had planned the whole thing, but perhaps the first suggestion came from Ruth Benedict. Of course Ruth and Louise and David had had a good deal to do with the getting of it all up.

Summerton church was a bower of beauty. The pulpit was a mass of evergreen and glossy leaves and feathery white blossoms. Every window held a bank of green. There were festoons of lovely ground pine hung from the center of the ceiling and draped to every corner and niche available. Nothing lovelier could have been imagined. Louise Clifton was an adept in decoration. Ruth had drilled and trained some little children in missionary exercises and recitations and singing. Summerton was to be astonished for once over what her children could do. But above all that there was to be a double surprise for the people. The two young volunteer missionaries were to be present and to speak.

It is wonderful what a change two years will make in two people. Ellen Haskins had not been at home since she left for college nearly two years before. It had happened that during her first college winter she had heard a great deal about a summer school where there was instruction for Christian workers and especially for young missionaries. Her heart longed to go, and her father gave his permission since if she chose to use some of his money in this way he was well satisfied. Her mother pursed up her lips and thought her daughter might as well come home and help with the canning and get a little of the winter sewing out of the way; but it was made easy for Ellen to go and everything seemed to point in that direction, and so she went. The summer had rushed by all too soon, and with her mind full of wonderful new thoughts and her note book and Bible filled with themes for future study this eager student went back to her college duties. But now they were to come home for an event which was to come off soon, and so Mother Haskins was to have her desire at last, and her pride would not be obliged to live entirely upon the first threadbare glory of her daughter's stated intention for distinction.

And they came. Not even Mrs. Haskins knew that Ellen was to speak. Ruth had written her and had persuaded her to put her eager earnestness into words for her home people to hear. Ruth had received from Ellen many long letters full of eager enthusiasm for missions. She felt certain that Ellen could speak about this theme so dear to her heart, and Ellen, after prayer and consideration, had consented.

But not even Ruth had counted on the changes that two years away from home and the contact with the college girls and books and all the world she had met since she had left them would make in her. She knew that Ellen's letters had changed, that they were better expressed and better written, and that there was in them an earnest tone which meant much for the future work of the girl.

By some mistake or delay of trains Ellen did not arrive until an hour or two before the hour for the meeting. Indeed they began to fear that she would not reach them at all that night and their surprise would not come off after all. But she came just in time to make a hasty toilet and go to the church. There was, of course, no opportunity to see her or note any changes. Robert Clifton had been dubious about allowing her to speak at this important meeting before they had tested her in a smaller one, but Ruth had thought it a good thing and so he had yielded, for in truth he had come to feel that Ruth was generally right. However, she began to feel just the least bit nervous for the girl herself, as the time drew near and she had no opportunity to talk with her. She could only sit and pray for her while the music of the grand missionary hymn rolled down the aisles. There was a great crowd out that night. All Summerton knew that "Joe Benedic'" was home from college and they wanted a good chance to watch him. They also knew that some strangers were to speak. The church people were out in full force. The "Brower boys," who still retained that name together with their former reputation, were there. They had not been to church much of late. They had interests in other directions, but the prospect of a lot of strangers from out of town was alluring. They lounged into the back seats and eyed the speakers as they came upon the platform. There were four or five men with the minister, a young woman with some music in her hand who was to sing, and another woman, tall and almost stately in her carriage and with an unmistakable "style" in her plain, perfectly-fitting, and becoming gown.

"I say, she's a stunner!" ejaculated Bill Brower, pursing up

his lips in a disgusting pucker to squirt some tobacco juice
in just the right spot under the dress of the lady who sat in
front of him. "I wonder who she is!"

"Well, I'll be eaten alive if that ain't Joe Benedic'," said
his brother in answer as he sat and stared in open-mouthed
wonder.

Joseph was greatly changed as well as Ellen. It was quite
astonishing to hear him introduced as a "student volunteer," to be told what that mystical title meant, and then to
look at Joe Benedict, whom they had known since he was in
long clothes and as a barefoot boy, and see him a handsome,
graceful, well-dressed young man and hear him talk the
smooth easy English of the minister. What was he saying?
Deacon Meakins took out his red cotton handkerchief and
blew his nose very loud after the first few sentences. Was
this really his friend, Mr. Benedict's boy, talking? Why, he
was so enthusiastic that the old deacon almost felt he would
like to go to a foreign field himself. The hard lines around
Mrs. Chatterton's mouth relaxed and even Deacon Chatterton himself nodded his approval in a series of jerky, severe
bobbings of his head.

Joseph had early decided to study for the ministry and
had not been long in finding out that the foreign field was
where his heart would fain carry him. He had been in many
meetings ever since he first entered college and he had
made a point to hear all the missionaries and good speakers
on the subject that came in his way, so he had plenty of
experience and knowledge to speak from. He told the
audience some of those interesting facts concerning the
amount of money spent for luxuries, necessities, drink, and
tobacco in this country, and then showed them how little
they gave to missions. He had a rod with lengths of colored
ribbons representing these different facts. When he came
to the black one—close beside the white one indicating the
money expended in missions—representing the amount of
money spent for liquor in this country and flung the end far
out into the audience, Bill and Ed Brower looked in amaze,
and Bill said, "I'll be gormed." Just exactly what that
epithet meant nobody ever knew, but Bill always used it
when he was particularly overcome and wished to be

reverent. He hardly ever swore during his remarks in the church. This word was used to take its place when swearing was inappropriate.

When Joseph sat down Ruth wished with all her heart that his speech had been put last, as she felt sure it would make a good impression which would bear fruit if left in the minds of the hearers. She had insisted in preparing the programme for this meeting, and had urged that Ellen be put at the end, for something had told her Ellen would be impressive and helpful as well. Now she began to fear that she had overestimated the girl and that she might fail and spoil the whole. She half wished that Ellen would, even at this late hour, whisper to the minister that she could not speak, Joseph had done so well. Ruth was proud indeed of her brother.

Joseph sat down and bowed his head a moment, as it was his custom, to ask the Master's blessing when he had finished a message. The young woman with the music was singing now:

> Hark! the voice of Jesus calling,
> Who will go and work to-day?

It was strange indeed that Joseph Benedict had not been told that Ellen Haskins was to address the meeting that night. No one had thought to mention the matter to him. He had been much with David during the few hours he had been at home, and David never dreamed it would be of any particular interest to him, nor would it except as it would arouse a kind curiosity. As Joseph began to listen to the singing and raised his eyes to the singer, he became aware of an annoyingly loud whisper. It was just behind him, one of the West Winterton ministers and a stranger whispering together, and Joseph could not but hear what they were saying inasmuch as they were mentioning his name and did not seem to try to speak quietly.

"You say the young woman who is to speak next is the wife of this Mr. Benedict who has just spoken? She is a remarkably fine-looking woman. If she can speak as well as she looks she will make a splendid helper for a man in a foreign field."

"No," said the West Winterton minister, who had a loud wheezy whisper, "I only said they both came from Summerton and from this church. No, she is a single lady. She attended our academy some time since."

"Oh, indeed," said the stranger, who was an elderly gentleman and seemed to know a good deal about missionary matters. "Well, it is a pity. They won't succeed near so well. They'd better make up their minds to marry. It is a great deal better. I'm told the Board is advising it in all cases. They can do more good."

And then the singing ceased and Joseph looked up, indignation in his heart, to see who was the yong woman whose fate was being so summarily disposed of at the direction of a Board.

Robert Clifton was introducing the tall young woman. Joseph had only noticed her casually as they had been coming in. He did not in the least know who she was. What did the minister mean? He was saying she was one of their own number, and—Miss Haskins! What Miss Haskins? Not Ellen Amelia, surely! Why, she was—she did not look like that! And what a voice! So rich and full and strong, and not the least bit self-conscious. She was in earnest too. She meant every word she said. She was ready to throw every bit of her magnificent energy and talent into the work. Joseph sat up straight and listened, and wondered, and his heart throbbed over the stories she had to tell. Where had she found all this information? What she had to say was new and original. It almost seemed as if she must have been at work in Africa or China or some of the other places she talked about, so familiar was she with their needs.

Joseph was not the only one who listened to Ellen's words in wonder and surprise and joy. Her old father sat with the tears streaming down his cheeks, glad to his weak old heart's core that his little Ellen had turned out so beautiful and grand, able to talk as well as the minister. Her mother sat beside him, her lips very stiffly shut, her eyes drooping with humility and pride as if she thought all Summerton was looking at her in admiration that she had brought up such a child. She would not let them think she was over-awed by it, and so she tipped her neck back uncomfortably and her head forward, and would not look up to watch her darling, though she confided to her husband on the way home that she was "jest all of a tremble, lest Ellen'melia should break down and forget her piece."

It is needless to say that Summerton was astonished and that the minister and his sister, and his sister's future husband, and his sister and brother were delighted and charmed beyond measure, and greeted Ellen with overwhelming joy when the meeting at last was over and they had her to themselves. Joseph, it is true, was not very demonstrative. He had shaken hands cordially, and then stepped back to give the others a chance, and while he waited had watched.

At home, in his palm-surrounded room he sat alone, later, upon his couch, and thought of the words of the stranger back of him on the platform. At last he said, as he began to prepare for rest, "I shouldn't wonder if that was good advice. I'll follow it."

Knowing Joseph as you do, do you think it was strange that he should stand, the very next evening, at the Haskins door, seeking admission, and asking for the daughter?

Ellen came in, the same and yet a new Ellen. She greeted him kindly, not effusively. That was new for her. She used to gush. Ellen's time to thank her first helper had not yet come, and until then she must abide behind a calm reserve. This she well knew.

Joseph told his errand at once. Perhaps his language was a little more blunt than that his brother had used some time before, on a similar occasion. He had come to ask her to join hands with him and go to the foreign field. And he had not learned any better in all his two years at college, and his many meetings, and his intensity, he did not know any better than to tell her a part of the conversation he had heard on the platform the night before. Ellen's color came and went. Her heart throbbed painfully, but she kept her self-control. She had not borne this young man's stunning blows of truth several times before in her life for nothing. Presently she gained control of her voice.

"No, Mr. Benedict," she said in a clear voice which seemed to herself to be speaking away off in the clouds somewhere, "it is not necessary for you to do that. We shall both work well where we are put, and we shall not make marriages of convenience, either, for the Master's cause. You remember," and here her voice tried to be light and playful, but there was a suspicious tremble in it, "you remember I 'know you do not care anything for me except for your sister's sake, and the promise,' and this cannot possibly affect either of those."

Joseph looked at her a moment in amazement and alarm, and then it all came over him what she meant, and he saw himself in just the light he was.

"I am a fool and a blunderer," he said, "and I must have been a boor. I ought to go down upon my knees and beg your pardon for that brutal speech I made in that long time ago. But you see, Ellen, I love you, though I don't seem to know how to tell you of it, and it *will* affect both my sister and my promise, for I couldn't possibly live and work unless you will work with me. Ellen, I believe in my heart I loved you then. I remember thinking it was queer I cared to go out of my way for you when I had never done such things before. I believe I loved you then and didn't know it. Can you forgive me? And will you love me just a little? Cannot we go out to some far land together and work for Him? You know we started the promise together, and we can surely work better if we help each other. Will you, Ellen?"

And Ellen answered, "Yes, I will."

And the next day was the marriage of David Benedict and Louise Clifton.

CHAPTER XXVII

David and Louise were married and gone on a year's trip to the Holy Land. It had been David's deep desire ever since he had been a Christian to wander over the places where the Master had trod, and Louise found that it was her desire as well. Indeed, she wanted nothing apart from what her husband wished.

Ruth was glad and sad together to see them depart. She was very happy over David's marriage, for she had come to love Louise dearly, and she saw they were well fitted for one another, but they were gone, and Joseph was still in college and was to go to the seminary, and she was alone in the great farmhouse. They had wanted her to go to Palestine with them, but she would not. She had a feeling that people who were just married needed to be by themselves for a while without any third person there to meddle, so that they might become adjusted to one another's ways of living and thinking. Moreover she loved her work in Summerton and could not be persuaded to leave it. Nevertheless, when she saw them depart she shed a few tears and wondered what the Lord would have of her now that she was again bereft of family and alone in the world.

What she did immediately was to ask a dear old lady who had been a mother in Israel to her ever since she came to Summerton, to come and live with her that winter, and so she made a pleasant home for one who was alone in the world and needed beauty and help and comfort, and who in turn was rich in Bible wisdom and good sound advice and a blessing to all who came near her. Her name was Mrs. Brown, just plain Mrs. Brown, but her face was a benediction in itself.

The minister closed and locked the parsonage door on the day after the wedding and started out on a walk by himself toward the country. His mother had left earlier in the morning for a visit to her sister near New York, and a rest to her soul after the various labors of persuading to wear this, and have that, and not do this or that fanatical thing at the wedding. The one servant left to care for the minister was out, telling her most intimate friend about the wedding and all the extra work, and the house seemed unusually desolate to the minister. His heart ached. He wanted something and he knew what it was he wanted. Was it any use to try? He had been reading the twenty-fourth chapter of Genesis, preparatory to his next Sunday's sermon. It had seemed to affect him strangely. He had taken a sudden determination. "I will ask the Lord to show me," he said; "I will ask a sign of the Lord as the men of old did," and he had knelt beside his study table and prayed long and then had gone out. And ever there came to him as he walked these words: "The Lord will send his angel with thee and will prosper thy way."

Out beside the little wood road not far away from the Benedict place he saw her. She was picking flowers of ferns or some sweet growing thing, and he went to meet her. She smiled and held out her hand to him, and he thought, he was sure, there had been tears in her eyes. He asked her to walk with him and they went on into the woods and there they sat down upon a mossy log. "Is your name Rebecca?" he asked her, and then he told her all that was in his heart; how she had blessed him ever since he had first met her and how he had loved and feared to tell it because he felt sure his love was not returned; and now he had read the chapter and it had led him to seek a sign of the Lord, and he had come feeling that he would be led in some way and helped; and how he would like to take her back home to the parsonage as his wife just as soon as she would let him. And then he waited for an answer.

And Ruth looked up with glad tears shining in her sweet eyes and said, "I will go."

As they rose to leave the woods that afternoon Robert Clifton quoted the text which had led him out to find her. "I being in the way, the Lord led me." "It is strange," he said, "how true that is. Every time when I have made up my mind to surrender my own way and follow what seemed to be pointed out as his way, I have been led to something great and sweet and beautiful, something that I wanted very much. And now at last it is you."

And Ruth, looking into the eyes of the man she loved said, "That text is true of me also. I certainly have been led into brighter and better things than I ever dreamed. Let us take it for our life motto, '*I being in the way*, the Lord led me.'"

As they came near to the house they heard through the open window the quavering voice of Mrs. Brown as she sang to herself a hymn that was dear to her and to them:

> "His wisdom ever waketh,
> His sight is never dim,
> He knows the way He taketh,
> And I will walk with him."

Novels of Enduring Romance and Inspiration by

GRACE LIVINGSTON HILL

☐	23361	**DAWN IN THE MORNING #43**	$2.50
☐	23856	**THE HONOR GIRL #57**	$2.50
☐	23558	**CHRISTMAS BRIDE #62**	$2.50
☐	20286	**MAN OF THE DESERT #63**	$2.25
☐	20911	**MISS LAVINIA'S CALL #64**	$2.50
☐	24736	**AN UNWILLING GUEST #65**	$2.50
☐	24799	**THE GIRL FROM MONTANA #66**	$2.50
☐	24876	**A DAILY RATE #67**	$2.50
☐	24981	**THE STORY OF A WHIM #68**	$2.50
☐	25124	**ACCORDING TO THE PATTERN #69**	$2.50
☐	25253	**IN THE WIND #70**	$2.95

Prices and availability subject to change without notice.

Buy them at your local bookstore or use this handy coupon for ordering:

Special Offer
Buy a Bantam Book
for only 50¢.

Now you can order the exciting books you've been wanting to read straight from Bantam's latest listing of hundreds of titles. *And* this special offer gives you the opportunity to purchase a Bantam book for only 50¢. Here's how:

By ordering any five books at the regular price per order, you can also choose any other single book listed (up to $4.95 value) for only 50¢. Some restrictions do apply, so for further details send for Bantam's listing of titles today.

Just send us your name and address and we'll send you Bantam Book's SHOP AT HOME CATALOG!

THE LATEST BOOKS
IN THE BANTAM
BESTSELLING TRADITION

DON'T MISS
THESE CURRENT
Bantam Bestsellers